THE COLLAPSING EMPIRE

John Scalzi is one of the most popular and acclaimed SF authors to emerge in the last decade. His debut, *Old Man's War*, won him science fiction's John W. Campbell Award for Best New Writer. His *New York Times* bestsellers include *The Last Colony, Fuzzy Nation, Lock In* and *Redshirts*, which won the 2013 Hugo Award for Best Novel. Material from his widely read blog *Whatever* (*whatever.scalzi.com*) has earned him two other Hugo Awards. He lives in Ohio with his wife and daughter.

BY JOHN SCALZI

The Old Man's War Series

Old Man's War
The Ghost Brigades
The Last Colony
Zoe's Tale
The Human Division
The End of All Things

Other Novels

Agent to the Stars
The Android's Dream
The God Engines
Fuzzy Nation
Redshirts
Lock In
The Collapsing Empire

Praise for John Scalzi

'Political plotting, plenty of snark, puzzle-solving, and a healthy dose of action . . . Scalzi continues to be almost insufferably good at his brand of fun but think-y sci-fi adventure'
Kirkus Reviews

'Polished and powerful . . . Scalzi knows just how to satisfy his fans, providing tense, thrilling action scenes while turning a critical eye on the interstellar equivalents of the military-industrial complex'   *Publishers Weekly* **(starred review)**

'It gladdens the reader's heart . . . great fun'   *Daily Telegraph*

'Scalzi's imagined interstellar arena is coherently and compellingly delineated . . . His speculative elements are top-notch. His combat scenes are blood-roiling. His dialogue is suitably snappy and profane'   *Washington Post*

'If anyone stands at the core of the American science fiction tradition at the moment, it is Scalzi'
The Encyclopedia of Science Fiction

'Scalzi's prose harkens back to the Golden Age of science fiction while still remaining fresh and vibrant'   *Strange Horizons*

'Punchy and cleverly executed'   *BiblioSanctum*

THE
COLLAPSING
EMPIRE

JOHN SCALZI

TOR

First published 2017 by Tom Doherty Associates, LLC

First published in the UK 2017 by Tor
an imprint of Pan Macmillan
20 New Wharf Road, London N1 9RR
Associated companies throughout the world
www.panmacmillan.com

ISBN 978-1-5098-3507-2

1 3 5 7 9 8 6 4 2

A CIP catalogue record for this book is available from the British Library.

Printed and bound by CPI Group (UK) Ltd, Croydon, CR0 4YY

Visit
and to   d
news
s

To Tom Doherty, specifically, and everyone at Tor generally.
Thanks for believing in me.
Here's to the next decade.
(At least.)

THE
COLLAPSING
EMPIRE

PROLOGUE

The mutineers would have gotten away with it, too, if it weren't for the collapse of the Flow.

There is, of course, a legal, standard way within the guilds for a crew to mutiny, a protocol that has lasted for centuries. A senior crew member, preferably the executive officer/first mate, but possibly the chief engineer, chief technician, chief physician or, in genuinely bizarre circumstances, the owner's representative, would offer the ship's imperial adjunct a formal Bill of Grievances Pursuant to a Mutiny, consistent with guild protocol. The imperial adjunct would confer with the ship's chief chaplain, calling for witnesses and testimony if required, and the two would, in no later than a month, either offer up with a Finding for Mutiny, or issue a Denial of Mutiny.

In the case of the former, the chief of security would formally remove and sequester the captain of the ship, who would face a formal guild hearing at the ship's next destination, with penalties ranging from loss of ship, rank, and spacing privileges, to actual civil and criminal charges leading to a stint in prison, or, in the most severe cases, a death sentence. In the case of the latter, it was the complaining crew member who was bundled up by the chief of security for the formal guild hearing, etc., etc.

Obviously no one was going to do any of that.

Then there is the way that mutinies *actually* happen, involving weapons, violence, sudden death, the officer ranks turning on each other like animals, the crew trying to figure out what the fuck is going on. Then, depending on the way things go, the captain being murdered and tossed out into the void, and then everything backdated after the fact to make it look all legal and pretty, or the mutinous officers and crew being shown the other side of an airlock and the captain filing a Notice of Extralegal Mutiny, which cancels the mutineers' survivors benefits and pensions, meaning their spouses and children starve and are blackballed from guild roles for two generations, because apparently mutiny is in the DNA, like eye color or a tendency toward irritable bowels.

On the bridge of the *Tell Me Another One*, Captain Arullos Gineos was busy dealing with an *actual* mutiny, not a paper one, and if she was going to be really honest about it to herself, things didn't look like they were going very well for her at the moment. More to the point, once her XO and his crew burned their way through that bulkhead with their hull welders, Gineos and her bridge crew were on their way to being the victims of an "accident" to be named later.

"Weapons locker is empty," Third Officer Nevin Bernus said, after checking. Gineos nodded at that; of course it was. The weapons locker was coded to open for exactly five people: the captain, the officers of the watch, and Security Chief Bremman. One of the five had removed the weapons on a previous watch; logic pointed to Executive Officer Ollie Inverr, who was currently cutting his way through the wall with his friends.

Gineos wasn't entirely unarmed. She had a low-velocity dart pusher that she kept in her boot, a habit she picked up when she was running with the Rapid Dogs gang in the warrens of

Grussgott as a teenager. Its single dart was meant for close-contact use; from a distance farther than a meter, all it would do is just piss off whoever got hit with it. Gineos was not under the illusion her dart pusher was going to save her or her command.

"Status," Gineos said to Lika Dunn, who had been busy contacting the other officers of the *Tell Me*.

"Nothing from Engineering since Chief Fanochi called in," Dunn said. Eva Fanochi was the one who had first raised the alarm about her department being taken over by armed crew led by the XO, which had caused Gineos to lock down the bridge and put the ship on alert. "Chief Technician Vossni isn't answering. Neither is Dr. Jutmen. Bremman has been sealed into his quarters." That would be Piter Bremman, *Tell Me*'s security chief.

"What about Egerti?" Lup Egerti was the owner's representative, useless as the proverbial tits on a boar in most circumstances, but who probably would not have been in on a mutiny, as mutinies were bad for business.

"Nothing. Nothing from Slavin or Preen, either," the latter two being the imperial adjunct and the chaplain. "Second Officer Niin also hasn't checked in."

"They're almost through," Bernus said, pointing to the bulkhead.

Gineos grimaced to herself. She was never happy with her XO, who had been pushed on to her by the guild with the endorsement of the House of Tois, the *Tell Me*'s owner. The second mate, Niin, had been Gineos's choice for her second in command. She should have pushed harder. Next time.

Not that there's going to be a next time now, Gineos thought. She was dead, the officers loyal to her would be dead if they weren't already, and because the *Tell Me* was in the Flow and would be for another month, there was no way for her to launch the ship's black box to tell anyone what had really happened. By the time the *Tell Me* exited the Flow at End, the mess would be cleaned up, evidence rearranged and stories gotten straight. *Tragic what happened to Gineos*, they would say. *An explosion. So many dead. And she courageously went back to try to save more of her crew.*

Or something like that.

The bulkhead had been burned through and a minute later a slab of metal was on the deck, and three crew members armed with bolt throwers stepped in, swiveling to track the bridge crew. None of the bridge crew moved; what was the point. One of the armed crew gave a "clear," and Executive Officer Ollie Inverr ducked through the hole of the bulkhead and onto the deck. He spied Gineos and came over to her. One of the armed crew trained his bolt thrower on her specifically.

"Captain Gineos," Inverr said, greeting her.

"Ollie," Gineos said, returning the greeting.

"Captain Arullos Gineos, pursuant to Article 38, Section 7 of the Uniform Code of the Mercantile Shipping Guilds, I hereby—"

"Cut the shit, Ollie," Gineos said.

Inverr smiled at this. "Fair enough."

"I have to say you did a pretty good job with the mutiny. Taking Engineering first so that if everything else goes wrong you can threaten to blow the engines."

"Thank you, Captain. I did in fact try to get us through this transition with a minimum of casualties."

"Does that mean Fanochi is still alive?"

"I said 'a minimum,' Captain. I'm sorry to say Chief Fanochi was not very accommodating. Assistant Chief Hybern has been promoted."

"How many of the other officers do you have?"

"I don't think you need to worry about that, Captain."

"Well, at least you're not pretending you're *not* going to kill me."

"For the record, I'm sorry that it's come to this, Captain. I do admire you."

"I already told you to cut the shit, Ollie."

Another smile from Inverr. "You never were one for flattery."

"You want to tell me *why* you've planned this insurrection?"

"Not really, no."

"Indulge me. I'd like to know why I'm about to die."

Inverr shrugged. "For money, of course. We're carrying a large shipment of weapons meant for the military of End to help them fight their current insurrection. Rifles, bolt throwers, rocket launchers. You know, you signed off on the manifest. I was approached when we were at Alpine about selling them to the rebels instead. Thirty percent premium. That seemed like a good deal. I said yes."

"I'm curious how you planned to get the arms to them. End's spaceport is controlled by its government."

"They would never have made it there. We come out of the Flow, and we're attacked by 'pirates' who offload the cargo. You and the other crew who don't go along with the plan die in the attack. Simple, easy, everyone who is left makes a bundle and is happy."

"The House of Tois won't be happy," Gineos said, invoking the *Tell Me*'s owner.

"They've got insurance for the ship and cargo. They'll be fine."

"He won't be happy about Egerti. You'll have to kill him. That's Yanner Tois's son-in-law."

Inverr smiled at the name of the House of Tois's patriarch.

"I have it on good authority that Tois would not be entirely put out to make his favorite son a widower. He has some other alliances a marriage could firm up."

"You have this all planned out, then."

"It's not personal, Captain."

"Getting murdered for money feels personal, Ollie."

Inverr opened his mouth to respond to this, but then *Tell Me Another One* dropped out of the Flow, triggering a set of alarms that no one on the *Tell Me*—not Gineos, not Inverr—had ever heard outside of an academy simulation.

Gineos and Inverr stood there for several seconds, gaping at the alarms. Then both of them went to their stations and got to work, because *Tell Me* had unexpectedly dropped out of the Flow, and if they didn't figure out how to get back into it, they were, without a doubt, irretrievably fucked.

Now, some context, here.

In this universe there is no such thing as "faster-than-light" travel. The speed of light is not only a good idea, it's the law. You can't get to it; the closer you accelerate toward it, the more energy you need to keep going toward, and it's a horrible idea to go that fast anyway, since space is only *mostly* empty, and anything you collide with at an appreciable percentage of the speed of light is going to turn your fragile spaceship into explody chunks of metal. And it would *still* take years, or decades, or centuries, for the wreckage of your spacecraft to zoom past wherever it was you originally planned to go.

There is no faster-than-light travel. But there is the Flow.

The Flow, generally described to laypeople as the river of alternate space-time that makes faster-than-light travel possible across the Holy Empire of the Interdependent States and Mercantile Guilds, called "the Interdependency" for short. The Flow, accessible by "shoals" created when the gravity of stars and planets interacts just right with the Flow, to allow ships to slip in and ride the current to another star. The Flow, which ensured the survival of humanity after it had lost the Earth, by allowing trade to thrive between the Interdependency, assuring that every human outpost would have the resources they'd need to survive—resources that almost none of them would have had on their own.

This was, of course, an absurd way of looking at the Flow. The Flow is not anything close to a river—it is a multidimensional brane-like metacosmological structure that intersects with local time-space in a topographically complex manner, influenced partially and chaotically *but not primarily* by gravity, in which the ships accessing it don't move in any traditional sense but merely take advantage of its vectoral nature, relative to local space-time, which, unbounded by our universe's laws regarding speed, velocity, and energy, gives the *appearance* of faster-than-light travel to local observers.

And even *that* was a crap way of describing it, because human languages are crap at describing things more complex than assembling a tree house. The accurate way of describing the Flow involved the sort of high-order math probably only a couple hundred human beings across the billions of the Interdependency could understand, much less themselves use to describe it meaningfully. You likely would not be one of them. Nor, for that matter, would Captain Gineos or Executive Officer Inverr.

But Gineos and Inverr knew this much: it was nearly impossible—and almost never heard of, over the centuries of the Interdependency—for a ship to exit the Flow unexpectedly. A random rupture in the Flow could strand a ship light-years from any human planet or outpost. Guild ships were designed to be self-sustaining for months and even years—they had to be, because the transit time between Interdependency systems

using the Flow ranged between two weeks to nine months—
but there's a difference between being self-sustaining for five
years or a decade, as the largest guild ships were, and being self-
sustaining *forever*.

Because there is no faster-than-light travel. There is only the
Flow.

And if you're randomly dumped out of it, somewhere between the stars, you're dead.

"I need a reading for where we are," Inverr said, from his
station.

"On it," Lika Dunn said.

"Then get the antennas up," Gineos said. "If we got dumped,
there's an exit shoal. We need to find an entrance shoal."

"Already deploying," Bernus said, from his console.

Gineos flipped open communications to Engineering. "Chief
Hybern," she said. "We've experienced a rupture exit from the
Flow. We need engines online immediately and I'm going to
need you to make sure we have sufficient push field power to
counteract extreme high-G maneuvers. We don't want to turn
into jelly."

"Uuuuhhhhh," came the reply.

"For fuck's sake," Gineos said, and looked over to Inverr.
"He's your minion, Ollie. *You* handle him."

Inverr flipped open his own communication circuit. "Hybern,
this is XO Inverr. Is there a problem understanding the captain's
orders?"

"Weren't we having a mutiny?" Hybern asked. Hybern was
an engineering prodigy, which advanced him through the guild
ranks. But he was very, very young.

"We just dropped out of the Flow, Hybern. If we don't find a
way back to it soon, we're all screwed. So I'm ordering you to
follow Captain Gineos's directives. Understood?"

"Yes, sir," came the reply, after a moment. "On it. Starting emergency engine protocol. Five minutes to full power. Uh, it's probably going to mess up the engines pretty badly, sir. And ma'am."

"If they get us back to the Flow we'll figure it out then," Gineos said. "Ping me the second they're ready to go." She flipped off the communication link. "You picked a very bad time to have a mutiny," she said to Inverr.

"We have a position," Dunn said. "We're about twenty-three light-years out from End, sixty-one out from Shirak."

"Any local gravity wells?"

"No, ma'am. Closest star is a red dwarf about three light-years away. Nothing else significant in the neighborhood."

"So how did we come out if there's no gravity well?" Inverr asked.

"Eva Fanochi probably could have answered that for you," Gineos said. "If you hadn't murdered her, that is."

"Now's not a great time for that discussion, Captain."

"Found it!" Bernus said. "Entrance shoal, a hundred thousand klicks from us! Except . . ."

"Except what?" Gineos asked.

"It's moving away from us," Bernus said. "And it's shrinking."

Gineos and Inverr looked at each other. As far as either of them knew, entrance and exit shoals for the Flow were static in size and location. That's why they could be used for everyday mercantile traffic at all. For a shoal to move and shrink was literally a new thing in their experience.

Figure it out later, Gineos thought to herself. "How fast is it moving relative to us, and how quickly is it shrinking?"

"It's heading away from us at about ten thousand klicks an hour, and it looks like it's shrinking about ten meters a second," Bernus said, after a minute. "I can't tell you if those are constant rates, either for the velocity or the shrinkage. It's just what I'm seeing now."

"Send me the data on the shoal," Inverr said to Bernus.

"Would you mind telling your lackeys to wait outside?" Gineos said to Inverr, motioning to the armed crew. "I'm finding it difficult to concentrate with bolt throwers aimed at my head."

Inverr glanced up at the armed crewmen and nodded. They headed over to the hole in the bulkhead and stepped through. "Stay close," Inverr said, as they exited.

"So can you plot a course to it?" Gineos asked. "Before it closes on us?"

"Give me a minute," Inverr said. There was silence on the bridge while he worked. Then, "Yes. If Hybern gives us the engines in the next couple of minutes, we'll make it with margin to spare."

Gineos nodded and flipped open communication to Engineering. "Hybern, where are my engines?"

"Another thirty seconds, ma'am."

"How are we for the push fields? We're going to be moving fast."

"It depends on how much you force the engines, ma'am. If you draw everything to drive the ship, it's got to take that last bit of energy from somewhere. It'll take it from everywhere else first, but eventually it'll take from the fields."

"I'd rather die fast than slow, wouldn't you, Hybern?"

"Uhhhh," came the reply.

"Engines are online," Inverr said.

"I see it." Gineos punched at her screen. "You've got navigation," she said to Inverr. "Get us out of here, Ollie."

"We have a problem," Bernus said.

"Of course we do," Gineos said. "What is this one?"

"The shoal is picking up speed and is shrinking faster."

"On it," Inverr said.

"Are we still going to make it?" Gineos asked.

"Probably. Some of the ship, anyway."

"What does *that* mean?"

"It means that depending how big the shoal is, part of the ship might get left behind. We've got the stalk and we've got the ring. The stalk is a long needle. The ring is a klick across. The stalk might make it through. The ring might not."

"That'll destroy the ship," Dunn said.

Gineos shook her head. "It's not like we're hitting a physical barrier. Anything not inside the shoal circumference will just get left behind. Sliced off like with a razor. We seal the bulkheads to the ring spokes and we survive." She turned her attention back to Inverr. "That is, if we can shape the bubble." The bubble was the small envelope of local space-time, surrounded by an energy field generated by *Tell Me*, that accompanied the ship into the Flow. Technically there was no *there* inside the Flow. Any ship that didn't bring a pocket of space-time with it into the Flow would cease to exist in any meaningful sense.

"We can shape the bubble," Inverr said.

"Are you sure?"

"If I'm not, it won't matter anyway."

Gineos grunted at this and turned to Dunn. "Put a ship-wide alert to get everyone out of the ring and into the stalk." She turned back to Inverr. "How long do we have until we reach the shoal?"

"Nine minutes."

"A little longer than that," Bernus said. "The shoal is still speeding up."

"Tell them they have five minutes," Gineos said, to Dunn. "After that we seal off the ring. If they're on the wrong side of the seal, they might get left behind." Dunn nodded and made the announcement. "I assume you'll let out some of the people you sealed into their quarters," she said to Inverr.

"We welded Piter into his," Inverr said, of the security chief. He was looking at his monitor and making tiny adjustments to the path of the *Tell Me*. "Not much time to fix that one."

"Lovely."

"It's going to be a close thing, you know."

"Making the shoal?"

"Yes. But I meant if we leave the ring behind. There are two hundred of us on the ship. Nearly all the food and supplies are in the ring. We're still a month out from End. Even in the best of circumstances, we aren't all going to make it."

"Well," Gineos said. "I assume you're already planning to eat my body first."

"It will be a noble sacrifice you'll be making, Captain."

"I can't tell whether you're joking or not, Ollie."

"At the moment, Captain, neither can I."

"I suppose this is as good a time as any to tell you I never really liked you."

Inverr smiled at this, but still didn't turn his attention away from his monitor. "I know that, Captain. It's one reason I was okay with a mutiny."

"That and the money."

"That and the money, yes," Inverr agreed. "Now let me work."

The next several minutes were Inverr showing that, whatever his deficiencies as an XO, he was possibly the best navigator that Gineos had ever seen. The entrance shoal was not retreating linearly from the *Tell Me*; it appeared to dodge and skip, jumping back and forth, an invisible dancer traceable by the barest of radio frequency hums where the Flow pressed up against timespace. Bernus would track the shoal and call out the latest data;

Inverr would make the adjustments and bring the *Tell Me* inexorably closer to the shoal. It was one of the great acts of space travel, possibly in the history of humanity. Despite everything Gineos felt privileged to be there for it.

"Uuuuuhhh, we have a problem," Interim Chief Engineer Hybern said, over the communication lines. "We're at the point where the engines have to start taking energy from other systems."

"We need push fields," Gineos said. "Everything else is negotiable."

"I need navigation," Inverr said, still not looking up.

"We need push fields and navigation," Gineos amended. "Everything else is negotiable."

"How do we feel about life support?" Hybern asked.

"If we don't do this in the next thirty seconds it won't matter whether we breathe or don't," Inverr said to Gineos.

"Cut everything but navigation and push fields," Gineos said.

"Copy," Hybern said, and immediately the air in *Tell Me* began to feel cooler and more stale.

"Shoal is almost down to two klicks across," Bernus said.

"It'll be close," Inverr agreed. "Fifteen seconds to shoal."

"One point eight klicks across."

"We're fine."

"One point five klicks across."

"Bernus, shut the fuck up, please."

Bernus shut the fuck up. Gineos stood up, adjusted her clothing, and went to stand by her XO.

Inverr counted down the last ten seconds, abandoning the countdown at six to announce he was shaping the space-time bubble, resuming it at three. At zero, Gineos could see from her vantage point behind and just to the side of him that he was smiling.

"We're in. We're all in. The whole ship," he said.

"That was some amazing work, Ollie," Gineos said.

"Yeah. I think it was. Not to toot my own horn or anything."

"Go ahead and toot it. The crew is alive because of you."

"Thank you, Captain," Inverr said. He turned to face Gineos, still smiling, and that's when she jammed the barrel of the dart-pusher she'd just retrieved from her boot into the orbit of his left eye and pushed the trigger. The dart unloaded into his eye with a soft *pop*. Inverr's other eye looked very surprised, and then Inverr slumped to the ground, dead.

From the other side of the bulkhead, Inverr's lackeys shouted in alarm and raised their bolt throwers. Gineos held up her hand, and by God, they stopped. "He's dead," she said, and then put her other hand on Inverr's station monitor. "And now I've just armed a command that will blow every airlock the ship has into the bubble. The second my hand goes off the monitor, everyone on the ship dies, including you. So now you get to decide who is dead today: Ollie Inverr, or everybody. Shoot me, we all die. If you don't drop your weapons in the next ten seconds, we all die. Make your choice."

All three dropped their bolt throwers. Gineos motioned to Dunn, who went over and collected them, handing one to Bernus and then handing the other to her captain, who took her hand off the monitor to take it. One of the lackeys gasped at this.

"For fuck's sake, you're gullible," Gineos said to him, flicked the bolt thrower setting to "nonlethal," and shot all three of them in rapid order. They fell, unconscious.

She turned to Dunn and Bernus. "Congratulations, you're promoted," she said to them. "Now, then. We have some muti-neers to deal with. Let's get to work, shall we."

PART ONE

1

For the week leading up to his death, Cardenia Wu-Patrick stayed mostly at the bedside of her father, Batrin, who, when he was informed that his condition had reached the limits of medical competence and that palliative care was all that was left to him, decided to die at home, in his favorite bed. Cardenia, who had been aware for some time that the end was close, had cleared her schedule until further notice and had a comfortable chair installed near her father's bed.

"Don't you have better things to do than to sit around here?" Batrin joked to his daughter and sole surviving child, as she sat to begin her morning session with her father.

"Not at the moment," she said.

"I doubt that. I'm pretty sure every time you leave this room to go to the bathroom, you're accosted by minions who need your signature on something."

"No," Cardenia said. "Everything right now is in the hands of the executive committee. Everything is in maintenance mode for the foreseeable future."

"Until I die," Batrin said.

"Until you die."

Batrin laughed at that, weakly, as that is how he did everything at this point. "This is, I'm afraid, all too foreseeable."

"Try not to think about it," Cardenia said.

"Easy for you to say." They both lapsed into a quiet, companionable silence for a few moments, until Batrin grimaced silently at a noise and turned to his daughter. "What is that?"

Cardenia cocked her head slightly. "You mean the singing?"

"There's *singing* going on?"

"You have a crowd of well-wishers outside," Cardenia said.

Batrin smiled at that. "You're sure that's what they are?"

Batrin Wu, Cardenia's father, was formally Attavio VI, Emperox of the Holy Empire of the Interdependent States and Mercantile Guilds, King of Hub and Associated Nations, Head of the Interdependent Church, Successor to Earth and Father of All, Eighty-seventh Emperox of the House of Wu, which claimed its lineage to the Prophet-Emperox Rachela I, founder of the Interdependency and Savior of Humanity.

"We're sure," Cardenia said. The two of them were at Brighton, the imperial residence at Hubfall, the capital of Hub and her father's favorite residence. The formal imperial seat lay several thousand klicks up the gravity well, at Xi'an, the sprawling space station that hovered over the surface of Hub, visible to Hubfall like a giant reflective plate flung out into the darkness—or would be, if most of Hubfall were anywhere near the planet surface. Hubfall, like all the cities of Hub, was first blasted, then carved, into the rock of the planet, with only occasional service domes and structures peppering the surface. Those domes looked out on an eternal twilight, waiting for a sunrise the tidally locked planet would never offer, and which, if it did, would bake Hub's citizens, screaming, like potatoes in a broiler.

Attavio VI hated Xi'an and never stayed there longer than

absolutely necessary. He certainly had no intention of dying there. Brighton was his home, and outside it, a thousand or more well-wishers pooled near its gate, cheering for him and occasionally breaking out into the imperial anthem or "What Say You," the cheering song for the imperial football team. All of the well-wishers, Cardenia knew, had been thoroughly vetted before they were allowed within a klick of Brighton's gate and within earshot of the emperox. Some of them didn't even have to be paid to show up.

"How many did we have to pay?" Batrin asked.

"Hardly any," Cardenia said.

"I had to pay all three thousand people who showed up to cheer my mother on her deathbed. I had to pay them a lot."

"You're more popular than your mother was." Cardenia had never met her grandmother, Emperox Zetian III, but the tales from history were toe-curling.

"A rock would be more popular than my mother," Batrin said. "But you shouldn't fool yourself, my child. No emperox of the Interdependency has ever been that popular. It's not in the job description."

"You were more popular than most, at least," Cardenia suggested.

"That's why you only had to pay some of the people outside the window."

"I could have them dismissed, if you like."

"They're fine. See if they take requests."

Presently Batrin napped again and when Cardenia was sure he was asleep, she got up from her chair and exited into her father's private office, which she had commandeered from him for the duration and which would be hers soon enough in any event. As she exited her father's bedroom she saw a squadron of medical professionals, headed by Qui Drinin, imperial physician, descend upon her father to clean him, check his vitals, and make sure he was as comfortable as someone who was dealing with a painful and incurable disease from which he would never recover could be.

In the private office was Naffa Dolg, Cardenia's recently appointed chief of staff. Naffa waited until Cardenia had reached into the office's small refrigerator, acquired a soft drink, sat down, opened the drink, had two swallows from the container, then set the drink down on her father's desk.

"Coaster," Naffa said to her boss.

"Really?" Cardenia said back.

Naffa pointed. "That desk was originally the desk of Turinu II. It is six hundred fifty years old. It was a gift to him by the father of Genevieve N'don, who would become his wife after—"

Cardenia held up a hand. "Enough." She reached over on the desk, grabbed a small leather-bound book, pulled it over to her, and set her drink on it. Then she caught Naffa's expression. "What now?"

"Oh, nothing," Naffa said. "Just that your 'coaster' is a first edition of Chao's *Commentaries on the Racheline Doctrines,* which means it's nearly a thousand years old and unspeakably priceless and even thinking of setting a drink can on it is probably blasphemy of the highest order."

"Oh, for God's sake." Cardenia took another swig of her drink and then set it on the carpet next to the desk. "Happy? I mean, unless the carpet is also unspeakably priceless."

"Actually—"

"Can we stipulate that everything in this room except the two of us is probably hundreds of years old, originally gifted to one of my ancestors by another immensely famous historical personage, and that it is priceless or at least worth more than most humans will make in their lifetimes? Is there anything in this room that does not fit that description?"

Naffa pointed to the refrigerator. "I think that's just a refrigerator."

Cardenia finally found a coaster on the desk, picked her drink up off the carpet, and set it on it. "This coaster is probably four hundred years old and the gift of the Duke of End," she said, then looked at her assistant. "Don't tell me if it is."

"I won't." Naffa pulled out her tablet.

"But you *know*, don't you."

"You have requests from the executive committee," Naffa said, ignoring her boss's last comment.

Cardenia threw up her hands. "Of course I do." The executive committee consisted of three guild representatives, three ministers of parliament, and three archbishops of the church. In other times, the committee was the emperox's direct link to the three centers of power in the Interdependency. At the moment they were charged with maintaining the continuity of government during these final days of the emperox's reign. They were driving Cardenia a little batty.

"First, they want you to make an appearance on the networks to, as they put it, 'calm the fears of the empire' regarding your father's situation."

"He's dying, and quickly," Cardenia said. "I'm not sure that's calming."

"I think they'd prefer something a little more inspiring. They sent over a speech."

"There's no point reassuring the empire. By the time my speech reaches End he'll have been dead for nine standard months. Even Bremen is two weeks away."

"There's still Hub and Xi'an and associated nations in-system. The furthest of those is only five light-hours out."

"They already know he's dying."

"It's not about him dying. It's about continuity."

"The Wu dynasty stretches back a thousand years, Naffa. No one is really *that* worried about continuity."

"That's not the continuity they're worried about. They're worried about their day-to-day lives. No matter who would become emperox, things change. There are three hundred million imperial subjects in-system, Cardenia. You're the heir. They know the dynasty won't change. It's everything else."

"I can't believe you're on the side of the executive committee here."

"Stopped clock. Twice a day."

"Have you read the speech?"

"I have. It's awful."

"Are you rewriting it?"

"Already rewritten, yes."

"What else?"

"They wanted to know if you've changed your position on Amit Nohamapetan."

"My position on what? Meeting with him or marrying him?"

"I would think they're hoping the first will lead to the second."

"I've met him once before. It's why I don't want to meet with him again. I'm definitely not going to marry him."

"The executive committee, perhaps anticipating your reluctance, wishes to remind you that your brother, the late crown prince, had agreed in principle to marry Nadashe Nohamapetan."

"I would rather marry her than her brother."

"Anticipating that you might say that, the executive committee wishes to remind you that option would also probably be acceptable to all parties."

"I'm not going to marry *her* either," Cardenia said. "I don't like either. They're terrible people."

"They're terrible people whose house is ascendant in the mercantile guilds and whose desire for an alliance with the House of Wu would allow the empire a lever with the guilds it hasn't had in centuries."

"Is that you talking or the executive committee?"

"Eighty percent executive committee."

"You're at twenty percent on this?" Cardenia offered mostly feigned shock.

"That twenty percent recognizes that political marriages are a thing that happens to people, like you, who are on the verge of becoming emperox and who, despite having a millennium-long dynasty to fall back on for credibility, still need allies to keep the guilds in line."

"This is where you tell me of all the times in the last thousand years the Wu emperoxs were basically puppets for guild interests, isn't it?"

"This is where I remind you that you gave me this position not just out of personal friendship and experience with court politics but because I have a doctorate in the history of the Wu dynasty and know more about your family than you do," Naffa said. "But sure, I could do that other thing, too."

Cardenia sighed. "We're in no danger of becoming guild puppets, though."

Naffa peered over at her boss, silently.

"You're kidding," Cardenia said.

"The House of Wu is its own mercantile family and it has the monopoly on ship building and military weaponry," Naffa said. "Likewise, control of the military runs through the emperox, not the guilds. So, no, it would be difficult for the guilds or any of the houses who control them to make short-term inroads into control of the house or of the empire. That said, your father has been very lax in controlling the mercantile houses and has allowed several of them, including the Nohamapetans, to build power centers that are unprecedented in the last two hundred years. This is, of course, leaving out the church entirely, which is its own power center. And you can expect to see all of these try to grab more power for themselves because you are expected to be a weak emperox."

"Thanks," Cardenia said, dryly.

"It's not personal. Your ascendance to the crown was unexpected."

"Tell me about it."

"No one knows what to think of you."

"Except the executive committee, who wants to marry me off."

"They want to preserve an existing potential alliance."

"An alliance with terrible people."

"Really nice people don't usually accrue power."

"You're saying I'm kind of an outlier," Cardenia said.

"I don't recall saying you were nice," Naffa replied.

• • •

"None of this was supposed to be your problem," Batrin said to Cardenia, later. She was back in his bedroom, sitting in the chair. The medical staff that had worried on him while he was asleep had retreated to nearby rooms. It was just the two of them again, plus an array of medical equipment.

"I know," Cardenia said. They'd had this conversation before, but she knew they were about to have it again.

"It was your brother who was groomed for all of this," Batrin continued, and Cardenia nodded as he droned on slowly. Her brother, Rennered Wu, was actually her half brother. He was the son of the imperial consort Glenna Costu, while Cardenia was the result of a brief liaison between the emperox and

Cardenia's mother, Hannah, a professor of ancient languages. Hannah Patrick met the emperox while giving him a tour of the rare books collection of the Spode Library at the University of Hubfall. The two corresponded on academics after that and then, a few years after the sudden death of the imperial consort, the emperox gifted Hannah Patrick first with a rare edition of the *Qasīdat-ul-Burda*, and subsequently, not too long thereafter, and a bit to the surprise of both, with Cardenia.

Rennered was already the heir and Hannah Patrick, upon reflection, decided that she would rather step out of an airlock than become a permanent fixture of the imperial court. As a result, Cardenia's childhood was pampered but far removed from the trappings of actual power. Cardenia was acknowledged as a child of the emperox and saw her famous father regularly but infrequently. She would occasionally be teased by classmates, who might call her "princess," but not too often or too viciously, because as it turns out she *was* a princess and her imperial security detail was sensitive to slights.

Her childhood and early adult years were as normal as they could be when one is the daughter of the most powerful human in the known universe, which was to say not very but close enough that Cardenia could see normal, distantly, from there. She attended the University of Hubfall, received degrees in modern literature and education, and upon graduation gave serious thought to becoming a professional patron of some arts-related programs and initiatives for the underadvantaged.

Then Rennered had to go get himself killed while racing, slamming himself and his charmingly retro automobile into a wall during a charity exhibition race with actual race car drivers and basically decapitating himself in the process. Cardenia never watched the video of the crash—that was her brother, why would she—but she read the forensics report afterward, which while clearing the event of any suspicion of foul play, noted the safety features of the automobile and the unlikelihood of the accident being fatal, much less one that ended in decapitation.

Cardenia later learned that at the charity auction after the race Rennered was supposed to have publicly announced his engagement to Nadashe Nohamapetan. The confluence of those two events stayed firmly connected in her mind afterward.

Cardenia had never been very close to Rennered—Rennered was a teenager when she was born and their circles never meshed—but he had treated her kindly. As a child she idolized him and his playboy ways from afar, and as she grew older and saw how much of the crush of imperial fame had passed by her to land on his shoulders, was quietly relieved he was there to shoulder it. He seemed to enjoy it more than she ever would.

He was gone and then suddenly the empire needed another heir for emperox.

"I think I lost you there," Batrin said.

"I'm sorry," Cardenia said. "I was thinking of Rennered. I wish he were still here."

"So do I. Although perhaps for different reasons."

"I would be happier if he were succeeding you. A lot of people would be."

"That's certain, my child. But Cardenia, listen to me. I don't regret that you are succeeding me."

"Thank you."

"I mean it. Rennered would have made a perfectly good emperox. He was literally born for the role, just as I was. You weren't. But that's not a bad thing."

"I think it's a bad thing. I don't know what I'm doing," Cardenia confessed.

"None of us knew what we were doing," Batrin said. "The difference is that you know it. If Rennered were here, he'd be just as clueless but more confident. Which is why he'd faceplant right out of the gate, just like I did, and my mother, and my grandfather. Perhaps you'll break the family tradition."

Cardenia smiled at this.

Batrin cocked his head, almost imperceptibly. "You still don't know what to make of me, do you?" he asked.

"No," Cardenia admitted. "I'm glad we've come to know each other better, these last few months. But—" She opened her hands, palms up. "All the rest of this."

Batrin smiled. "You want to get to know your father, but you have to focus on getting ready to rule the universe instead."

"It sounds ridiculous. But yes."

"That's on me. You know you were an accident. At least on my part." Cardenia nodded at this. "Everyone, including your mother, told me that it would be better to keep you at a distance. And I was happy to agree with them."

"I know. I never blamed you for that."

"No, you didn't, and you have to admit that was odd," Batrin said.

"I don't know what you mean."

"You are a literal princess, but you didn't live like one. I think it's fair to say most people in your situation would have resented that."

Cardenia shrugged. "I liked it being optional. When I was eight, I resented it a little. When I was old enough to know what being a princess meant, I was glad I got to miss most of it."

"It caught up to you anyway."

"Yes, it did," Cardenia agreed.

"You don't still want to be emperox, do you?"

"No, I don't. I would have rather you had given it to a cousin or nephew or someone else."

"If Rennered had married earlier and had a child, that would have solved your problem. But he didn't. And anyway if he had married that Nohamapetan woman, and she'd produced an heir, then she would have been regent. That seems like a bad idea, to have her running things unchecked."

"You pushed him to marry her."

"Politics. You're being pushed to marry the brother already, I assume."

"Yes."

"It's politically advantageous."

"Do you want me to?"

Batrin coughed, extensively. Cardenia poured him a glass of water and held it to his lips to let him sip. "Thank you. And no. Nadashe Nohamapetan is heartless and vicious, but Rennered was no innocent, either. He reminded me of my mother that way. He would have kept her in check, and he would have enjoyed the challenge and so would she. You're not like Rennered, and Amit Nohamapetan doesn't have his sister's saving grace of being brilliant."

"He's a bore."

"A much more succinct way of putting it."

"But you just said it's a politically advantageous match."

Batrin gave the very slightest of shrugs. "It is, but so what? You'll be emperox soon enough."

"And then no one can tell me what to do."

"Oh, no," Batrin said. "*Everyone* will tell you what to do. But you won't always have to listen."

$$\bullet \quad \bullet \quad \bullet$$

"How much more time does he have?" Cardenia asked Qui Drinin, at dinner. More accurately, Cardenia was having dinner in the residential apartment private dining room, which was only ridiculously sumptuously decorated rather than appallingly so, in delightful contrast to the rest of the residential apartments. Drinin was not eating but rather was standing, waiting to give his report. Cardenia had asked him if he would like to eat, but he'd refused so quickly that she wondered if she had unwittingly breached some bit of imperial protocol.

"No more than a day, I think, ma'am," Drinin said. "His renal system has basically failed, and while we can help with that, that system is running just slightly ahead of everything else. Pulmonary, respiratory, and other systems are at critical milestones. Your father understands that heroic measures could be taken but those would prolong his life by days at best. He's opted not to take them. We're really just making him comfortable at this point."

"He's still lucid," Naffa said. She was also not eating.

Drinin nodded at this and turned to address Cardenia. "You shouldn't expect this to continue, ma'am, especially as the toxins continue to accumulate in his blood. At the risk of sounding presumptuous, if you have anything very important to say to your father, you should do it sooner than later."

"Thank you, Doctor," Cardenia said.

"Of course, ma'am. And may I also ask how you are doing?"

"Personally, or medically?"

"Either, ma'am. I know you had your network installed a few weeks ago. I want to be sure you have no side effects from that."

With the hand not currently holding a utensil, Cardenia reached back to the spot on her neck, just at the base of her skull, where the seed of the imperial neural network had been implanted, to grow into her brain over the course of a month or so. "I had some headaches a week after it was implanted," she said. "It's fine."

Drinin nodded. "Very well. Historically, headaches are not

uncommon. If you experience any other side effects let me know, of course. It should be fully implanted by now, but you never know."

"Thank you, Doctor," Cardenia said.

"Ma'am." Drinin nodded and moved to leave.

"Dr. Drinin."

Drinin stopped and turned. "Ma'am?"

"After the transition I would be pleased if you and your staff were to remain in the service of the emperox."

Drinin smiled and bowed deeply. "Of course, ma'am," he said, and departed.

"You know you don't have to ask every member of the imperial staff to stay," Naffa said, after he had gone. "You'd spend your first month doing that."

Cardenia motioned to where the doctor had departed. "That man is going to be giving me physical examinations for decades," she said. "I think it's okay to ask him personally to stay." She looked up at her aide. "It's weird, you know. You not eating with me right now. Just standing there with your tablet, waiting to tell me things."

"Staff doesn't eat with the emperox."

"They do if the emperox tells them to."

"Are you commanding me to eat whatever disgusting thing you're eating with you?"

"It's not disgusting, it's a cinnamonfish bouillabaisse. And no, I'm not commanding you. I'm telling you that you may, if you like, have something to eat with your friend Cardenia."

"Thanks, Car," Naffa said.

"The last thing I need right now is you being staff all the time. I do actually still need friends. Friends who don't get worked up about who I am. You were the only kid I knew when we were growing up who didn't make a big deal out of me being a princess."

"My parents are republicans," Naffa reminded her friend. "If I treated you differently because of who your father was, they'd've disowned me. They're still mildly scandalized that I'm working for you now."

"That reminds me that when I become emperox, I'll be able to give you a title."

"Don't you dare, Car," Naffa said. "I'll never be able to go home for holidays."

" 'Baroness' has a nice ring to it."

"I'll dump your fish soup on your head if you keep this up," Naffa warned. Cardenia smiled at this.

• • •

"I saw the video you made," Batrin said, once he had woken again. Cardenia observed that Drinin had been correct; her father's demeanor was fuzzy and wandering now. "The one where you were talking about me."

"What did you think?" Cardenia asked.

"It was nice. It wasn't written by the committee, was it?"

"No." The executive committee had complained about Naffa's rewritten speech until Cardenia informed them that it was either Naffa's words or none at all. She enjoyed her first victory over the tripartite political forces counterbalancing the emperox. She did not pretend that there would be many more of those once she came into power.

"Good," Batrin said. "You should be your own emperox, my daughter. No one else's."

"I'll remember that."

"Do." Batrin closed his eyes for a moment and appeared to

drift off. Then he opened them again and looked at Cardenia. "Have you chosen your imperial name yet?"

"I thought I might keep my own," Cardenia said.

"What? No," Batrin said. "Your own name is for your private world. For friends and spouses and children and lovers. You'll need that private name. Don't give it away to the empire."

"Which of your names did my mother call you?"

"She called me Batrin. At least long enough to matter. How is your mother?"

"She's fine." Three years prior, Hannah Patrick had accepted a position of provost at Guelph Institute of Technology, ten weeks from Hub via the Flow. By now news of the emperox's worsening condition would have reached her. She wouldn't know her daughter had become emperox until well after the fact. Cardenia knew her mother was deeply ambivalent about her ascension.

"I considered marrying her," Batrin said.

"You've told me." Cardenia had heard a different story from her mother but this was not the time to bring it up.

The emperox nodded and changed the subject. "May I suggest a name to you? For your imperial name."

"Yes, please."

"Grayland."

Cardenia furrowed her brow. "I don't know this name."

"When I die, look her up. And then come talk to me about it."

"I will."

"Good, good. You will be a good emperox, Cardenia."

"Thank you."

"You'll have to be. The empire is going to need it, in the end."

Cardenia didn't know what to say to that, so she just nodded, and reached out for her father's hand. He seemed surprised by it, and then gave it the smallest of squeezes.

"I think I'll go to sleep now," he said. "I'll go to sleep and then you'll be emperox. Is that all right?"

"It's fine," Cardenia said.

"Okay. Good." Batrin gave Cardenia's hand a squeeze so light it barely registered. "Farewell, Cardenia, my daughter. I'm sorry I didn't make more time to love you."

"It's all right," Cardenia said.

Batrin smiled. "Come see me."

"I will."

"Good," Batrin said, and then drifted off.

Cardenia sat with her father and waited to become emperox. She didn't have to wait long.

Kiva Lagos was busily fucking the brains out of the assistant purser she'd been after for the last six weeks of the *Yes, Sir, That's My Baby*'s trip from Lankaran to End when Second Officer Waylov Brennir entered her stateroom, unannounced. "You're needed," he said.

"I'm a little busy at the moment," Kiva said. She'd just finally gotten herself into a groove, so fuck Waylov (not literally, he was awful) if she was going to get out of the groove just because he walked into it. Grooves were hard to come by. People have sex, and he was unannounced. If this was what he walked into, it was his fault, not hers. The assistant purser seemed a little concerned, but Kiva applied a little pressure to make it clear festivities were to continue.

"It's important."

"Trust me, so is this."

"We've got a customs official who won't let us take any haver-fruit off the ship," Brennir said. If he was shocked or scandalized by Lagos's activities he was doing a good job of hiding it. He mostly looked bored. "Offloading our haverfruit is why we came to End. If we don't sell it, or develop licenses, we're screwed. You're the owner's representative. You're going to have to explain to your mother why this trip was the cause of the financial ruin of your family. So perhaps you might like to join Captain Blinnikka in talking with this customs official *right now* to see if you can resolve this problem. Or you can just go on fucking that junior crew member, ma'am. I'm sure those are equivalent activities as regards your future, and the future of this ship, and your family."

"Well, shit," Kiva said. Her groove was definitely gone, and the assistant purser, her little project, looked pretty miserable at the moment. "That was a pretty impressive jab you just gave to someone who can fire your ass, Brennir."

"You can't fire me, ma'am," Brennir said. "I've got tenure with the guild. Now, are you coming or not?"

"I'm thinking."

"I should go," the assistant purser said. "I mean, I can go. Maybe I should go?"

Kiva sighed and looked down at her conquest. "When are you on duty again?"

"Three hours."

"Then you stay right here." She untangled herself from the assistant purser, put on something acceptable for the outside world, and then followed Brennir out of her stateroom and through the ship.

The *Yes, Sir, That's My Baby* was a fiver, a ship whose size and design meant that theoretically it could support a full complement of crew from its own resources for roughly five standard years before everything began to go bad, internal biological and support systems began to fail, and the crew collapsed into a brief spasm of unspeakable horror toward each other before the end, as all crews marooned in the vast emptiness of space with no hope of rescue eventually did.

As a practical matter, however, within the Flow streams of

the Interdependency, no one human outpost was more than nine months from any other. Fivers and tenners, their larger siblings, typically dedicated enough of themselves to support their crews for a year—a three-month margin for error—and the rest of their space and systems were given over to cargo and, in the case of the *Yes, Sir,* astroponics, growing the agricultural products that the ship's owners had a monopoly on and traveled from outpost to outpost to deliver.

The House of Lagos, the owners of the *Yes, Sir,* had a monopoly on citrus. The entire genus, from root to fruit, from the heirloom species like lemons and oranges to more recent hybrids like gabins, zestfists, and haverfruit. It was the last of these that the *Yes, Sir* had come to End to do business in—to sell the fruit it had grown and harvested on the trip out to End directly, and to negotiate licensing for local agribusiness to grow it on End on behalf of the Lagos family.

That was the plan, anyway. Except now some asshole customs official was trying to fuck them all.

Kiva entered the *Yes, Sir* conference room where Captain Tomi Blinnikka, Chief Purser Gazson Magnut, and some miserable shitfuck of an imperial customs official waited. Kiva nodded to Blinnikka and Magnut and took a seat at the table they were at. Blinnikka dismissed Brennir, who slid the door closed behind him as he left.

"All right, what's the problem?" Kiva said, when Brennir was gone.

"Lady Kiva, I am Inspector Pretan Vanosh, assistant head of imperial customs for End," the miserable shitfuck began.

"Charmed," Kiva said, cutting him off. "What's the problem?"

"The problem is a closterovirus," Vanosh said. "That's a type of virus—"

"My family has had the monopoly on citrus fruits for eight

hundred years, Mr. Vanosh," Kiva said. "I know what a clostero-virus is. I also know it's been two hundred years since we've had a confirmed case of a citrus closterovirus affecting any of the crops we either sell or license. We genetically engineer our crops for resistance."

Vanosh smiled thinly and offered up a physical folder to Kiva, who took it. "That clock has been reset, Lady Kiva," he said. "Nine months ago your sister ship, *No, Sir, I Don't Mean Maybe*, arrived with a shipment of grapefruit graft stock that carried a new strain of virus. It spread through your licensed orchards and devastated your client's crops."

"All right, but so what?" Kiva said. "If it did happen, and I'm not going to stipulate it did until we have our own people take a look, then we'll compensate the clients and plow under the orchards. It doesn't have anything to do with this shipment of haverfruit."

"It's not that simple," Vanosh said. "The virus is cross-compatible with some of End's local crops, including banu, a staple down there. We've had to quarantine entire provinces to halt its spread. Food prices are through the roof. People are concerned about the possibility of famine. The Duke of End was already battling an insurgency. This has made it worse." Vanosh leaned forward on the table, toward Lagos. "To put it bluntly, Lady Kiva, the House of Lagos has helped to destabilize this entire planet."

Kiva stared at this official fuckwit in disbelief. "You can't think we intended—"

Now it was Vanosh's turn to cut off Lagos. "Lady Kiva, it doesn't *matter* what your house intended, what matters is what it *did*. What it did in this case is pour oil onto a fire. Until this is resolved in a court of law, I'm afraid your trade rights for End are suspended."

"I don't know about any of this," Kiva said.

"Everything about the virus is in the report."

"Not about the fucking *virus*. About the destabilization and the famine or any of the rest of that crap. You can't pin it on us."

"It's not all pinned onto your family, Lady Kiva, I assure you. But enough can be pinned to your family to have caused this suspension."

"Is this is a squeeze?" Kiva asked.

Vanosh blinked. "I beg your pardon?"

"You heard me. Is this a squeeze? Are you hitting us up for a bribe?"

"A bribe?"

"Yes."

"I'm not sure what part of this discussion suggested to you that I was fishing for a bribe, Lady Kiva."

"Oh, for fuck's sake, don't be coy," Kiva said, irritably. "Let's pretend we're all adults here and we don't have to get cute about a business transaction. Tell me what you *want*"—she jabbed a thumb at Magnut, whose expression suggested he couldn't believe this particular conversation was actually happening— "and Magnut here will take care of the rest."

Vanosh turned to Magnut. "Do you bribe imperial customs officers often, Chief Purser Magnut?"

"Don't answer that," Captain Blinnikka said, to Magnut. Magnut looked visibly relieved to be told to stay quiet. Blinnikka turned to Vanosh. "My apologies, Inspector. Our owner's representative is understandably frustrated at the moment and chose her words foolishly. I assure you that it is not our policy to attempt to bribe imperial officials, nor should Lady Kiva's outburst suggest that any of us believe you are bribable. Isn't that correct, Lady Kiva?"

Kiva gave her starship captain a long look of *you have to be fucking kidding me, pal* and then, having received an *I am so not fucking kidding you, you asshole* look back from the captain, turned her attention back to Vanosh. "Yes. I made a bad joke. Sorry about that."

"Perhaps you should stay out of the field of comedy, Lady Kiva," Vanosh said.

"That's a hot tip, thanks for that."

"In any event, Lady Kiva, Captain Blinnikka, you appear to be under the impression that *I'm* the reason your goods are sequestered and your trade privileges suspended."

"Aren't you?" Kiva asked.

Vanosh smiled, again thinly, which made Lagos wonder if he could smile any other way. "If it were up to me, Lady Kiva, I would have taken the bribe and then threatened to have all three of you arrested, and then pocketed the even larger second bribe."

"I *knew* it," Kiva said. "You shifty little fucker."

Vanosh nodded his head slightly in acknowledgment. "However, in this case, the directive comes from over my head. In point of fact, Lady Kiva, the ban on your haverfruit and any trade your ship and your family might conduct on End comes from the duke himself." Vanosh handed over another document, this one a traditional folded letter on heavy parchment, sealed in wax with the ducal signet, which meant the Duke of End was very much not fucking around on this one. "You will have to take it up with him," Vanosh continued.

Kiva took it. "Well, this is just fucking perfect, isn't it," she said.

"Indeed," Vanosh said. "If I may offer a suggestion, Lady Kiva."

"Yes?"

"The Duke of End owns most of the planet. Maybe don't try to bribe him."

•   •   •

Arranging a meeting with the Duke of End took a day. The Port of Endfall wasn't allowing direct shuttle flights from ships— "We had some shot at when they came in for a landing"—so Kiva had to shuttle to Imperial Station, the massive space station where the empire kept the majority of its business, and take the beanstalk, heavily fortified from insurgent attack, down to port. There she was met by a local family lackey, who welcomed her and led her to her car.

"What the hell is this?" Kiva asked when she saw it. The car was less of a car than a small tank.

"In order to reach the duke's palace, we're going to have to go through some rough neighborhoods, Lady Kiva," the lackey said.

"You don't think this looks a little conspicuous? That it doesn't have 'shoot at me' blinking over it in bright lights?"

"Ma'am, at the moment, pretty much anything that moves is being shot at." The lackey opened the passenger compartment door. "For that matter, anything that stays still for too long is shot at, too." He motioned her inside. Kiva took the hint.

The inside of the passenger compartment of the little tank was reasonably luxurious, at least. Kiva sat down and strapped in and acknowledged the other two people in the compartment with her, executives for the family here on End.

One of them extended her hand to Lagos. "Lady Kiva, I'm Eiota Finn, your local executive vice president for the House of Lagos." Kiva shook it, and Finn used her other hand to motion to the third occupant. "This is Jonan Rue, head of your legal department here." Rue nodded.

"Hi," Kiva said, to both.

"You won't remember, but you and I have met before," Finn said, to Kiva. "Before I was assigned to End, I worked in your mother's office in Ikoyi. You were a child then, of course."

"Right. Well, that's a great story, Finn, but at the moment you'll forgive me if I don't really give a shit if you met me when I was six. I want to know what the fuck is going on with this ban."

Finn smiled. "You're definitely your mother's child," she said. "She was also blunt and to the point."

"Yes, we're a family of assholes," Kiva said, and the car lurched forward. "Now, explain."

Finn nodded to Rue. "We have two problems right now, Lady Kiva, and they're related. The first is the ban. The second is the rebellion."

Kiva furrowed her brow at this. "What does the rebellion have to do with us?"

"Politically, nothing. It's just another rebellion."

" 'Just another'? How many rebellions does this goddamned planet have?"

"One or two a decade," Finn said. "The planet's called 'End' for a reason, Lady Kiva. It's the farthest human outpost in the Interdependency and the most difficult to get to, and the only one where the residents don't have guaranteed travel privileges. It's been the dumping ground for all the empire's rebels and dissidents for centuries. They don't all just start playing nice when they get here."

As if to accentuate the point, there was a loud *thock* from one of the side panels.

"What was that?" Kiva asked the driver.

"Exploratory shot, ma'am. Nothing to worry about."

"Being shot at is nothing to worry about?"

"If they'd been serious, they would have hit us with a rocket."

Kiva looked back to Finn. "You people do this once a decade."

"Once or twice a decade, yes."

"You don't have other things to take up your time? Sport teams? Board games?"

"Usually the rebellions are confined to outer provinces," Rue said. "They pop up, the reigning duke sends in the Home Guard, it's over in a couple of months. This one is different."

"This one is organized," Finn said. "It's got some firepower behind it."

"Yeah, I figured that part out on my own," Kiva said. "But I'm still not hearing what it has to do with us."

"As I said, politically, nothing," Rue continued. "But this particular rebellion has been expensive to fight. Tax revenues are dropping because of business disruption. That money's got to come from somewhere."

"From us?"

"From us," Rue agreed.

"Not just us," Finn amended. "He's putting the squeeze on all guild interests here. Higher taxes and tariffs, for a start. The duke pushed them up to the imperial legal limit."

"But that wasn't enough," Rue said. "So at that point, the duke started getting creative."

"When the virus was reported on the grapefruit, the duke froze the banking accounts of the House of Lagos," Finn said. "Theoretically they're in escrow pending legal determination of damages to End in the spread of the virus to native crops."

"How are we responsible for that?" Kiva asked.

"We might not be," Rue said. "That'll need to be decided in court. But if the duke can prove that the virus was introduced into the End ecosystem due to negligence on our part, he's entitled by imperial law to compensation and penalties."

"And in the meantime, to keep us from repatriating profits to Ikoyi and potentially out of the reach of the duke, our accounts are in escrow here," Finn said.

"But they're not really in escrow, are they?" Kiva said, and pointed out the small, thick, bulletproof window. "The duke is using them to fund the fight against these rebels."

Rue smiled, thinly. Everyone on End, apparently, smiled that way. "As it happens, when the duke declared the current state of emergency, he nationalized the banks. The official line is that it's to tamp down on financial panics and speculations. But the executives at the guild banks tell us he's raiding accounts."

Kiva snorted. "Well, *that's* nice."

"It's not a bad plan, at least as it relates to the House of Lagos," Finn admitted. "If he beats the rebellion, he has all the time it will take for the litigation to run to replace the funds he's stolen. That will be years."

"And if he loses then it won't matter anyway, because he'll probably be dead," Rue said.

Kiva grunted at this and looked out the window. End's capital city of Inverness rolled by, run-down, unhappy, a few sooty fires in the distance. "Will he?"

"Will he what?" Finn asked.

"Will he lose?"

Finn and Rue looked at each other. "It wouldn't be the first time a Duke of End has been deposed," Finn said.

"Fine, but what about *this* one?" Kiva asked. "Are we wasting our fucking time going to talk to this asshole?"

"It's not looking great for the duke, no," Rue said, after a minute. "We've heard rumors of desertions in the provinces, and of military commanders changing sides and taking their soldiers with them. We'll probably know within the next week how things are going to shake out."

Kiva pointed upward. "And what about *those* assholes? The imperials? The duke is a goddamned noble, after all. They would probably see it as *bad optics* to have him dragged out in the street and shot."

"This is End, Lady Kiva," Rue said. "As long as the Interdependency gets its percentage of trade, everything else is an internal matter."

"Including the death of a duke?"

"It wouldn't be the first time a Duke of End has been deposed," Finn repeated.

"We're about to arrive at the palace," the driver said. "It'll take a few minutes to get through the security checkpoints. Ma'am, may I have your invitation to the palace?"

Kiva passed it forward and then turned her attention back to her underlings. "So basically what I do now is go in and beg this motherfucker to let me sell my haverfruit, and if he does, expect him to put any profit into this so-called escrow and never see it again."

"Not for years, no," Finn said. "Best-case scenario."

"Why the fuck didn't you see this coming?" Lagos asked Finn, and jabbed a finger toward the heavily fortified palace, visible through the front windshield. "We're sitting here grabbing our own tits while this asshole is using our cash to play whack-a-mole with insurgents."

"As it happens, I *did* see it coming," Finn said. "Which is why the accounts that are escrowed were only about half as full as they were the minute the first reports of the virus started coming in."

"Where's the rest of the money? Did you bury it in the backyard?"

"In a manner of speaking. The House of Lagos has become, through a number of intermediaries, owners of quite a lot of property."

Kiva motioned around. "Not *here*, I hope. This fucking town is on fire."

"No. Mostly in the provinces of Tomnahurich and Claremont. Particularly Claremont. The local count there was keen on offloading a number of very nice properties. He wanted to achieve liquidity, fast."

"Of course he did. Nobles don't tend to be popular during revolutions."

"No, they don't, Lady Kiva."

The car started moving forward again. "There are two other things you should know going into this meeting with the duke," Rue said, to Kiva.

"Tell me."

Rue handed over a sheet. "One, we did as you asked and followed up on that virus. There was absolutely *no* evidence of viral infection on those grapefruit grafts until after they made it to orchards here on End. Nothing in the stock or fruit in the warehouses, and nothing on the samples that were tested on the *No, Sir* before she left."

Kiva took the sheet and looked at it. "So you think it's sabotage."

"Pretty sure of that, yes. Whether we can prove that to the satisfaction of a court is another matter. Which brings us to the other thing. The duke has an advisor from one of the guild houses. You're not going to like which house it is."

Kiva looked up. "Oh, don't you even fucking say it."

"It's the House of Nohamapetan."

• • •

The name of the ducal castle was Kinmylies. It was overly plush in a manner that suggested that the residents had confused excess for elegance. Kiva, who came from a line of immensely wealthy people who didn't give a shit whether their wealth impressed you or not, immediately felt twitchy within its walls. *This place needs a cleansing fucking fire*, she thought, as she was led down one interminable hallway after another, on her way to the Duke of End's office.

"One thing," Finn said to Kiva as the page came to retrieve her. "The duke finds profanity a mark of a lesser intellect. Try to avoid it with him if you can."

What an asshole, she thought, as she stepped into the duke's office, as vomitiously ornate as any other part of the palace. The family legend had it that Kiva Lagos's very first word as an infant was "fuck," a legend that was entirely liable to be true, given the swearing propensity of the Countess Huma Lagos, Kiva's mother and head of the House of Lagos. It would have been more surprising if it wasn't, frankly. Kiva couldn't remember ever not swearing, and of course as the daughter of Countess Lagos, even as the sixth child with no shot at the title, no one was ever going to tell her to stop.

And now *this* prick, who had a jabong up his ass about it.

The prick in question, the one with the rectally stored jabong, was standing at his office bar, a tumbler of some amber liquid in his hand, tall with a beard that could hide birds in it, laughing. Standing next to him, also with a tumbler, also laughing, and in his family's pretentiously simple black, was none other than Ghreni Nohamapetan.

The page cleared his throat and the duke looked up. "The Lady Kiva Lagos," the page said, and departed.

"My dear Lady Kiva," said the Duke of End, coming away from the bar. "Welcome. Welcome."

"Your Grace," Kiva said, and gave a bare nod. As the daughter of a house head and ranking representative of the house on the planet, Lagos could have simply addressed him as "Duke" and gotten away with it. But she was here to kiss ass, so might as well get to the puckering early.

"Allow me to introduce my advisor, Lord Ghreni, of the House of Nohamapetan."

"We've met," Ghreni said, to the duke.

"Have you now?"

"We went to school together," Ghreni said.

"What a small world," remarked the duke.

"Isn't it just," Kiva replied.

"Yes, well. Sit down, Lady Kiva," the duke said, motioning to the left-hand chair in front of his desk. Lagos took it, an over-stuffed monstrosity she nearly disappeared into, with Ghreni taking the chair on the right. The duke sat down in his own fucking parody of a chair, behind a desk a poor family could make a house out of. "I do regret that the circumstances of our meeting could not be better."

"I understand, sir. It is challenging when you have insurgents almost knocking on your door."

"What? No," the duke said, and Kiva saw Ghreni twitch out the very smallest of smiles. "No, not that. I meant the difficulty with this virus your house brought to us."

"Truly," Kiva said. "Are you sure that we brought it, sir?"

"What do you mean?"

"I mean our investigators here did not find it in any of the samples in our warehouse, or on the *No, Sir*. It only showed up in the orchards."

"This is news to us," Ghreni said.

"Is it?" Kiva replied, looking at him directly. "Well, if it is, my representatives have made a report." She looked over to the duke. "They've filed it with your secretary's office, along with the notice of an appeal for the lifting of our trade ban."

"I don't think lifting that ban would be wise," Ghreni said.

"With all due respect to your representatives and their investigators, Kiva, until that study can be thoroughly examined, the duke, for the safety of the citizens of End, has to assume that any other product you carry is likewise infected."

"I'm afraid your friend is correct about that," the duke said, to Kiva. "You've heard about how the virus crossed over to our banu. Wiped out the crop in entire areas. We can't risk another event like that. The banu failure is one of the reasons we have this rebellion in the first place."

"I understand your concern, sir, and that is why the House of Lagos is willing to assist you."

The duke squinted at Kiva. "How do you mean?"

"I understand you have placed our accounts in escrow, pending resolution of a court case regarding the virus."

Kiva watched the duke's eyes flicker, briefly, over to Ghreni's before coming back to her own. "So I have. It was the prudent course of action."

"Allow me to formally offer those sums to you as a loan from the House of Lagos to assist you in resisting this rebellion. We would be happy to offer you excellent terms."

"That's . . . generous of you," the duke said.

"It's business," Kiva replied. "It does the House of Lagos no good to have you out of power, sir. And this allows you access to funds that you would not otherwise have at your disposal. Why should that money sit and do you no good? Put it to use."

"I'm afraid it's not that simple," Ghreni said.

"Actually it *is* that simple," Kiva retorted. "We can write it into the loan that if the House of Lagos is found liable, the loan represents the damages and that any remainder plus interest on the loan constitutes penalties."

"It's not a matter of legalities, it's the matter of perception," Ghreni said.

"The perception of the duke robustly defending his people looks bad? Worse than the perception of a duke being overthrown because he's too daintily concerned about looking bad?"

Ghreni turned to the duke. "Sir, it looks like a bribe."

"A bribe for *what*?" Kiva exclaimed.

"Well, that's the question, isn't it?" Ghreni said.

"Lady Kiva, in exchange for this generosity by the House of Lagos, what would you expect?" asked the duke.

"Again, and with respect, sir, it's not generosity. If the suit fails, the House of Lagos would expect to get our loan back. That's business."

"But you want something else, too, don't you?" Ghreni asked.

"Of course I do. I want to be able to sell my god—" Kiva caught herself at the last moment. "—blessed haverfruit, sir. And when I do, the money we make on the sale and licensing will *not* go with the *Yes, Sir* when we leave. It'll stay here, with you, as part of the loan."

"Along with any additional viruses your crop might be carrying," Ghreni said.

Kiva looked over to the duke. "Sir, there are inspectors at Imperial Station. They do random sampling of our cargo anyway. I'm happy to have them do an in-depth inspection of the haverfruit to assure it's clean and poses no threat to the End biome."

The Duke of End at least appeared to think about it, but then he stared over at Ghreni, who sat impassively, and shook his head. "Lady Kiva, you have been kind, both with your offer and your concern. But I don't believe that such measures will be necessary. I believe this rebellion will be contained presently. As such your offer will be unneeded. As for your haverfruit, until we have time to thoroughly examine your report, I need to err on the side of caution. I'm afraid I'm unable to lift your trade ban until the conclusion of the trial. I know you understand."

"You bet your ass I do," Kiva said, and stood.

"Excuse me?" the duke said, standing. Ghreni stood as well.

"Thank you for your time, sir. Will you call me a page so I can find my way out of this goddamned maze?"

"Allow me to walk the Lady Kiva out, sir," Ghreni said, to the duke, smoothly.

"Yes, of course." The duke nodded his good-bye to both of them and headed back over to his bar.

"You motherfucker," Kiva said, to Ghreni, as soon as they exited his office.

"It's nice to see you too," Ghreni said.

"You better hope I don't find you or the House of Nohama-petan is behind this fucking virus. Because if I do, I will come all the way back to End to feast on your fucking heart."

"You're always welcome to visit me, of course."

"So, are you?"

"Behind the virus?"

"Yes."

"Obviously I am not, but even if I were, I don't think you're foolish enough to believe I would tell you."

"You could save me a trip."

"Now, why would I want to do that?"

"You haven't changed, Ghreni."

"And you shouldn't feel too bad, Kiva." Ghreni motioned back toward the duke's office. "You almost had him with that offer of a loan. That was smart, by the way. As a guild house any loan you make to a noble in the defense of the imperial system is backed by the empire itself. A fine way to cover your ass."

"Until you screwed me."

"I'd think you'd be used to that by now."

Kiva snorted at this. "Don't think I didn't notice *that*, Ghreni. 'We went to school together,' my ass."

"It was much more politic than how you would have put it. 'I fucked his brains out whenever he went to visit his sister in her dormitory at university.'"

"I wouldn't have said it like that," Kiva said. "I was told not to swear. How is your asshole sister, anyway?"

"Not happy. She was going to be crown princess of the empire, but then Rennered Wu lost his head in a racing accident."

"A real tragedy for her."

"She thinks so. It was bad for Rennered as well, of course. I understand the emperox's bastard daughter is now the heir. So my brother will take a run at her, I imagine."

"There's the Nohamapetan family I remember. Full of romantics."

"You didn't complain, once."

Kiva stopped and looked at Ghreni, who also stopped. "Well, once I was a fucking idiot. Now I'm not."

"That would be a first for a Lagos, then," Ghreni said.

"What scam do you have running on this dipshit duke?"

"One, his name is Ferd, and not 'dipshit.' Two, I'm offended you think I'm running a scam on him."

"You got him to shake off a multimillion-mark bribe."

"See, I told you it was a bribe. I was right."

"No one passes up that much unless they've got something better on offer."

"I can't possibly speak to that, Kiva. Certainly not to you."

"Come on, Ghreni. This isn't about the virus. And we're on fucking End. It's going to take me nine months to get back to Hub and another three from there to Ikoyi. Anything you tell me now is going to be dead news then."

Ghreni looked around, and then started walking again. Kiva caught up. "Tell me. Tell me what you have planned for End."

"Your first error, Kiva, is assuming that anything I'm doing *here* has to do with just this planet."

"I don't follow."

"I know you don't. I didn't intend for you to." Ghreni stopped again, and then pointed. "Take this hall. Then the second left, and then the first right after that. You'll be back to the same lobby you came in from."

Kiva nodded. "You were never one to go all the way to the end of things, were you, Ghreni?"

"You might be surprised." He leaned in and gave Kiva a peck on the cheek. "Good-bye, my dear Kiva. I wasn't ever expecting to see you again, you know. No one important really ever comes to End. And I don't expect to see you again after this. But I am fond of you, in spite of everything. So I'm glad we got a moment for this."

"Whatever this is."

Ghreni smiled. "You'll have a name for it soon," he said, and walked off.

•   •   •

"Hit me with it," Kiva said, back on *Yes, Sir*, with Captain Blinnikka and Gazson Magnut.

"We were supposed to take receipt of roughly sixty million marks' worth of licensing fees and royalties here on End," Magnut said. "We're going to come away with zero, all in escrow, and we probably won't get it back. We estimated that the haverfruit would generate twenty million marks for the product on hand and another ten million marks in initial license fees and stock sales. We're coming away with another zero for that. We have another roughly ten million marks in miscellaneous cargo picked up at other stops that we're not being allowed to unload and sell, so zero for that, too. There's about a million marks' worth of cargo being sent to End that we're acting as shipping for, and that was allowed to be unloaded, but has been placed in quarantine for several weeks in a hold open to the vacuum of space. We'll be gone when the delivery happens and the fees will be held for the next Lagos ship to arrive. Which is the *I Think We're Alone Now*, which will be along in twenty standard months."

"So, a hundred-million-mark loss," Kiva said.

"We netted forty million marks on the last three stops, so it's a net sixty-million-mark loss, more or less. And this is the last stop on the itinerary. Then back to Hub to transfer to Ikoyi."

Lagos nodded. Using the Flow there were several ways to get to End, but only one way to get back—the Flow stream from End to Hub. Sooner or later, all streams flowed into Hub. But what that meant was there was no other chance to recoup losses between End and Hub.

"I'm open to ideas, here," Kiva said. "Tomi?"

"The whole point was to introduce haverfruit to End," the captain said. "Everyone else in the Interdependency is already full up on it. We can harvest what we have—we're going to have to, at this point—vacuum flash out the water and sell the concentrate at Hub. But your family already has licensees there. They could complain to the imperial trade commission if we came in and undersold them."

"The captain's right," Magnut said. "And even if we matched prices we'd create a glut. We'd pick up a few million marks at most, and piss off the licensees the House of Lagos needs for long-term profits."

"So what we're saying is we're fucked."

"That would be the gist of it, yes, ma'am."

Kiva put her head in her hands for a couple of moments, then looked over to Blinnikka. "When do we leave End?"

"We have some ship maintenance we're taking care of while we're here at Imperial Station, and Gazson here is taking on some additional crew to make up for the ones we lost at Lankaran. We're here for another week."

"Can we stretch that?"

"Not really," Blinnikka said. "Our current dock is claimed nine days from now. Imperial Station needs a full day for cargo clearance and reset. We have seven days and then we have to move."

"Then seven days it is."

"Seven days for what?" Magnut asked.

"For a fucking miracle to happen and save our asses," Kiva said. "That's not too much to ask for, is it?"

Technically speaking, upon the moment of the death of Emperox Attavio IV, Cardenia became the new emperox. Realistically speaking, nothing is ever that simple.

"You are going to have to officially declare a period of mourning," Naffa Dolg said to her, in what had suddenly and officially become her office. It was now only moments after her father had died; his body was currently being removed from his bedroom—her bedroom—via a litter that had borne the bodies of nearly all the emperoxs who had been lucky enough to actually die at home. Cardenia had seen the litter, stored away in one of the other rooms in the private apartment, and thought it a ghastly bit of business, and realized that one day, it was very likely her bones would be carted out on it too. Tradition had its downsides.

Cardenia laughed to herself.

"Car?" Naffa said.

"I'm having morbid thoughts," Cardenia said.

"I can give you a couple of minutes for yourself."

"But only a couple."

"The transition of emperoxs is a busy time," Naffa said, as gently as possible.

"How long is the official mourning period supposed to be?"

"It's traditionally five standard days."

Cardenia nodded. "The rest of the Interdependency gets five days. I get five minutes."

"I'm going to come back," Naffa said, getting up.

"No." Cardenia shook her head. "Keep me busy, Naf."

Naffa kept her busy.

First: the official declaration of mourning. Cardenia went down the hall to the office of Gell Deng, her father's (and now, unless she chose otherwise, her) personal secretary, who would transmit the order. Cardenia was worried that she would have to dictate something that sounded official, but Deng had the declaration already ready for her—which shouldn't have surprised her. Many emperoxs had come and gone during the time of the Interdependency.

Cardenia read over the declaration, its contents hallowed by time and consecrated by tradition, found the language ossified and musty, but was in no condition mentally to revise. So she nodded her assent, took a pen to sign, and then hesitated.

"What is it, Your Majesty?" Deng said, and some part of Cardenia's brain noted that this was the first time anyone had called her that officially.

"I don't know how to sign this," Cardenia said. "I haven't chosen my official name yet."

"If you prefer, you may simply sign it with the imperial seal for now."

"Yes, thank you."

Deng got out wax and seal, melted the wax, and gave the seal to Cardenia to press. She did, the seal lifting off the imperial green wax, revealing the crest of the Wu family with the imperial crown above it. Her crown.

Cardenia handed the seal back to Deng and noticed he was

crying. "This makes it official," he said to her. "You are the emperox now, Your Majesty."

"How long did you serve my father?" Cardenia asked.

"Thirty-nine years," Deng said, and looked about to break down. Impulsively Cardenia reached over and hugged him, and after a moment broke the hug.

"I'm sorry," she said. "I shouldn't have done that."

"You're the emperox, ma'am," Deng said. "You can do anything you want."

"Keep me from inappropriate familiarity from now on, please," Cardenia said to Naffa, after they left the secretary's office.

"I thought it was sweet," Naffa said. "That poor old man. He's had a rough day."

"His boss died."

"Yes, but he also assumes he lost his job. Normally by this time the new emperox's set of cronies are busy installing themselves into positions of power. His is a position of power, nominally."

"I don't have any cronies," Cardenia said. "I mean, besides you."

"Don't worry, you'll have volunteers."

"What do I have next?"

"You're meeting with the executive committee in half an hour."

Cardenia frowned at this. "We can't get to Xi'an that quickly." The executive committee, as with nearly all of the imperial apparatus of state, did its work in the immense space station above Hub.

Naffa arched her eyebrow at this. "*You* don't have to go anywhere," she said. "You are emperox now. They come to you. Dr. Drinin informed them several hours ago that your father was fading. The committee had hoped to be present to comfort you when he passed. Those are their words, by the way."

Cardenia thought of the nine members of the executive committee hovering over her father's deathbed, robbing the two of them of their final, as-intimate-as-possible-under-the-circumstances moments together and suppressed an itchy feeling. "I'll have to remember to thank them."

Naffa's eyebrow arched again but she said nothing. "They're in the formal ballroom at the moment. That's on the other side of the building."

"Thank you."

"Of course. What would you like to do now?"

"I think I want to pee."

Naffa nodded and walked Cardenia to her suite of rooms. "I'll be back in fifteen minutes," she said to her boss.

"What will you do with your free time?"

"Same thing as you, in a slightly less luxurious commode." Cardenia smiled at this, and Naffa walked off.

Inside her rooms, part of Cardenia's brain noted everything she was doing as a first. *This is the first time in this room as emperox,* it said. *This is the first time picking up a tablet as emperox. This is the first time in this bathroom as emperox. This is the first time I've unzipped my pants as emperox. First time sitting on the toilet as emperox. Aaaaaaand now this is my first pee as emperox.*

So many firsts.

"Tell me about Emperox Grayland," Cardenia said, to her tablet, as she sat on the toilet.

"Emperox Grayland reigned from 220 to 223 FI," her tablet said, in a pleasant voice, popping up a search page. The Interdependency started its calendar from the founding of the empire by Prophet-Emperox Rachela I, which was arrogant—there had already been a perfectly good calendar system in use, in which the founding of the Interdependency took place in the late twenty-sixth century—but Cardenia suspected it was no less arrogant than what any empire did, given the chance. "Notable events in her reign include the founding of Lamphun, the disappearance of Dalasýsla, and the emperox's assassination by Gunnar Olafsen in 223."

"Why was she assassinated?"

"At his trial, Gunnar Olafsen maintained the emperox did not do enough to rescue the citizens of Dalasýsla."

"Was this true?"

"I am a search function. I do not have opinions on political matters."

Cardenia crossed her eyes in irritation. *Fair point, faceless computer,* she thought. "How was Dalasýsla lost?"

"The Flow stream access to it disappeared in 222," the tablet said.

Oh, right, Cardenia thought. Her elementary school Interdependency history lessons came back to her now. Dalasýsla was one of several early settlements that had met with a bad end before the Wu emperoxs and the religious and social tenets of Interdependence had entirely locked down most opposition. Most of those settlements, however, had been lost to war or famine or disease. Dalasýsla was lost because suddenly there was no way to get to it, or from it, through the Flow. It had just . . . disappeared, off the map entirely.

Cardenia called up an encyclopedia article on the assassination, complete with a photo of Olafsen, a ship engineer from Dalasýsla, who had been stationed on the *Toun Sandin,* the imperial tenner. He had assassinated the Emperox Grayland, along with more than a hundred of her retinue, by sealing off the ring segment her staterooms were in, and, while the *Toun Sandin* was in the Flow, returning from a state visit from Jendouba, jettisoning the ring segment out of the time-space bubble surrounding the ship, into the Flow itself, where it promptly stopped existing.

"Well, *this* is cheerful," Cardenia said to herself. She was not entirely sure why her father had suggested the name Grayland to her, unless he was confident she would be assassinated by a disgruntled minion. This discomfited her somewhat. She skimmed through the rest of the entry and noted that Grayland had apparently actually ordered the evacuation of Dalasýsla, based on data provided to her by scientists, but that the evacuation had been opposed in parliament, including by Dalasýsla's own ministers, and by the guilds, which delayed an evacuation until it was too late. Olafsen blamed the emperox for the delay, when the blame should have properly set elsewhere.

But there is only one emperox, Cardenia thought. *And she was on his ship.*

"Hey," Naffa said, from the other room. "Are you about done?"

"Almost," Cardenia said. She finished her business, washed up, and walked out of her bathroom, to see Naffa holding up a very serious uniform, tailored to Cardenia's measurements.

"What is that?" Cardenia asked.

"You're about to meet the nine most powerful humans in the universe, not counting yourself," Naffa said. "You might want to dress up a bit."

• • •

The Very Serious Uniform chafed, but not nearly as much as the executive committee.

As Cardenia entered the cavernous ballroom, the nine members of the committee approached her and bowed deeply. "Your Majesty," said Gunda Korbijn, archbishop of Xi'an and nominal head of the executive committee, from the depth of the bow. "Our deepest sorrow and sympathy this day, on the passing of your father, the emperox. He will undoubtedly be seated with the Prophet in the Beyond."

Cardenia, who knew of the emperox's utter lack of religiosity, despite being the official head of the Church of the Interdependency, suppressed the smallest of wry smiles. "Thank you, Your Eminence."

"I speak for the entire council when I say to you that we pledge our unending allegiance to you, the Imperial House of Wu, and the Interdependency."

"Sure, and we thank you," Cardenia said, using for the first time the imperial "we," and the somewhat more formal imperial style of address she'd been coached in over the last year. *That's going to take some getting used to*, she thought. She glanced over at Naffa, who offered no arched brow at the switch. She would no doubt offer it later.

The committee remained in a deep bow, which confused Cardenia until she realized they were waiting on her to release them. "Please," she said, only a little flustered, motioning for them to rise. They rose. Cardenia motioned to the long table that had been set in the center of the ballroom. "Let us sit and proceed with business."

The committee sat, senior-most closest to the emperox's chair at the head of the table, with the exception of Archbishop Korbijn, who sat opposite of Cardenia. Cardenia noted the dress of each—the church bishops in fine red robes lined in purple, the guild representatives in their formal black and gold, the parliamentarians in somber blue business suits. Her own Very Serious Uniform was imperial green, dark with emerald piping.

We look like a box of crayons, Cardenia thought.

"You're smiling, Your Majesty," Archbishop Korbijn said, as she sat.

"We were remembering our father, who often spoke of meeting with this committee."

"He spoke well of us, I hope."

No, not really. "Yes, of course."

"Your Majesty, the next few days are critical. You must set forth a period of mourning—"

"We have already done so, Your Eminence. We shall observe the traditional five days."

"Very good," Korbijn said, giving no sign of fluster at being interrupted. "During that time you yourself will unfortunately be quite busy." She nodded to Bishop Vear of Hub, sitting to Cardenia's right, who produced a leather folder and from it, a thick sheaf of papers, and offered them to Cardenia. "We have produced a proposed schedule for you, to assist you. It includes a number of briefings, plus formal and informal meetings with the guilds, parliament, and the church."

Cardenia took the papers but did not look at them, handing them over to Naffa, standing behind her chair. "We thank you."

"We wish to assure you that during this time of transition, everything will be handled smoothly and with the utmost care and respect. We know this is a difficult time for you, and much of this is new. We want to be able to help you transition smoothly into your new role, Your Majesty."

You want to help me transition, or to manage me? "Once more, we thank you, Archbishop. We are warmed by your concern and solicitousness."

"We have other concerns as well," said Lenn Edmunk, one of the guild representatives. The House of Edmunk held the commercial monopolies on cows and pigs and all products deriving thereof, from milk to pig leather. "Your father left unresolved a number of issues with the guilds, including monopoly transfers and trade route clearances."

Cardenia noted Archbishop Korbijn pursing her lips; clearly Edmunk was speaking out of turn. "We have been led to understand that these matters must be sent through parliament, then for us to give our assent or refusal."

"Your father gave assurances these matters would be dealt with, Your Majesty."

"Would this be in a way that circumvents the privileges of parliament, Lord Edmunk?"

"Of course not, ma'am," Edmunk said, after a moment.

"We are glad to hear that. One of the things we would like not to do at this early juncture is to give the parliament the opinion that their role is merely an advisory one, subject to the whims of the emperox." She turned to Upeksha Ranatunga, the ranking parliamentarian on the committee, seated to her left, who nodded her thanks. "Our father believed in the balance of power that has allowed the Interdependency to thrive: the parliament for the laws and justice; the guilds for trade and prosperity; the church for spirituality and community. And above them, the emperox, mother of all, for order."

"With that said, ma'am—"

"Do not forget that the House of Wu also has a guild," Cardenia said, interrupting Edmunk, who was clearly put out by this point. "We would not thereby discount the interests of the guilds. We are also mother of the church and a simple member of parliament. We have interest in all, to be fair to all. We shall address guild matters in their time, Lord Edmunk. But we are not our father. His assurances to you are not unheard. But neither am I bound to them. *I* am emperox now, not my father."

There, Cardenia thought, and stared levelly at Edmunk. *Suck on that for a while.*

Edmunk dropped his head in a bow. "Ma'am," he said.

"With regard to parliament, ma'am, there is another, serious issue," Ranatunga said. "Word has come to us that the rebellion on End has moved to a new and more dangerous phase. The Duke of End has sent assurances that everything is under control, but the assessment of the Imperial Marines commander stationed there is rather less optimistic. He expects the duke to fall within two standard years. Of course this note was sent nine months ago. Who knows what the situation there is now."

"Have our marines intervened?"

"It was your father's policy, and the policy of the several emperoxs before him, to let End handle End. The marines are mostly there to keep anyone from leaving the planet without permission. The commander tells us the only watch they have set from the emperox—the previous emperox—was to monitor the safety of the Count of Claremont."

"Who is that?"

"I remember him, ma'am," Korbijn said. "A minor noble from Sofala, whom your father enlarged. A friend of your father's from university. A physicist who studied the Flow."

"Why did our father exile him?"

"Your father offered the title to him just prior to his marriage to the Lady Glenna."

Well, that was an unsubtle hint, Cardenia thought. The archbishop was all but implying that her dad and this count were an item prior to Batrin's marriage, which was very much one of those dynastical marriages, the House of Costu heading one of the most powerful guilds.

The idea was mildly surprising to Cardenia, since in all the time she knew her father, he never came across as anything other than blandly heterosexual. But there was a time and place for everything, and it was called "university," and in any event this count wouldn't be the first inconvenient lover an emperox shunted out of the picture with a title upgrade, somewhere very far away. It would also explain the marine watch.

Cardenia nodded her understanding. "For now we will continue our father's posture, but we will want a full briefing."

"It's one of the briefings listed on your proposed schedule," Korbijn said. "And while we are at least tangentially on the subject of marriage—"

"You are going to bring up Amit Nohamapetan, aren't you?" Cardenia said, in a somewhat less formal tone than she'd previously been managing.

"The Nohamapetans are being insistent," Korbijn said, almost apologetically.

"We are not our brother. We made no assurances to marry a Nohamapetan."

"With respect, ma'am, the House of Nohamapetan believes the assurance was not between your brother and Lady Nadashe, it was between the House of Wu and the House of Nohamapetan. And precedent suggests their argument has validity. In 512, Crown Princess Davina was engaged to a member of the House of Edmunk and died before the wedding. Her brother, who would become Chonglin I, married a cousin of the original betrothed on the reasoning that the arrangement had already been set into motion."

Cardenia turned to Naffa. "How did Crown Princess Davina die?"

"Suicide, your majesty," Naffa said. Cardenia knew that she would know off the top of her head, or would look it up instantly. "Out of an airlock at Xi'an. Her suicide note suggests she did not believe the betrothal to be in her best interests."

Cardenia turned to Lenn Edmunk. "We hope you do not believe this sets you in any negative light, Lord Edmunk."

"Thank you, ma'am."

"Ma'am, may I also suggest to you that you at least consider Amit Nohamapetan's suit," Korbijn persisted. "Aside from any theoretical agreement between your houses, the House of Nohamapetan is a power among the guilds." Korbijn glanced over at Edmunk, who, as he was looking at the emperox, was unaware. "Many potential problems and issues with the guilds could be dealt with expeditiously with this alliance."

Cardenia smiled grimly at this. "And there are no houses who object to this pairing?"

"No, ma'am," Edmunk said.

"Well," Cardenia said, impressed. "This is a rare show of unanimity among the guilds. Almost unprecedented in a millennium."

"I believe everyone agrees it is in the interest of the Interdependency to have any questions of succession settled sooner than later," Korbijn said.

This rankled Cardenia. "We are pleased, Archbishop, that this committee appears unanimous that the most important part of us is our uterus."

Korbijn had the good grace to blush at this. "Apologies, Your Majesty. Nothing could be further from the truth. But surely the emperox must be aware that should something happen to you, there will be contesting claims to the throne within the House of Wu from your many cousins. Many of them were less than pleased when you were—rightfully—put into the line of succession behind your brother. A clear line of succession staves off any questions."

"Staves off a civil war," Ranatunga said.

"Do we agree that it seems unlikely that we will be dead prior to our coronation?" Cardenia asked the committee.

"That seems reasonable, ma'am," Korbijn said, smiling.

"Then may we suggest that we table it until after then. If you like," Cardenia nodded to Korbijn, "you may give the House of Nohamapetan excellent seats to the coronation and we will speak to Amit Nohamapetan afterwards."

"Yes, ma'am."

"Emphasis on 'speak.' We hope we are understood on this matter and not otherwise represented to Lord Nohamapetan."

"Yes, ma'am."

"Good. Then is there anything else?"

"One small thing," Korbijn said. Cardenia waited. "We need to know your imperial name."

"We are Grayland," Cardenia said, after a pause. "Grayland II."

• • •

"I hate the imperial 'we,'" Cardenia confessed to Naffa.

After the meeting with the executive committee, the two of them had lifted to Xi'an, the heart of the Interdependency, in order for Cardenia, now Grayland II, to begin the formal transfer of authority from her late father to her. Upon arrival Grayland II was immediately surrounded by advisors, courtiers, flatterers, and assistants, all with their own agendas and plans. Cardenia was tired of it in the first hour and there was all the rest of her life yet to go.

"What bothers you about it?" Naffa asked.

"It's so pretentious."

"You *are* the emperox," Naffa pointed out. "You are literally the only person in the universe who may use it without pretension."

"You know what I mean."

"I do. I just think you're wrong."

"You think I should use it all the time, then."

"I didn't say that," Naffa said. "But you have to admit it's a pretty fantastic power move. 'Oh, you have an opinion? Well, screw you, because *my vote counts as two*.'"

Cardenia smiled at this.

The two of them were alone, finally, in the cavernous private apartments of the imperial palace of Xi'an. All the assistants and courtiers and advisors had been shoved out the door by Naffa. There was only one more thing Cardenia had to do with her day, and it lay behind a door here in the private apartments. A door that could be opened and entered only by the emperox.

Or so Cardenia explained to Naffa, who frowned. "Only the emperox."

"Yes."

"What happens if anyone else enters? Are there dogs? Lasers that will burn you to ash?"

"I don't think so."

"Can your servants go in there? Or technicians? Are you, as emperox, responsible for tidying up? Is there a small vacuum cleaner in there? Are you made to dust the place?"

"I don't think you're taking this very seriously," Cardenia said.

"I take it seriously," Naffa promised. "I'm just skeptical of how it's being presented."

They both looked at the door.

"Well?" Naffa said. "You might as well get it over with."

"Where are you going to be?"

"I can stay here if you like and wait for you to be done."

Cardenia shook her head. "I don't know how long this will take."

"Then I'll be in my quarters, the ones across the palace, you know, where the palace majordomo has exiled me."

"We'll get those changed."

"No, don't," Naffa said. "You need your time away from everyone, including me." She got up. "We're still in the same house. I'm just sixteen wings away, is all."

"I don't think the palace has sixteen wings."

"It has twenty-four major sections to it."

"Well, you would know."

"Yes, I would," Naffa said. "And soon so will you." She bowed. "Good night, Your Majesty." She left, smiling. Cardenia watched her go, and then turned her attention to the door.

The door was ornate, like everything in the palace, and Cardenia realized that "ornate" was a design motif she was probably stuck with now; she couldn't just burn everything down and start with clean lines and spaces, tempting as it might be. She was emperox but even they had their limits.

The door had no knob or access panel or anything else that suggested that it could be opened. Cardenia, sheepishly, put her hand on it to feel for a secret button.

The door slid open.

Keyed to my fingerprints? Cardenia wondered, and then walked through. The door slid closed behind her.

The room inside was large; as large as the bedroom in the imperial quarters, which made this single room larger than the apartments Cardenia grew up in. The room was bare, except for a single bench that jutted out from the wall to her left. Cardenia went and sat on it.

"I'm here," she said, to no one in particular.

A figure of light appeared in the center of the room and walked toward her. Cardenia looked up as the figure approached; microprojectors in the ceiling were creating the image walking over to her now. Cardenia idly wondered at the physics behind it, but only for a second, because now the image was directly in front of her.

"Emperox Grayland II," it said, and bowed.

"You know who I am," Cardenia said, skipping the imperial "we."

"Yes," the image said. It had no identifiable signs of gender or age. "I am Jiyi. You are in the Memory Room. Please tell me how I may assist you."

Cardenia knew why she was there but hesitated. "Does anyone other than the emperox come in here?"

"No," Jiyi said.

"What if I invite someone?"

"Focused light and sound waves would make it unbearable for anyone other than the reigning emperox to come through the door."

"Can't I override that?"

"No."

"I am the emperox." *And I am arguing with a machine*, Cardenia thought but did not say.

"The injunction was made by the Prophet," Jiyi said, "whose order is inviolable."

This took Cardenia aback. "This room dates to the reign of the first emperox," she said.

"Yes."

"Xi'an didn't *exist* then."

"The room was moved from Hubfall, with other elements of the palace, when Xi'an was founded. The rest of the palace was built around it."

The image of the space station of Xi'an being built around the imperial palace popped into Cardenia's mind, so absurd as to be almost comical. "So you are a thousand years old," she said, to Jiyi.

"The information I store dates back to the founding of the Interdependency," Jiyi said. "The physical machinery it is stored on is regularly updated, as are the functional elements of this room and the manifestation you see in front of you."

"I thought you said no one may enter this room but the emperox."

"Automated maintenance, ma'am," Jiyi said, and Cardenia thought she heard just the slightest edge of humor in the voice. Which made her first feel a bit stupid, and then curious.

"Are you alive, Jiyi?" she asked.

"No," Jiyi said. "Nothing you encounter in this room is alive, excepting you, ma'am."

"Of course," Cardenia said, only a little disappointed.

"I sense we have carried this specific conversation to an end," Jiyi said. "May I assist you otherwise?"

"Yes," Cardenia said. "I would like to speak to my father."

Jiyi nodded and faded out. As it did so, another form coalesced, in the center of the room.

It was Cardenia's father, Batrin, lately Emperox Attavio VI. He appeared, looked toward his daughter, smiled, and walked over to her.

The Memory Room was established by the Prophet-Emperox Rachela I not long after the foundation of the Interdependency, and her ascendance as its first emperox. Each emperox was fitted with a personal network of sensors running through their body that captured not only every sight seen, and every sound heard or spoken by the emperox, but every other sensation, action, emotion, thought, and desire apprehended or produced by them as well.

Within the Memory Room were the thoughts and memories of every emperox of the Interdependency, dating back to the very first, the Prophet-Emperox Rachela I herself. If Cardenia wanted, she could ask any one of her predecessors any question, about them, about their reign, about their time. They would answer from memory, from the thoughts and recordings and the computer modeling of who they were, girded on decades of every single thing about their internal lives recorded for this very room.

There was only one destination for this information: the Memory Room. There was only one audience for it: the current emperox.

Cardenia subconsciously touched the back of her neck again, in the place where the network seed was implanted, to grow inside her. *One day, everything I do as emperox will be in here,* she thought. *For my own child and their children to see. Every emperox will know who I was, better than history will.*

She looked at the apparition of her father, now directly in front of her, and shuddered.

The apparition noticed. "Are you not happy to see me?" it asked.

"I saw you just a few hours ago," Cardenia said, standing up from the bench, and looking over the apparition of her father. It was perfect. Almost touchable. Cardenia did not touch it. "You were dead then."

"I still am," Attavio VI said. "The consciousness that was me is gone. Everything else was stored."

"So you're not conscious now?"

"I'm not, but I can respond to you as if I were. You may ask me anything. I will tell you."

"What do you think of me?" Cardenia asked, blurting it out.

"I always thought you were a nice young lady," Attavio VI said. "Smart. Attentive to me. I don't think you'll make a very good emperox."

"Why not?"

"Because right now the Interdependency has no need of a *nice* emperox. It never does, but it can tolerate one when nothing consequential is going on. This is not one of those times."

"I wasn't particularly nice to the executive committee today," Cardenia said, hearing how defensive the words sounded coming out of her mouth.

"I'm sure that in the wake of my death, for your very first meeting with them, the executive committee made a fine show of being restrained and deferential. Also, they are seeing at what length of chain you're most comfortable, in order for them to get every single thing they want from you. They'll yank on that chain presently."

"I'm not sure I like this entirely honest you," Cardenia said, after a moment.

"If you like we can adjust my conversational model to be more like I was in life."

"You're telling me you lied to me in life."

"No more than to anyone else."

"That's comforting."

"In life I was human, with an ego, just like anyone else. I had my own desires and intentions. Here I am nothing but memory, here for the purpose of assisting you, the current emperox. I have no ego to flatter, and will flatter yours only if ordered to. I would not suggest it. It makes me less useful."

"Did you love me?"

"It depends on what you mean by love."

"That sounds like an evasive, ego-filled answer."

"I was fond of you. You were also inconvenient until the moment you were needed for succession. When you became the crown princess I was relieved you didn't hate me. You couldn't have been blamed if you had."

"When you died you said you wished you had had time to love me better."

Attavio VI nodded. "That sounds like something I would say. I imagine I meant it in the moment."

"You don't remember it."

"Not yet. My final moments have not yet been uploaded."

Cardenia dropped the subject. "I chose the imperial name of Grayland II, as you suggested."

"Yes. That information, at least, is in our database. And, good."

"I read up on her."

"Yes, I had planned to ask you to."

"You did, before you died. Why did you ask me to name myself for her?"

"Because I hoped it would inspire you to take seriously what's coming next, and what it would require from you," Attavio VI said. "Do you know about the Count of Claremont, on End?"

"I do," Cardenia said. "An old lover of yours."

Attavio VI smiled. "No, not at all. A friend. A very good friend, and a scientist. One who brought me information that no one else had, and that no one else would have wanted to see. One who needed to do his work and research insulated from the stupidities of court, and government, and even of the community of scientists in the Interdependency. He's someone who has been collecting data for more than thirty years now. He knows more about what's coming next than anyone else. A thing you must be prepared for. A thing you are not in the least prepared for, now. And a thing I worry that you will not be strong enough to see through."

Cardenia stared at the apparition of Attavio VI, which stood there, a small, pleasant, distracted smile on its face.

"Well?" Cardenia said, finally. "What is it?"

4

"Who here knows what the Interdependency is?" Marce Clare-mont asked, from the well of the planetarium.

From the chairs of the planetarium, the hands of several eight-year-olds shot upward. Marce scanned the hands, looking for the one who seemed to most urgently need to answer the question. He picked a hand sitting in the second arc of chairs. "Yes? You."

"I have to go to the bathroom," the child said. Behind the child, Marce saw one of the adult chaperones roll her eyes, get up, grab the child by the hand, and start walking him to the bathrooms. Then he picked another kid.

"It's the nation of systems we all live in," said the girl.

"That's right," Marce said, and pressed a button on his tablet to dim the lights and start his presentation. "It's the nation of systems in which we live. But what does that really mean?"

Before he could continue, the planetarium rocked slightly as what sounded like two interceptors buzzed the university science center the planetarium was part of. The children started at the noise, the chaperones trying to hush them and telling them everything would be all right.

Marce doubted everything was actually going to be all right.

The University of Opole, which housed the science center, was far from the capital and the focus of the fighting. But in the last week things had taken a decisive turn against the duke and his loyalist forces, and now even the far provinces had sprouted rebels, and the violence that came with revolution.

He'd been surprised when this bus full of children had showed up at the science center today; he had assumed that all the schools had canceled their classes, like the university had. Then he saw the look on the faces of the adults who had brought the children. They appeared grimly determined to give the kids as commonplace an experience as they could, for as long as they could.

Marce, who was in point of fact the only member of the non-janitorial staff to show up on this particular morning, and then only to collect some materials that were not already on the network, didn't dare let them down. He brought them all down to the planetarium and dug into his brain to remember the standard presentation about the Interdependency that the tour docents usually gave.

"It's all right," he said, to the children. "Those aircraft were just passing by. We're just on their flight path, that's all. The university is safe." This was also probably not true, since the University of Opole had more than its share of rebel sympathizers, ranging from stoned students looking for a movement to join, to reflexively contrarian professors who enjoyed sticking it to the duke while still retaining tenure. Most of them, students and faculty, were probably down in a cellar at the moment. Marce, who was personally resolutely apolitical, for all the good it did him, did not blame them at all.

Be that as it may, there was no point panicking eight-year-olds about the possibility of the university being occupied either by rebels or by the duke's troops. Right now, Marce's job was keeping them distracted. Today might be the last relatively normal day they'd have for a while. Might as well make the most of it.

Marce touched his tablet again, and a star field leapt out of the projector into the empty space above the well of the planetarium, accompanied by soothing, tinkling music. The eight-year-olds, apprehensive just five seconds earlier, oohed and aahed at the sight. So did the adults.

"What you're seeing now are all the stars that exist in the area that holds the Interdependency," Marce said. "From Hub to End, all of the stars we live around are here. Does anyone want to guess which one we are?"

The children shot out their fingers, all at entirely different points of light. From his tablet, Marce tapped on one of the stars. The projected image zoomed in toward a single star and when it stopped, showed a solar system of five planets; two terrestrial, three gas giants. "This is us," he said. "The second planet out from our sun. This is End, called that because it's located as far away from anything else in the Interdependency as you can go."

Marce pulled back out into the full star field. "Now, all of these stars are in the space the Interdependency claims for its own, but not all of them have systems that humans can live in. In fact, of these more than five thousand star systems, only forty-seven of them have humans in them." He made the star systems of the Interdependency glow more brightly, so the children could see them. The systems were not generally close to each other in space; they seemed randomly distributed, diamonds among grains of sand.

"Why are they all so far apart?" asked one of the children, rather conveniently, for the purposes of the next part of the standard presentation.

"Excellent question!" Marce said. "Now, you might think that all the human systems would be huddled close together so they would be easy to travel to, but all the systems are connected not in space, but by the Flow."

A bunch of lines arched out of the human systems, connecting them to each other system, prompting another set of appreciative coos from the children.

"The Flow is like a super shortcut through space," Marce said. "Normally, it would take years or even centuries for humans to get from one star system to the next. Even the closest systems are a few light-years away from each other, and using regular drives, even that relatively short distance would take twenty or thirty years for us to cross. Even our most advanced starships, called 'tenners,' can't make that trip. With the Flow, we can travel between systems in weeks or months at most. But, here's the catch: We can only travel to the systems where the Flow is nearby."

He zoomed in to another system, this one with ten planets, and zoomed in further. "Does anyone know which planet this is?" There was no answer. "This is called Hub, and it's the capital of the Interdependency. Does anyone want to guess why?"

"Because that's where the emperox lives?"

"Well, yes, but the emperox lives there for a reason, and the reason is this." Marce tapped his tablet and the planet of Hub was surrounded by what looked like a whirlpool of lines, swirling in the space above the world. "Hub is the one place in the Interdependency where *all* the Flow streams converge—it's the only place you can get directly from and to nearly every system in the Interdependency. That makes it the most important planet for trade and travel. If we couldn't travel through Hub, some systems in the Interdependency would be years away from each other. That's why the planet is called 'Hub.' It's the center of our universe, so to speak."

"Can't we just make a path in the Flow between planets?" This question was from one of the adults, who apparently had gotten so sucked into the presentation that he forgot question time was for the children.

"We'd like to but we can't," Marce said, answering anyway. "The Flow isn't something that we control, and really, if we're honest with ourselves, it's something that we don't understand very well. It's like a natural feature of the universe. We can access it but we can't really do anything with it but go where it's going anyway. In fact, that makes for one of the really unusual features about the Interdependency."

Marce zoomed out, wiped the star field, and put up a grid of the forty-seven systems of the Interdependency. The systems featured stars ranging from red dwarfs to sun-like yellow stars, harboring anywhere between one and a dozen major planets. The images of the systems were not to scale and showed the planets zooming along in their orbits, some so quickly it was comical. A few of the children laughed.

"Humans live in all of these star systems, but the planets in most of these star systems aren't the kinds that are good for human life." Marce zoomed into Hub again. "Hub, for example, is airless and tidally locked. That means one side of the planet is always facing the sun, so it's super-hot, and the other side is facing away, which makes it frozen. Humans on Hub have to live under the ground to survive."

He zoomed out and picked another system. "Here in the Morobe system, the only planets are gas giants—huge planets that don't even have a surface to land on. We couldn't live on those. These planets have moons but most of them aren't very suitable for humans either. So here we live in space habitats, positioned in spots called Lagrange points, or in other places that can be made stable. So that's how most humans live now:

underground on rocky planets or on large space habitats. There's only one place in the Interdependency where humans live on the surface of the planet."

Marce zoomed out and in again, back to End, which hovered on the screen, a blue-green marble, clouded in white. "That's us. That's End."

"What about Earth?" one of the children asked, as one of them always did.

"Good question!" Marce said. "Earth is where humans originally come from, and like on End, you could walk around on its surface. But the Earth isn't part of the Interdependency. We lost contact with the Earth over a thousand years ago when the single Flow stream to it disappeared."

"How did that happen?" It was the adult again, who was immediately shushed by one of the other adults. Marce smiled at this.

"It's complicated," he said. "The best nontechnical answer I can give you is that everything in the universe is constantly moving, including star systems, and that movement sometimes affects the Flow. Basically, the Earth moved, we moved, and the Flow stream went away."

"Can it happen again?"

"Bint!" someone said, to the adult asking questions, admonishing him.

"Look, I want to know," Bint said.

"It's all right," Marce said, holding up a hand. "In fact, it *did* happen again, more than seven hundred years ago, when we lost contact with a system called Dalasýsla. This was before the local Flow streams were as extensively mapped as they are now. The Flow stream to Dalasýsla was apparently already collapsing when it was first colonized, it just took a couple hundred years to close entirely. Now, as it happens, the rest of the Flow streams in the Interdependency have been robust and mostly unchanged for the last several hundred years."

This seemed to satisfy Bint, and Marce was happy this fellow hadn't noticed he didn't actually answer the question.

From a distance, a low *crummp* made it into the momentary silence of the planetarium. One of the adults in the audience started to take in a sharp breath, and then stopped.

"And I think that's about all the time we have for today," Marce said. "Thank you all for coming, and I hope you'll come again another time. We'd love to see you." *A day when someone isn't clearly shelling someone else only a few klicks away.* He flicked up the house lights and waved good-bye to the children as the adults filed them out of the room. One of the adults looked back and mouthed the words *thank you* to him. Marce smiled and waved again.

"Still giving tours in the middle of a war," said someone new, in the back of the planetarium. "That's noble. Stupid, but noble."

Marce looked up, saw who it was, and smiled again. "Well, technically, we *are* nobility, aren't we, sis?"

Vrenna Claremont, in her full constable uniform, smiled back and started walking down toward her brother. "Being a noble on End is like being the richest person in a trash heap. It doesn't mean much. Especially now, when the duke is about to get his ass handed to him and rebels are running about liberating his property. It's not a stretch to assume other nobles will find their stuff similarly liberated."

"My stuff is a bunch of books in graduate housing," Marce said. "I think they'll be disappointed."

"You're a professor now. You should move out of graduate housing."

"I'm resident master. Saves on rent."

"A count's son, worried about rent," Vrenna said.

"We are really unimpressive nobility, it's true."

There was another *crummp* somewhere in the distance, and it didn't sound as distant as the last one.

"I'm doing a really good job of not panicking right now," Marce said.

"I noticed that," said Vrenna. "I mean, I wasn't going to mention it. But I noticed it."

"We can't all have ice water in our veins."

"I don't have ice water in my veins. I just know how far away those explosions are, so I'm not going to worry about them right now."

"How far away are they?"

"About five klicks. The docks, where the duke's forces are trying to bury a contingent of the rebels under shattered cargo containers. It probably won't work. Most of the rebels are long gone from there, moving to occupy strategic resources. You and I are going in the other direction anyway."

"We are?"

"Yes. Dad sent me to collect you."

"Why?"

"One, because there's a war on, and although I don't expect that shelling is going to get any closer, there's no guarantee the university, including your graduate housing, isn't going to be on fire by the time the sun sets today."

"That bad," Marce said.

Vrenna nodded. "Yup. You may not remember this, but the house has a watch set on it by the Imperial Marines. If a rebel comes within a klick of it they're likely to be vaporized from space. That makes it the safest place on the surface of the planet right now."

"Did Dad tell that to the duke?"

"You know, I think he might have skipped mentioning that to him."

Marce grinned again at that.

"Two, Dad wants to show you something."

"What is it?"

"Data."

"Anytime you want to be less ambiguous, Vren, that'd be great."

"He said you would know what it was, and that it wouldn't be something we'd talk about out loud in public."

"Oh," Marce said.

"Yup."

Another *crummp.*

"That sounded closer," Marce said.

"It wasn't. But we should leave anyway. We wait any longer, someone might take it into their heads to start taking potshots at the skimmer."

• • •

Someone took a potshot at the skimmer anyway, several times during the flight.

"Go faster," Marce urged his sister.

"Anytime *you* want to fly a skimmer just over the city rooftops, without crashing into some random chimney, you let me know," she replied.

In lieu of bothering his sister further, Marce looked out the skimmer bubble at the streets of Opole. Most of the residential streets were untouched, with only a few glimpses of people carrying things out to their cars, as if packing for a move. The main streets, however, were clogged with cars, and several were jammed to a standstill.

That took effort; Marce suspected some drivers had disabled

autodrive to take control of their cars directly, either in a panic or because they suspected the government was somehow going to disable their movement. The end result either way was that these newly independent cars were messing things up for everyone else.

And every now and again, Marce would see columns of soldiers moving along the streets, armored vehicles among them, off to secure and/or liberate one strategic element of the city or another.

"This isn't going to end well," Marce said to his sister.

"Does it ever?" she asked, banking toward the Warta, the wide river that ran through Opole. She flew the skimmer to the middle of it, far enough away from either bank to discourage any further potshots. Marce suspected that technically his sister was flying the skimmer illegally—skimmers were supposed to use automation and stick to specific air routes within the city to avoid problems with other air traffic. The middle of the Warta was not one of those routes. He also suspected that today local law enforcement had other things to worry about.

Presently the skimmer left Opole behind and the land rose into rolling hills, the Warta meandering gently between them, suburbs and then rural villages nestled up against their inclines. A small tributary of the Warta branched off, into another set of hills; Vrenna followed it and within minutes was at the house.

"The house" was technically Claremont Palace, named for the province district that their father had been made count of, nearly forty standard years earlier, and from which the family now took its name. There had been a previous count, whom Marce had never met, having not been born yet; he had been persuaded to give up the title by accepting an appointment to the imperial court. The story Marce had been told was that the fellow needed very little convincing. Better to be a functionary at court than a noble on a planet of exile. The previous count departed so quickly he left most of his furniture and at least a couple of pets, cats who had been perfectly fine with the new tenants, his father had told him, so long as the food kept coming.

"Come on," Vrenna said, as they stepped out of the skimmer, on the landing pad near the garage. "Let's not keep Dad waiting."

Their father, Jamies, Count Claremont, was in his office, watching the revolution on the wall monitor. He saw them enter and pointed to the monitor. "Look at this nonsense," he said to them.

"Welcome to the revolution," Vrenna said.

Jamies snorted. "It's not a revolution. The 'rebels' are probably funded by merchant guilds who want an import tax break. Or something. The duke wouldn't allow it. Or something. So the 'rebels' will take down the duke and install an ambitious noble in his place, who will cut the tariff. It'll be rubberstamped by the emperox, because no one out there cares what happens to End. And because they think in another twenty years we'll all just do it again."

"Won't we?"

"Not this time." Jamies went to his desk, retrieved a tablet, and handed it to Marce. "We finally got it. The smoking gun. And the last bit of data I needed for the prediction model."

Marce took the tablet and started scanning through the work there. "When did this happen?"

"Six weeks ago. A ship called *Tell Me Another One* experienced a Flow anomaly and then recorded a transient Flow shoal, consistent with my model. It's observed, recorded, verified, and tracked. Everything about it fits. Everything about it is exactly what we've been looking for. It confirms everything we've suspected about the Flow."

Marce stopped trying to scan the work, which would require hours for him to read and ingest, and looked to his father. "You're *sure* about this."

"Do you think I would tell you if I wasn't?" Jamies said. "Have you ever known me to be anything other than *exceptionally* careful about this hypothesis? Do you think I didn't throw everything I could at it to disprove it? Do you think I *want* it to be accurate?"

Marce shook his head. "No, Dad."

"Don't get me wrong, Marce. I need you to read it. I need you to tell me if there's anything I'm missing. Anything I've overlooked. Because as much as the scientist in me is thrilled to have made this leap in understanding the physics of the Flow . . ."

". . . as a human being you want to be wrong," Marce finished.

"Yes," Jamies said. "Yes, I very much do."

For as long as Marce could remember, Dad had called it "the Family Secret": his father's examination of navigation data from every ship that had ever come to End over the last four decades. Officially Count Claremont's role for the empire was chief imperial auditor for End. He examined the data to assure that none of the ships ever deviated from the imperially approved trade route—and thereby avoided the trade tariffs and other taxes that were required of them—that were often planned years or even decades in advance. In this, the count was one of dozens of chief imperial auditors, one in every system, who made sure money stayed where it was supposed to stay: in the pocket of the emperox first, guilds second, and everyone else somewhere rather further down the line.

In reality, Jamies, Count Claremont, didn't give a shit about any of that nonsense. He performed the role of chief imperial auditor well enough, primarily by delegating it to underlings with the admonition that any graft too obvious to be ignored would have to be punished. But that wasn't why he came to End, or why his friend, the Emperox Attavio VI, had sent him. He had been sent to examine the navigational data of the ships for discrepancies, but not of trade. He was looking for data that backed up his hypothesis, first formulated while he was still an undergraduate at the University of Hubfall, that the Flow streams that defined the Interdependency did not benefit from "robustness through resonance"—the theory that the unusual density and interaction of Flow streams within the Interdependency helped to create a stable waveform within the Flow that would keep those streams open and unchanging for millennia.

Jamies read the math behind the theory and surmised what others didn't, or did and preferred not to believe: that "robustness through resonance" was data-fudging nonsense, and that the collapse of the Flow streams to Earth and Dalasýsla were precursors, rather than the exceptions that modern Flow theory held them out to be. He said as much to his friend Batrin, the newly crowned Emperox Attavio VI, showed him the data, and warned him that a collapse could happen within the century.

Batrin saw the possibility of validity in the data. He also recognized that it represented a threat to the trade and stability of the Interdependency, and would likely be considered blasphemy by the church. So he did two things for his friend Jamies. First, he bribed him into silence by making him a count. Then he sent him to End, as far as he could be sent in the whole of the Interdependency, and gave him a job that would give him the data he needed to verify or dismiss his hypothesis, and told him to tell no one but him about the work.

Which Jamies did, mostly. First he told his wife, Guice, and then after their twin children Marce and Vrenna were old enough, told them too. He assumed the emperox wouldn't mind. Guice took the secret to her tragic, early grave. Vrenna kept the secret because she was good at secrets. Marce kept it because once he showed enough interest and aptitude in the physics of the Flow, Jamies relied on him to check his work.

Now, all the years of quiet, methodical data collection and interpretation had paid off. Jamies, Count Claremont, had verified the most important discovery in human experience since the discovery of the Flow itself. If it were known to other scientists, they'd shovel every single possible award they offered onto him.

That is, if the Interdependency were still around for them to do so.

"So it's true, then," Vrenna said, to her father and brother. "The Flow is collapsing."

"The Flow is the Flow," Jamies said. "It doesn't *do* anything. Our *access* to it, on the other hand, is definitely going away. The unusual stability of the Flow streams that have allowed the development of the Interdependency is coming to an end. One by one, the streams are going to dry up. One by one, the systems of the Interdependency are going to find themselves alone. For a long time. Possibly forever."

"How long do we have?" Vrenna asked.

"Ten years," Marce said. "At the outside." He glanced over to his father. "If Dad's models are perfectly accurate, less than that. Probably closer to seven or eight years before all the local Flow streams are gone. Most of them will be gone before then."

Jamies turned toward his son. "And that's why you must go."

"Wait, what?" Marce said.

"You have to go," Jamies repeated.

"Where?"

"To Hub, of course. You have to take this data to the emperox."

"I thought you were sending regular updates to the emperox," Vrenna said, to her father.

"I have been, obviously. The data is encrypted and sent monthly via outgoing ships."

"So send this the same way," Marce said.

Jamies shook his head. "You don't understand. It's one thing to keep the emperox updated when I'm just crunching through the data and refining the model. It's another thing entirely when the model is verified, and real, and a threat to the Interdependency. He's going to need someone to walk him through it all. And then walk everyone *else* through it. And then argue with everyone from scientists to politicians who want to poke holes in it for their own purposes. Someone needs to go."

"I agree," Marce said. "And that person should be you."

Jamies opened his mouth but then Doung Xavos, the count's secretary, poked his head into the room. "My lord, Lord Ghreni Nohamapetan is here to see you. He says he comes at the request of the duke."

"Bring him," Jamies said, and looked at his children.

"Should we go?" Vrenna asked.

"I'd rather you stayed." Jamies gestured at the monitor spilling out the news of the revolution; it switched itself off. Jamies sat at his desk and encouraged his children to sit as well. They did.

Lord Ghreni Nohamapetan entered the room, clad in black, and Marce watched as the noble went to greet his father. Ghreni and the Claremont siblings were of an age, but the two of them had never socialized extensively with the Nohamapetan scion; he'd arrived to End only a few years prior to handle his house's interests. They'd seen him once or twice at functions at the duke's palace and had once been formally introduced to him. Marce recalled Ghreni scanning the both of them quickly, to see if there was any political advantage in knowing either, and when the apparent answer was "no," politely ignoring them from there on out. Marce was still mildly annoyed by this; Vrenna found it amusing, because of course she would.

"Count Claremont," Ghreni Nohamapetan said, bowing.

"Lord Ghreni," Jamies said. "A pleasure." He gestured toward Marce and Vrenna, who stood. "You remember my children, no doubt."

"Of course. Lord Marce, Lady Vrenna." Ghreni gave a head nod to each, which they returned before sitting again. Formalities thus satisfied, he turned his attention back to their father. "My lord, my duke has sent me on a mission of some delicacy, and I wonder if it might be better if we spoke alone."

"My children are my foremost advisors and I don't keep secrets from them. You may speak to me in front of them with the same assurance of confidentiality as you would if we spoke alone."

Ghreni paused for a moment and Marce was certain he was going to insist on speaking alone with their father. He glanced over at Vrenna, who had a wry smile on her face. Then he nodded. "Yes, very well."

"What is your business, Lord Ghreni?"

"As you are no doubt aware, the duke is facing a serious challenge with the rebels."

Vrenna snorted at this. "You mean to say he's on the verge of losing his dukedom, my lord," she said.

"The duke is somewhat more optimistic than your daughter," Ghreni said, to Jamies. "Nevertheless, the challenge is real and the duke is now looking for ways to increase his tactical advantages."

"Such as?"

"Weapons, my lord."

"I have an antique bolt thrower left here by the previous count," Jamies said. "And I believe Vrenna carries a sidearm at all times. Other than that I don't believe we have any weapons."

"The duke is aware that you don't have weapons, my lord. But you do have money."

"Not really. The title 'Count of Claremont' comes with remarkably little rentable land and no local or larger monopolies. It's largely a courtesy title. I have my salary as chief auditor and an upkeep allowance for the palace. I recently sold some properties, but it's still not a lot."

Ghreni laughed. "Not *your* money, my lord. The emperox's. We want to use it to buy the weapons the duke needs."

Jamies's expression darkened at this. "Explain yourself, sir."

"The duke is aware that in your role as chief auditor, all imperial taxes and levies run through your office before they are sent forward to the treasury at Xi'an."

"My office doesn't send them forward. That's the role of the chief of the imperial bank here on End."

"Of course. And we have spoken to Chief Han, and she is willing to assist the duke in this endeavor. Chief Han also informed us that any transfer of imperial taxes or levies outside of their usual route to Xi'an must also be approved by your office."

"That's correct but simplistically presented. I may approve direct application of taxes and levies to imperially approved projects, like construction or infrastructure. Things that those taxes would go to anyway. That saves time, rather than sending the money away and then bringing it back."

"Yes. And if you consult your records, you'll see that two years ago, when this current uprising began, the duke asked for, and the imperial parliament approved, funding for the purchase of weapons to help suppress the uprising."

"I don't need to consult the records, Lord Ghreni, to be aware that the funds for those purchases were already allocated and the weapons purchased and shipped."

"Then you're also no doubt aware that the ship carrying those weapons, the *Tell Me Another One*, was attacked by pirates and boarded when it came out of the Flow. Its captain and crew fought valiantly to repel the attack but in the end many of the crew died, including the executive officer, security officer, and the owner's representative, and the ship's cargo was taken. The *Tell Me* barely limped into port intact."

"I'm aware of the *Tell Me*," Jamies said.

"The point is that the weapons are now in the hands of pirates. Pirates who intended to sell them to the rebels but who can be persuaded to sell them to the duke."

"That's what the duke's own treasury is for," Marce pointed out.

"Alas, Lord Marce, two years of fighting have depleted the duke's treasury and also made it more difficult to collect taxes and other revenues. He needs help."

"He got the help," Vrenna pointed out. "The parliament authorized the weapons. But it's also the duke's responsibility to patrol the space between the Flow shoal and the planet. If pirates are operating there, it's because the duke hasn't been doing his job."

Ghreni turned his attention back to the count. "The duke is aware that asking for this disbursement is unusual. His argument, and I think it's a good one, is that parliament intended those weapons for the duke, and therefore in allowing these additional funds to go to the duke to repurchase the weapons, you are following their intent."

"I don't think that argument is as good as the duke thinks it is," Jamies said. "As I'm also aware that the imperial garrison here has been told not to intervene in the matter."

This got a nod from Ghreni. "The duke knows full well that the only noble currently under the protection of the imperial military is you, Count Claremont. He finds that interesting."

"It's not interesting at all, Lord Ghreni. As you've noted, the Interdependency's money goes through my offices. The emperox values his money. Which is why I'm not convinced he will be happy to see it unexpectedly diverted. Nor would he be happy with me."

"The duke is prepared for that eventuality."

"That's nice," Jamies said. "Considering *he* will not be the one sent to prison for it."

"Come, now, Count Claremont. Give the duke credit for some intelligence. Remember that we are nine months away from Hub and Xi'an. In those nine months, the duke can crush this rebellion and return with interest any funds lent to him. He will lend his authority to yours to argue to the emperox that you and Chief Han were acting in the best interests of the Interdependency. And in the meantime the duke promises that your loyalty will be rewarded."

Jamies laughed at this. "There is irony in attempting to bribe someone who you are trying to get money *from*, Lord Ghreni."

"The duke believes that money is not the only coin for loyalty."

"And Chief Han was convinced by this argument."

"Yes, she was, my lord."

"So to sum up," Jamies said, "you wish me to illegally transfer imperial funds to the duke so he may buy the weapons he already bought but lost due to negligence, because the person whom you have already suborned cannot do it herself, and to compensate for executing several crimes against the imperial state, you offer me nebulous, so-called rewards to be determined later, which are not actual money. Is this correct?"

"I wouldn't put it that way," Ghreni said. "Nor would the duke."

"Of course you wouldn't put it that way. But that's what you're asking for."

"So this means you're unwilling to help the duke," Nohamapetan said.

"I didn't say that," Jamies said, and Marce, for one, was entirely surprised. A quick glance over to his sister found her unreadable. "I may help the duke. But I don't want either you or I, or the duke, for that matter, to pretend that we're doing anything other than this."

Jamies stood, signaling the interview was over. Marce and Vrenna stood as well. Nohamapetan picked up the hint and bowed. "What may I tell the duke?" he asked.

"You may tell him that I will have an answer for him in a week," Jamies said.

"With all due respect, my lord, right now, a week is a very long time."

"Not as long as the fifty years I'll spend in prison if this all goes sideways, Lord Ghreni," Jamies said. "That is, if the emperox doesn't simply decide to have me killed."

"May I humbly ask that I can say to the duke that he'll have an answer within five days. Five days, I am sure, would be acceptable to him."

Jamies appeared to think about this. "Very well, Lord Ghreni. Five days."

"Thank you, my lord." He bowed. "If the duke wishes to come see you himself, where may I tell him you will be, these next few days?"

"I'll be here," Jamies said. "As I always am. As I always have been."

Ghreni bowed again, turned, and exited. Marce waited until Vrenna went and closed the office door behind him before speaking.

"You can't seriously be thinking of doing that," he said to his father.

"Why not?" Jamies asked.

Marce was gobsmacked.

"You're buying time," Vrenna said, coming back up to both of them.

"I am," Jamies agreed.

"Buying time for what?"

"Until it doesn't matter anymore." Jamies pointed at the tablet that Marce was still holding. "I've modeled the collapse of the Flow streams, son. It will be years before they're all gone. But some of them are already about to fail." He tapped the tablet. "One of the first will be the stream from here to Hub. The model shows it's already collapsing."

"How long until it's gone?" Vrenna asked.

"Another year. But it's collapsing from the entrance shoal. The best-case scenario has it closing in a month. The worst case is in about a week. After that it will be entirely inaccessible. Any ship that's here at End will stay here. Forever." Jamies turned to his son. "Which is another reason you have to go, now. If you don't go now, you'll never be able to go."

"You should be the one to go," Marce repeated, to his father.

Jamies shook his head. "The duke's about to be deposed. All the sitting nobles are being watched to see if they're trying to abandon the planet ahead of his fall. And now I have to give Ghreni Nohamapetan an answer about the money. If I so much as leave this *house*, the assumption will be that I'm making a run for it. They're watching me. They're not watching you."

"It makes sense, Marce," Vrenna said. "You're the only one who can explain this stuff as well as Dad can. And they won't be paying attention to you."

"Especially since I've made Vrenna my heir," Jamies said.

"What?" Marce said.

"Yeah, what?" Vrenna said.

"I officially made Vrenna my heir as soon as I knew about the collapse of the Flow," Jamies said, to his son. "And now you have a public excuse to leave End because you won't inherit. Even right now no one would question it."

"I don't want to be countess," Vrenna protested. "And I sure as hell don't want to be imperial auditor."

"Relax," Jamies said. "There will be nothing to audit soon."

"That's . . . not encouraging."

Jamies smiled at his daughter and looked back to his son. "I sold some holdings recently. It should be enough to get you passage on a ship and get you set up at Hub when you get there."

"How much is it?" Marce asked.

"About eighty million marks."

"Good lord!"

"Yes," agreed Jamies. "I may have lied to that Ghreni Nohamapetan character about my net worth. The point is, Marce, now you have means, motive, and opportunity to leave End. Leave. Do it now. Tell the emperox what we know. If we're lucky, he may still have time to prepare."

"Prepare for what?"

"The collapsing empire," Jamies said. "And the darkness that follows."

5

Kiva Lagos didn't get a miracle, but as far as she was concerned over the next week she got the next best thing: Sivouren Donher.

"He's one of our franchisees," Gazson Magnut said, speaking of the pompous-looking man currently loitering on the floor of the hold the *Yes, Sir* was operating out of in the imperial station. The franchisee was standing by a stack of haverfruit crates, the fruit inside of which had now come close to peak ripeness. The entire hold was saturated with a heavy floral scent that in the next few days would rapidly descend into rancidity. Magnut and Lagos were in a spare office given over by the station to the hold's current occupants; they were staring down at the poor bastard.

"Okay," Kiva said. "So fucking what?"

"He wants to buy passage for himself and his family. On the *Yes, Sir*."

"Off of End? To where?"

"He said that he would figure that out later."

Kiva snorted at this. "It's not like there's anywhere in the Interdependency that isn't already maxed out in population.

They haven't built a new outpost or dug out a new city in decades."

"I pointed that out to him. He said that would be his problem."

Kiva looked at the man again. "We're not running a cruise line here, Gazson."

"No, ma'am," Magnut agreed. "But if I may say so, it wouldn't really do us any harm, either. We're not running a full crew at this point, and we're not recruiting as many new crew as I'd like here on End. If nothing else we can put him and his family on custodial detail and make them pay for the privilege."

"Why are you having trouble hiring?"

Gazson shrugged. "There's a war on."

Kiva pointed. "*He* wants to leave."

"It's not the same, ma'am. He wants to leave forever and take his family with him. Everyone who has family *here* wants to be with them right now. Down on the surface there are huge numbers of people moving away from the open war zones. There's a refugee crisis down there. Honestly, even if we hadn't been barred from selling the haverfruit we wouldn't have sold much anyway. There's almost no market right now."

"We still would have had our license fees and profits," Kiva noted. Then she stopped, looked again at the man in her hold. "What's this dude's name again?" she asked Gazson.

"Sivouren Donher."

"Has he been a good franchisee for us?"

"One of our most successful. It's one of the reasons why he's asking. I think he thinks we owe him."

"Does he," Kiva said. "Then I guess you better bring him up."

Gazson nodded and went to retrieve him.

Close up Sivouren Donher was middle-aged, a little puffy, and had a look on his face that twitched between arrogance and anxiety so quickly that Kiva was certain he wasn't aware his head was doing that. It was a look of someone who until the last few days was pretty sure he could ride out whatever nonsense this rebellion was about, and then suddenly realized he couldn't.

"Lady Kiva," Donher said, bowing. He looked at the seat Gazson Magnut had recently vacated in order to retrieve him. He clearly expected that he would be offered a seat, this meeting being between equals and all.

"You want off End," Kiva said, not offering the seat. Magnut, who stood in the corner of the room, also not taking the seat, raised his eyebrows ever so slightly at the intentional breach of courtesy.

"Yes, ma'am."

Kiva nodded in the direction of Magnut. "Gazson here tells me that you're one of our most successful franchisees."

Donher smiled and nodded. "I have done well for your family, Lady Kiva."

"Define 'well' for me."

"For this current payment period, House of Lagos received four million marks from my companies. Uh, *will* receive, once the current unpleasantness you are having with the Duke of End is resolved."

"Four million marks," Kiva said. "That's not bad. That's not bad at all."

"Thank you, ma'am."

"So why the fuck would I want to mess with that?"

Donher blinked. "Ma'am?"

"You're one of my biggest moneymakers. If you leave End, that money dries up. Logic dictates I tell you to go back to your orchards and factories and keep at it."

"Ma'am . . . there's a war on."

"And? My people here tell me you idiots do this shit on a regular basis. In a few months you'll all be back to life as usual."

"Not this time, ma'am. This one is different. The duke is about to be overthrown. People who are known to be in his favor are being targeted and killed. They and their families."

"And I suppose *you* are best friends with the duke, aren't you?"

"I am frequently at court, ma'am. As is my wife, who is especially close to the duchess. We have had them to our estate on occasion."

Kiva squinted. "But you're not noble yourself."

"No, ma'am." Donher shrugged. "There was some talk of knighting me this year. My wife and I made a considerable donation to the duke's hospital charity. But such things are up in the air right now."

"Uh-huh." Kiva looked this fearful little social climber up and down and figured she had his number, all right. "Four million."

"Excuse me, ma'am?"

"You're not just asking me for passage, Donher. You're also asking me to let you out of your franchise deal with the House of Lagos. To abandon *our* income on this planet. Fine. That'll cost you four million marks."

"I have reached an agreement with my senior vice president to continue operations—" Donher stammered.

Kiva cut him off. "Our agreement is with *you*, Donher."

"With my companies, ma'am—"

"They're not *your* companies anymore," Kiva said, cutting him off again. "You're getting your ass out of town. We never made an agreement with whoever the fuck this senior vice president is. We don't know if they're competent to find their asshole with a flashlight and a map. *We*, the House of Lagos, are going to have to vet your company again. *We* are going to have to assess whether this vice president is worth doing business with. If he's not, *we* are going to have to pull the franchise, which will inevitably lead to a bunch of legal stupidity and this asshole suing us, and then *we* are going to lose money because of it."

"Lady Kiva, I can assure you—"

"*You* can't assure me of a goddamned thing, Donher. Not anymore. You're already off the playing board. You're literally fucking useless to me right now. The only assurance here is money. A lot of it. In this case, four million marks. In cash, on the proverbial goddamned barrelhead. That's the deal."

It was interesting to watch color drain out of someone's face. Kiva had read about it in books, but had never seen it happen in real life until now. Donher's face went from ruddy and sweaty to pale and clammy. "I'm not sure I have that, ma'am," he said.

"Oh, I am entirely certain that you *do*," Kiva replied. "You were planning to leave the planet and never come back. You're going to have to start somewhere else, where you have no franchise and no assurance of having prospects. The only way you and your family will survive long enough to generate those prospects is with a heaping pile of ready cash." She stopped and considered Donher. "I'm going to guess you've probably got ten or fifteen million marks in a personal data crypt right now." She pointed. "It might even be in that vest pocket right there. Am I wrong?"

Donher said nothing to this.

Kiva nodded. "Then back to business. Four million to let you out of your franchise obligations."

"Yes, Lady Kiva." Donher bowed, signaling that he assumed the deal had been struck.

"We're not done," Kiva said. "How many people are you bringing with you?"

"Myself, my wife, and our children. My wife's mother. Two servants."

"How many children?"

"Three. Two girls and a boy."

"What a nice family. A half a million marks for each person we transport."

Kiva watched the color march back into Donher's face. "That's outrageous!" he finally managed to sputter.

"Probably," Kiva admitted. "But I don't care. Your little family unit will be with us for nine months while we travel to Hub. That's nine months of food, of oxygen, of *space*, on our ship."

"That's another four million marks!"

"Your math skills are impressive, Donher."

"I can't afford it."

"Oh, well."

"Surely we can come to some accommodation, my lady."

Kiva laughed. "I'm sorry, did you think this was a negotiation? It's not. You want off the planet. These are my rates. If you don't like them, you're welcome to look elsewhere. I understand the *Tell Me Another One* is departing soon."

"Actually ma'am, it's been detained," Magnut said. "The duke had its captain arrested. He seems to think she allowed pirates to board the ship and take a shipment of weapons."

"Is that so."

"Apparently the deal was originally with the executive officer, who attempted a mutiny and failed. The captain decided to follow up on the deal with the pirates anyway. Better money. Allegedly."

"Huh." Kiva turned back to Donher. "One less option for you, then."

"Lady Kiva, I can offer you three million marks for passage. With the four million marks you already require, that's more than half of what I have."

"Then I guess you're leaving your servants behind," Kiva said. "Unless you were planning to take one and leave your mother-in-law behind."

The color began to drain from Donher's face again.

"You *were*!" Kiva crowed. "You were going to ditch your mother-in-law! You utter dog."

"I was not," Donher protested, weakly.

"A word of advice for you, Donher. With that face of yours, you shouldn't play cards with anyone on this ship. You'll end up in debt. So, we're up to seven million marks. You planning to bring anything with you? Any cargo?"

"If you'll allow it, ma'am."

"Of course I'll allow it. One thousand marks a kilo, and I'll collect a half million marks up front to allocate the cargo space. Any mass allowance you don't use, we'll refund."

Donher had learned by this point not to argue. "Yes, ma'am."

She pointed to Magnut. "Gazson will collect before you leave here and otherwise make arrangements. All of it, in full. We depart in five days. Gazson will give you the exact time. If you and your family aren't on the ship twelve hours prior to that moment, you all stay here, and we keep the money. Do you understand?"

"Yes, ma'am."

"Then we're done. Go back to the floor of the hold and wait there for Gazson."

Donher bowed and left. Magnut closed the door behind him.

"That was impressive, ma'am," he said to Kiva, after Donher was back on the hold floor.

Kiva snorted again. Then, "What did we learn here today, Gazson?"

"That Sivouren Donher really wants off the planet?"

"We learned that he wants off the planet badly enough to pay seven and a half million marks for it," Kiva said. "And that means there are *other* people like him who are willing to pay just as much as he is, if not more so."

"Are you thinking of taking on more refugees, ma'am?"

"Refugees? No. Exiles? Yes."

"There's a difference?"

"Roughly half a million marks per head, Gazson."

"Ah. So we *are* running a cruise line, then."

Kiva smirked and pointed down at Donher, standing forlornly once more near a stack of haverfruit crates. "We just bagged seven and a half million marks off this one dumb bastard," she said. "That's twelve and a half percent of our financial loss for this entire fucking trip, erased. A few more like him and we'll actually make it into the black. That's worth putting up with their entitled asses for a few months."

Magnut motioned toward Donher with his head. "That one's actually got travel documents for his family and servants. Not everyone who wants to go with us and can afford it will have those documents. Even if they were allowed to leave, most government offices are closed, so they wouldn't be able to get them."

"This is our problem?"

"When we get to Hub and unload these . . . exiles, if they don't have travel documents, we can get fined for illegal conveyance. So, yes, it could be our problem."

"We can only be fined if they can prove we knew they weren't allowed to travel, right?"

"Sort of," Magnut said. "It's more complicated than that."

"But *basically*," Kiva said. "If they have travel documents and they just *happen* to turn out to be fake, but *we* weren't able to tell, then the house can probably get those fines dismissed."

"Yes, ma'am."

Kiva raised her eyebrows, signaling to Magnut without incriminating words ever being spoken that he should find and procure the services of someone who could make passable faked travel documents on an expedited basis, to make sure these forgers charged an outrageous amount for them, of which the House of Lagos would take a "finder's fee" cut, and that, of course, if the forged documents were ever to be traced back to them, Magnut himself would take the fall rather than implicate Kiva and by extension the House of Lagos.

Magnut's heavy sigh and curt nod signaled that he understood this perfectly well.

"Then send out the word that we're accepting exiles. If they want on the ship they better hurry. And they better bring cash."

• • •

A lot of exiles *did* want on the ship. And they were happy to bring cash.

Not all of them were the financial windfall of Sivouren Donher, of course. Not everyone was planning to bring a family of five with hangers-on. But they added up: the single exiles, the couples and occasional families of three or four, all at half a million marks a head, plus cargo charges, plus documents, plus additional sums if the refugees were Lagos franchisees or business associates, which many were because Kiva told Magnut to screen for those and to give them preferential treatment.

Within two days, Kiva was within five million marks of going into the black for the trip. "I'm a fucking financial genius," she said, to Captain Blinnikka, back on the *Yes, Sir*.

"Or you're war profiteering," Blinnikka said.

"I'm not selling anything to the combatants," Kiva said, taken aback, but then trying to shrug it off with some light snark. "I'm offering a service to those who wish to leave the theater of combat. That makes me a humanitarian, actually. I'm saving people."

"For half a million marks each."

"I didn't say I was a bleeding heart about it."

"Whatever you say."

"We might finish this trip making a profit," Kiva pointed out. "You don't object to that."

"No," Blinnikka admitted. "Even a small loss will be a win for us given the circumstances. I won't lose my command. You won't lose face in front of your mother and the House of Lagos. What you're doing makes sound financial sense."

"But."

"There's no but. You're right. It's just a reminder that war favors the rich. The ones who can leave, do. The ones who can't, suffer."

Kiva was silent for a moment. Then, "Fuck you for having a conscience, Tomi."

"Yes, ma'am."

Kiva's tablet pinged; it was Gazson Magnut. "You're about to have a visitor," he said when Kiva connected.

"Who is it?"

"A Lord Ghreni Nohamapetan. He says you know him."

"Oh, for fuck's sake," Kiva said. "What does that abject pile of shit want?"

"I think it has something to do with your exile plan. He was asking questions about it, anyway."

"And what did you tell him?"

"I told him that he would need to bring it up with you. He got snitty about it and tried to pull rank with me, at which point I started quoting Interdependency trade regulations at him until he got frustrated and left me alone. He turned to his flunky and told her to get him a shuttle to take him to the *Yes, Sir*. He'll be there presently."

"Got it," Kiva said, and closed the connection. She turned to the captain. "Ready to do some space lawyering?"

Blinnikka smiled. "Of course."

"Good. Let's go."

• • •

"Lady Kiva," Ghreni Nohamapetan said, once the shuttle bay had run through its cycle and put air back into the space. "So lovely to see you again."

"Is it?" Kiva said.

"As far as you know, yes." Ghreni nodded to the captain. "You are Captain Blinnikka, I assume."

"Yes, my lord." Blinnikka bowed.

Ghreni did a quick head bow in return and then focused on Kiva. "We should talk privately," he said.

"About what?"

"About your profit-taking on refugees."

"There's nothing to talk about."

"The duke disagrees."

"Captain," Kiva said, to Blinnikka.

"My lord, the Interdependency is quite clear on the rights of refugees during wartime and the leeway ships and their crew have in offering assistance to them. Indeed, it's one of the core rights of the Interdependency, handed down by the Prophet herself."

Ghreni gave a humorless smile to this. "That's a lovely sentiment, Captain, obviated by the fact that you're charging a half million marks a head for passage."

"Actually, the captain and I were just talking about the plight of the less advantaged," Kiva said.

"You?" Ghreni said, disbelieving.

"One, fuck you, and two, yes." Kiva looked over to Blinnikka. "Isn't that right?"

"There had been some discussion, yes."

"And I suppose now you're going to tell me that you charging half a million a head to leave End is meant to subsidize the poor you will also take on as a gesture of your concern for their plight."

"Maybe. I suppose that's hard for you to believe, Ghreni, but then, you've always been a condescending little shit."

"There was a time when you saw that as an endearing quality, Lady Kiva." Ghreni turned his attention to the captain. "Laws concerning refugees notwithstanding, you are aware that End has special status in the Interdependency. Many people here can't just leave. They are here on End for a reason."

"Our chief purser is well aware of the special nature of End and some of its citizens," Blinnikka said. "We won't take anyone from the planet who is not allowed to leave."

"You don't mind if we double-check that," Ghreni said.

"Of course not," Blinnikka said. "I am sure the imperial customs office here on End will supply you whatever information you desire."

"The duke would prefer to examine your passenger manifest directly."

Blinnikka shook his head. "Apologies, my lord, but by Interdependency regulation that information must come through a request to the customs office, not from the ship directly."

"Surely you may accommodate the duke as a courtesy."

"Are you asking my captain to go against Interdependency law?" Kiva said.

"There is substantial overlap between the duke's interests and Interdependency law."

"As I am well fucking aware, thanks to your duke's embargo of my cargo. But in this case there's not, is there, Captain?"

"No, my lady," Blinnikka said.

"Well, then." Kiva looked at Ghreni, steadily.

"As long as I'm here, I would love to see some of the ship," Ghreni said, after a moment.

"You want a fucking tour," Kiva said.

"If you wouldn't mind."

"Because three days out from departure we don't have better things to do than indulge your whims."

"You really don't."

"This is your subtle attempt to talk with me alone, yes?"

Ghreni held his hands open, as if to say, *You got me.*

Kiva nodded and turned to Blinnikka. "I'm taking him to the production floor. If I need you again to spout imperial law at him, I'll call."

Blinnikka nodded and left.

"Come on, let's get this over with," Kiva said, and motioned to Ghreni to follow her.

The shuttle bay was at the aft of the main body of the *Yes, Sir,* a long, segmented needle, off from which branched two separate rings, which held the farming and processing modules, among others. Each rotated to provide a baseline .5 standard G, with push fields employed to bring the internal effective gravity to 1 G. Variations could be employed within individual modules and areas for production and other purposes.

As Ghreni noted when they entered an agricultural module. "I'm bouncier in here."

Kiva nodded. "Haverfruit grow best at .8 G, so that's what these modules are kept at."

"End is slightly over 1 G. Were you going to tell the people you licensed to about that?"

"It's not like it won't grow at that gravity," Kiva said. "It'll grow just fine. And they'd be growing them off of actual haverfruit bushes rather than the hydroponic setup we're using here." She motioned to the growing racks, densely packed with lights and fruits arising out of the growth medium. "If you have anything on End, it's acreage. Not that it matters, thanks to the fucking duke."

"To be fair, the House of Lagos let loose a virus that wiped out a staple crop."

"To be fair, you can go fuck yourself because we had nothing to do with that and you know it."

"I've missed you, Kiva. You and your marvelous way with the word 'fuck.'"

"No you haven't, but thank you anyway."

Ghreni motioned to the haverfruit. "So what will you do with all of this?"

"Follow me to the next module and find out."

The next ring module was a processing module, set to 1.1 G for efficiency.

"You're juicing them," Ghreni said, looking.

Kiva nodded. "Juicing, concentrating, making fruit pastes from the remains, all that shit. Not that we'll be able to do much with them directly. It doesn't make sense for us to compete against our franchisees. We thought about it, but we'd just make them upset. So when I get back to Hub we'll see if we can sell it as surplus to the imperial government. They'll distribute it as part of their food assistance to poor families, or whatever, and the House of Lagos will get a tax deduction."

"So you'll finish the trip just fine, is what you're saying."

"It's a maybe. If the imperial government doesn't shove this shit into its food assistance program, we're on the hook for all of it."

"I'm sure the Lagos accountants are clever enough to find a way to bury the loss. Combine that with the extortion you're wrenching out from the people trying to leave End, you might even eke out a profit."

"You make it sound like a bad thing."

"Not at all. What are the guild houses if they don't make money? That is their point. Your point. My point."

"You haven't actually come to your point yet," Kiva said.

"Then here's my point, Kiva: The duke is concerned about some of the people you might be transporting off the planet."

"Okay. So what?"

"Some of them are people who are of interest to the duke, for various reasons."

"This is where I say 'so what' again."

"So, if certain people try to buy passage from you, the duke wants to know."

Kiva laughed at this. "You have to be fucking kidding me, Ghreni. The duke is the reason I'm resorting to making fruit paste and taking on rich assholes as cargo."

"The duke asks it as a favor, one noble to another."

"The duke can fuck himself with a loaded shotgun."

Ghreni nodded again. "I thought you might say that. So I've also been authorized to offer you a bribe."

"For what?"

"For letting us know if certain people try to book passage on your ship. And for telling us where to find them if they do."

"I'm asking for a lot of money for passage," Kiva said.

"The duke is willing to match what you're charging as the reward."

"Match, hell. If he wants my cooperation, it starts at two million marks per person."

"That doesn't strike you as perhaps a lot to ask?"

"The duke screwed me out of sixty million marks at least, so, no, in fact, it *doesn't* strike me as a lot to ask."

"One million marks per person."

"Look at you, Ghreni, acting like I actually *need* something from you."

"The duke could decide to make your departure difficult."

"Is he going to have my captain arrested, like he did with the *Tell Me Another One*?"

"You heard about that."

"Space is a small town. We've already received our clearances, Ghreni. Our departure's already been approved. And the duke already has his hands full with not being deposed and probably killed."

"One and a half million marks per person."

"Two and a half million marks, and every time you try to negotiate the price from here on out, the price goes up."

"The duke is not made of money."

"Maybe he can just *borrow* some out of the money of mine he's appropriated, the son of a bitch."

"That's actually not a bad idea."

"Fuck you. Now it's up to three million marks just because you're pissing me off."

Ghreni held up his hands, placatingly. "Kiva. Stop. We have a deal."

"Three million per."

"Yes."

"You'll put ten million in escrow *right now* so I know you won't fuck me."

"I'll do it the minute I get back on Imperial Station."

"Who are you looking for?"

"The Count of Claremont and either of his children."

"Kids?"

"The children? No. They're both about thirty, standard. Twins. One male and one female."

"Why do you want them?"

"I'll tell you for three million marks."

"Don't be an asshole."

"It's not important. What is important is that we know if any of them try to leave the planet."

"If they try to contact us, then what?"

"Then you contact me, and we'll come in and collect them from Imperial Station, just before they try to board the *Yes, Sir.*"

"So you'll take care of all of it."

"Yes."

"You going to shove them down a well or something?"

"I don't think you need to worry about that."

"I may be an asshole, Ghreni, but I don't want to be an active accomplice to murder."

"We have no plans to murder anyone. We just don't want them to go."

"Anyone else? I mean, as long as you're offering three million per."

"No. But I admire the flexibility of your moral grounding."

"You said it yourself. Who are we if we're not making money?"

As Ghreni left the *Yes, Sir*, Kiva pinged Gazson Magnut. "I need you to do something for me."

"We have quite a lot of things to take care of at the moment, ma'am." This was, Kiva knew, as close to *fuck you, I'm busy* as Magnut was ever going to get.

"Yes, I know, but this is a thing that needs doing."

"What is it?"

"I need you to get someone to discreetly—as in *actually* fucking discreetly, not just saying the word—tell me who the Count of Claremont is and why the duke would give a shit about him in any way. The count's children, too."

"Yes, ma'am. The time frame on this?"

"An hour ago would be great."

"Understood."

"And while you're at it, get someone to tell me why the hell Ghreni Nohamapetan is on this planet and what his relationship is with the duke."

"We already know he's an advisor."

"Right, and I know that twice in the last three days his ass has been the one crossing my path on matters involving the duke. And maybe you see that shit as coincidence, but I don't."

"The same time frame, ma'am?"

"Yes."

"That will take money."

"Spend it."

"How much?"

"Whatever it costs. Tack it onto the boarding price of the next person who wants passage."

"Yes, ma'am."

Kiva punched out of the conversation and used her tablet to access one of the *Yes, Sir*'s external cameras, right outside the shuttle bay. Ghreni Nohamapetan's shuttle was receding into the distance, toward the imperial station.

"What are you up to, you motherfucker?" Kiva said, out loud

to herself. "And what is your *family* up to?" Because whatever Ghreni was up to, it was just part of some larger Nohamapetan plan. And whatever *those* assholes were up to, it was no good for anyone else, including the House of Lagos. Or the imperial House of Wu, for that matter. Or the Interdependency as a whole, come to think of it.

Kiva looked at that shuttle, a speck now, and wondered whether she shouldn't just order the *Yes, Sir*'s defensive grid to launch a missile into it. Yes, there would be explaining to do. Yes, *technically* it would be murder. Yes, it would probably start a war between the House of Lagos and the House of Nohamapetan, which the House of Lagos, for all its power, would probably lose in the long run.

On the other hand, at this very moment, it would make Kiva feel *really good*.

Kiva reluctantly put down her tablet and decided to do something else with her time, a decision, by her own admission, that she would later come to regret.

6

The coronation robes were heavy, the anointing oil smelled like it had gone bad a century ago, the crown dug into her forehead and chafed, she was sweating, the coronational liturgy was nearly an hour long, and to top it all off, Cardenia's period had begun last night and right now her cramps were like someone with an iron glove had taken it, wrapped it around her uterus, and squeezed.

Yes, Coronation Day was going along just great for Emperox Grayland II, thanks for asking.

The cathedral in Xi'an—*her* cathedral, in point of fact, because in addition to being emperox she was the head of the Interdependent Church, technically the Cardinal of Xi'an and Hub, and thus had to have her own cathedral—was a vast space, made of stone and glass in the Early Interdependence style. Cardenia mused on the incongruity of a massive edifice of stone constructed inside of a space station, but not for too long, lest the incongruity of Xi'an entire, with its hills, streams, and forests, with administrative buildings, housing corridors, and commerce artfully tucked away to avoid the impression of clutter, send her into delirious giggles.

Xi'an Cathedral had room for thousands in its pews and

today of all days those pews were filled. Representatives from all of the interdependent states, guild families, celebrities, and princes of the Interdependent Church looked on, presumably reverently, as Archbishop Gunda Korbijn droned through the liturgy. At one point Cardenia noted that Korbijn had a speaker set into her left ear canal, revealing that even the archbishop couldn't be relied upon to know the entire ceremony by heart. This relieved Cardenia somewhat and made everything slightly more human-scaled.

Cardenia did not herself have a speaker in her ear, but then her role in the event was oddly limited: walk and sit. She had processed down the nave of Xi'an Cathedral in a relatively simple imperial green suit, stopped at the transept, and waited for Korbijn to offer her opening prayer and homily, and her invitation for Cardenia—for Grayland II, rather—to join her on the chancel. A stool for kneeling had been set in its center, above a mosaic of the imperial seal. Cardenia kneeled, bowed her head, and waited for things to be put on her by Korbijn and her assistants.

First, the aforementioned anointing oil, which almost made her gag with its smell. Then a ceremonial scarlet robe and a golden braid with a medallion, the braid being the symbol of the Interdependent Church and medallion featuring a phoenix, the personal symbol of the prophet. With that she was declared the cardinal of Xi'an and Hub, and thus, the head of the Interdependent Church.

Next came a key on a smaller golden chain, symbolizing access to the rooms of parliament, which resided at the other end of Xi'an from the imperial palace, symbolizing (in theory if not always in practice) the independence of the parliament from the emperox. This independence was in part belied by the fact that the emperox was always the minister of parliament for

Xi'an, a seat that was generally considered honorary and ceremonial but which in fact had the same voting privileges as any other. It was tradition for the emperox to abstain from voting on any legislation, including legislation they were known to favor (legislation they disliked they would simply veto). But every once in a while an emperox would record a vote, to the scandal of the rank-and-file parliamentarians.

After the key came a signet ring, the size of a small rock, which symbolized Cardenia's ascendance to the role of matriarch of the House of Wu. This was a role formally separate from Cardenia's role as emperox; while the House of Wu was the imperial dynasty, it was also a guild family, with monopolies on starship construction and military weaponry and services. One could very easily say that the House of Wu was the imperial house because of these particular monopolies. As emperox, Cardenia would not be actively involved in the day-to-day running of the house monopolies; those would be administered by a board of cousins who would resent her interference. But she was the one with the Wu signet nonetheless, worn on the left hand to leave room for the imperial signet on the right.

Which came next, a ring even larger than the one for the House of Wu, along with a ceremonial scepter tipped with an emerald the size of a fist, and a crown of rubies, diamonds, and emeralds, signifying the church, the parliament, and the imperial house, which was heavy as hell and which started chafing Cardenia almost immediately. The scepter, crown, and signet also marked her as Queen of Hub and the Associated Nations, a lesser title. Cardenia also held dukedoms and earldoms and a few baronies which were salted away among the various interdependent states, which she would have almost nothing ever to do with directly.

For each step Korbijn said something ceremonial, said more

as she was laying the object on Cardenia, and even more afterward, followed by a prayer or small homily, or both. After a certain early point Cardenia, sweating and cramping, started wishing that she could have just filed a form.

Korbijn turned and looked directly at Cardenia, and now, finally, she was required to do something besides kneel there.

"Arise, Grayland II, Emperox of the Holy Empire of the Interdependent States and Mercantile Guilds, Queen of Hub and Associated Nations, Head of the Interdependent Church, Successor to Earth and Mother of All, Eighty-eighth Emperox of the House of Wu, and proclaim your reign," Korbijn said, and then stood aside.

Cardenia took a breath and rose, using the scepter briefly to stabilize herself, the first and possibly last time the scepter would offer any practical use. Upon the completion of the ceremony, all the accouterment of the coronation would be (thankfully) stripped off her and sent back into their storage vault, to await the next coronation of the next emperox, whomever they might be. But for now they lay heavy on her.

That's not at all symbolic, she thought.

She turned, to face the assembly of nobles, notables, and representatives. The executive committee, save Korbijn, in the front row of pews. Behind them, representatives from the House of Wu, and among them, looking wildly out of place, her uncle Brendan Patrick and her cousins Moira and Justin, representing her mother. Hannah Patrick would not hear of her daughter's ascendance for weeks, and would hear it simultaneously to the news of her enlargement to become Baroness of Tacuarembó, a courtesy title from one of the emperox's own holdings. This title would probably simultaneously annoy and tickle her mother.

Several rows back sat Naffa Dolg, with her family of

republicans. Cardenia was touched that despite their opposition to imperial rule in a general sense, they still came out to support her, and their daughter. Between Naffa's row and the close pews with the Wus sat the matriarchs and patriarchs of various guild families, nobles all.

And, in the third row, Amit and Nadashe Nohamapetan, both of them staring fixedly at Cardenia as if she were a long-term project, or a side of meat.

Or both, Cardenia thought.

Behind her, Archbishop Korbijn cleared her throat quietly, as if to say, *Get on with it.*

"I, Cardenia Wu-Patrick, having accepted these instruments of church and state, as is my right, become Grayland II, emperox, queen, head of church, successor to Earth, and mother to all. May the tenets of Interdependency, laid forth by the Prophet, bring continued peace and prosperity to all."

"Long live the emperox," came the reply, from the first pew to the rafters, followed by immense cheering, which Cardenia, through the sweat and cramps, still managed to enjoy.

Music swelled; the "March of the Prophetess" by Higeliac, written in the third century FI, swelled, performed by a chamber orchestra cleverly hidden in one of the transept alcoves in order to allow more pews to be placed in the cathedral. The boxed-up orchestra had its efforts played through speakers; the coronation audience stood, still cheering, as Grayland II took her first steps, down from the chancel, down the nave, and quickly down a side corridor, where assistants were waiting to escort her to a small office to divest her of crown, scepter, and other nonsense, and the imperial bodyguards to post themselves by the door.

"I thought that went well, Your Majesty," Naffa said to her.

Cardenia looked up, confused, as she was being stripped down. "I just saw you in the audience."

"That's because I was just in the audience."

"How did you get here so quickly?"

"Because it's my job," Naffa said, and magically a clipboard appeared. "How are you doing?"

"Tell me I never have to do this again."

"It's exceedingly rare for an emperox to have two coronation ceremonies, so, yes. You will never have to do this again."

"Now tell me I can go home."

"As the emperox owns Xi'an itself, technically speaking you are home."

"There's a terrifying thought."

"In more prosaic fashion, however, you may not go home yet. In the next ten minutes, you must change into the formal uniform Dochae here is now showing you—" Naffa nodded toward the assistant, who indeed had a very formal uniform at the ready. "—and then you must go to the presentation balcony to wave to the tens of thousands of people who are currently ruining the lawn of the cathedral in the hope of seeing you. You'll be up there for five minutes and then we go back to the palace where you will have an hour's worth of five-minute audiences with a minute between them, and another hour of ten-minute audiences with two minutes between them. Then you are to arrive at your coronation celebration, at which point you will give a short address—"

Cardenia groaned.

"—which I have already prepared for you and which no one will listen to anyway because it is not of consequence, and then for the rest of your celebration you'll spend three hours in a receiving line, shaking hands and having pictures and video taken with everyone, which I suspect is exactly the hell you imagine it will be. Then and only then will you be able to relax and eat something, so I suggest that while Dochae here helps you into that new uniform, that you also eat the protein bars she has for you. And maybe drink some water."

"Do I get to relieve myself?"

"There's a lavatory here. Door to your left. Before you ask, it's stocked with everything you need at the moment."

"Thank you. I'm glad someone remembers I am still actually a human."

"Of course. Take your time as long as your time is under a minute."

Cardenia groaned again and headed toward the lavatory.

Seven minutes later Cardenia's coronation outfit was packed, her post-coronation outfit was on and surprisingly comfortable, and her phalanx of bodyguards was surrounding her in the elevator taking her up to the cathedral's observatory deck, where her presentation balcony awaited. Cardenia looked around her and realized that outside of the palace itself, she was likely never to be alone in an elevator ever again.

The elevator door opened and there was Naffa again, standing in front of the alcove that was the presentation balcony.

"You have to stop doing that," Cardenia said. "It's creepy."

"Relax. I took up the elevator on the other side. It has its own set of bodyguards."

"Welcome to my world."

"I've been in it a while. I hope you noticed."

Cardenia laughed, stepped to exit the elevator, and then was knocked back into the elevator as the presentation balcony exploded. She was unconscious before her body slammed into the elevator's back wall.

• • •

"There's a very real possibility that the Flow streams that connect the Interdependency will collapse during your reign," Attavio VI, Cardenia's father, or rather the computer projection of him, said to Cardenia in her dream.

Cardenia was aware she was dreaming; Cardenia was also aware that the dream was, for the moment at least, replaying her first conversation in the Memory Room. She was not aware of how or when it was that she fell asleep, and the part of her brain that was lucid enough to register that she was in a dream was strongly shying away from thinking about it that much. *Go with this conversation. It's safe*, that part of her brain seemed to be saying, so Cardenia did, saying her part of the conversation again as if reading off a script.

"How will that happen?" Cardenia asked.

"I'm not a scientist," Attavio VI said. "But the Count of Claremont is. He's been collecting data for three decades now. He sends me updates from time to time. The data he's collected suggests that the stability of the Flow is an illusion and that over a long enough timescale everything shifts, and that we're about to enter a period of shifts. He says it's already been happening slowly, and it's about to start happening very quickly indeed. It's happened before."

"To Dalasýsla. When the first Grayland was emperox."

Attavio VI nodded. "Yes. She was given information, just like I have been given information—information you'll now have access to."

"She had information, but why didn't she act on it? If she knew they were about to lose the stream to Dalasýsla, why didn't she do something about it?"

"I could tell you, but you can ask her yourself."

Cardenia blinked at this. "She's in here?"

"Of course."

"She was lost in the Flow. I didn't think she *existed*."

"She updated before her final trip. Everything but those last few days is in here."

This took Cardenia aback. On one hand it made sense. On another, the idea of a person being . . . *incomplete* was odd. "Jiyi, show me Emperox Grayland I."

A shimmer and a tall, wide woman appeared and walked toward Cardenia.

"You're Emperox Grayland I," Cardenia asked.

"Yes," the woman said.

"You . . . know what happened to you? How you died?"

"I'm aware of the information, yes."

"How do you feel about it?" This was all an aside, but Cardenia had to know.

"I don't feel anything about it. I'm a computer simulation of a person. That said, given what I know about it, I imagine the actual Emperox Grayland I was exceptionally pissed about it."

This made Cardenia smile. Then she got back on track. "You knew the Flow stream for Dalasýsla was collapsing."

"I was given models by scientists that suggested that the stream was in danger of collapsing, yes. Given the data and my understanding of it, I thought it was possible, and likely."

"But you didn't evacuate the Dalasýsla system."

"No."

"Why not?"

"Politics," Grayland said. "Evacuating the twenty million people who lived in the Dalasýsla system would have required immense planning and capital on the part of the Interdependency. There was no will for it."

"The parliament didn't want to save the lives of twenty million people?"

"They didn't see it as a matter of saving those lives. They considered it a matter of someone they saw as a weak emperox trying to manufacture a crisis, as a way of shifting the balance of power away from the parliament. They also saw it as a threat to trade and the economy, since a large number of ships would need to be committed to an evacuation, at a huge cost."

"What about the data showing the possibility of a collapse?"

"They held a commission which featured other Flow physicists poking holes in the findings, introducing enough doubt to undermine any political drive to do anything. Even the representatives from Dalasýsla voted down my recommendation to begin an evacuation. What eventually passed was a recommendation for further study. But money wasn't appropriated in the imperial budget for that further study, so nothing came of it."

"So—" *So you did nothing,* Cardenia was going to say, but then stopped because it would be rude and would make Grayland almost instantly defensive. Then she remembered she was talking to a computer who didn't have feelings. "So you did nothing."

"I sent the local duchess an advisory, and told the military and local imperial bureaucrats to assist, on an expedited basis, any Dalasýslans who wanted to leave."

"And did they?"

"We don't know. The Flow stream collapsed almost immediately after I sent the advisory."

"So twenty million people died because of politics and bureaucracy."

"Yes. Not immediately, of course. But the intentional nature of the Interdependency is that each system is reliant on the others for essentials. Remove one system, and its ruling house and monopoly, and the dozens of other systems will survive. But that one system will not. Over time it will begin to fail. The habitats in space and outposts on otherwise uninhabitable planets and moons will fall into disrepair and over time will become harder to fix. Farms and food production factories will also start to fail. Social networks will break down predictably, commensurate to failures of the physical plant and the realization that ultimately nothing can save the people in the cut-off system. Between the physical and social failures that will follow the collapse of the Flow stream, system-wide death is inevitable."

"How long did it take?"

"When the Dalasýsla collapse happened, I ordered radio observatories in the Kaipara system to train in on Dalasýsla. Kaipara was the closest system by physical distance, seventeen light-years away. I was dead before they heard anything."

"But they heard something."

"Briefly. Most in-system communication in my era was through focused streams of data, so it would have been difficult to eavesdrop randomly. When I ordered the radio telescopes to listen I hoped someone at Dalasýsla would have the presence of mind to point a wide-spectrum transmitter at Kaipara. And as I understand it, someone did, for about a month, two years after the collapse."

"What did it say?"

"Basically: civil war, murder, violence, sabotage of life-support systems and food production, the rise of cults of personality. There's a classified report that was prepared by my son and successor, Bruno III."

"Classified?" Cardenia turned to Attavio VI. "Is it still classified?"

"I didn't unclassify it, no," Attavio said.

"Why not? Especially if you believe the Flow is in danger of collapsing?"

"Because the problems that existed in Grayland's era exist in ours, or mine, I should say. The parliament would still see raising the concern as a political move to marginalize them. No one wants to disrupt trade or the privileges of the guild houses. And in this case it won't be just one system, like Dalasýsla. It will be all of them. There won't be anywhere to run. What happened at Dalasýsla will happen everywhere. Unless I was absolutely sure, I wasn't going to open that particular box of trouble."

And here is where Cardenia, in her dream, departed from her script. "This is all stupid," she said, to Attavio VI and Grayland I. "We're doomed only if we keep doing what we're doing. If we know a collapse is coming, we have to reform the Interdependency. End the house monopolies. Help every system prepare for the collapse."

"It won't happen," Attavio VI said.

"You don't know that."

"Of course I know that. I'm the emperox. Or was."

Cardenia turned to Grayland I. "You saw a collapse happen. In your time, they must have responded."

"I was assassinated," Grayland I said. "And after a brief vogue for entertainment about the lost system of Dalasýsla, everyone decided to forget about it. The other Flow streams looked stable, and thinking about Dalasýsla was inconvenient."

"No one wants the Interdependency to end. Including the House of Wu. There's too much money and power at stake," Attavio VI said.

"And the survival of humanity doesn't matter?" Cardenia asked, incredulously.

"Not if it means the end of the Interdependency."

"The survival of humanity was the *point* of the Interdependency!" Cardenia shouted, at the computer simulation of her father.

And this is where, in her dream, both Attavio VI and Grayland I laughed in her face.

"My child, that's *never* been the point of the Interdependency," Attavio VI said.

"It's just the excuse we gave for it," Grayland I affirmed, nodding.

"Then what is the point?" Cardenia asked, still shouting. "What *is* the Interdependency?"

And here there was another shimmer, and another figure walked toward Cardenia, a figure that Cardenia knew was meant to be Rachela I, prophet-emperox, the legendary founder of the Interdependency. It was meant to be Rachela I but looked like Naffa, Naffa who had been caught in the explosion of the presentation balcony, Naffa, the last sight of whom that Cardenia would ever have was her being torn apart by the blast, Naffa, covered in blood, who stood in front of Cardenia now, as Rachela I, to tell her what the Interdependency was and is.

"It's a scam," she said.

And then Cardenia, who even dreaming could no longer pretend not to know what had happened, willed herself awake, to find herself in a bed in her own very small, very secure private hospital, surrounded by imperial bodyguards, a phalanx of doctors led by Qui Drinin, and a small contingent of imperial guards, including the one, right there, who would tell her what she already knew, that her friend Naffa Dolg was dead.

PART TWO

The fighting near the University of Opole had subsided enough that Marce Claremont had been able to return to his apartment in graduate housing to pack for a trip from which he would likely never return.

Which did bring up the question: If you are leaving forever, what do you take with you?

Marce's triage was helped by certain factors. With regard to clothing, Marce was already packed; he had enough clothes at home in Claremont that he didn't need any from his apartment in Opole. The only thing his apartment had to offer in that regard were some casual shirts with clever astrophysics comments silkscreened on them. Marce was reasonably sure he could leave those behind. The clothing he did pack was mostly neutral in color and design. His father pointed out that fashion on Hub would be so dramatically different that he would have to restock anyway.

All the music, books, pictures, entertainment, and much of the personal communication that Marce treasured was stored in a thumb-sized data crypt, along with what appeared to be close to one hundred thousand marks of spending money, the latter accessible only through Marce's biometrics, theoretically. Marce wouldn't have to waste space on any of those.

That left things—objects of sentimental value. The large majority of these sorts of objects also resided in Claremont Palace, both because that's where Marce had lived most of his life, and also because the apartment in graduate housing was ridiculously small. Of the objects that were at the apartment, Marce chose four. Two were books, given to him by his father, one on his thirteenth standard birthday, and one when he received his doctorate.

The third was an obsolete music player given to him by Vrenna, who took the player to a Green Gods concert and managed to get it signed by three of the four members of the band. The player didn't work anymore and the Green Gods had broken up years ago, members dispersing into oblivion and/or ill-advised solo careers. But he kept it to remember that time in his life, and to remind him that Vrenna, despite often being a pain in his ass as they grew up, was occasionally capable of being thoughtful and kind.

The final object was a threadbare stuffed pig named Giggy, bought for Marce on his first birthday by his mother, who had given Vrenna a stuffed bear named Howie at the same time. Howie had disappeared years before—there was reason to believe Vrenna may have launched him into the sky using a homemade rocket—but Giggy survived and accompanied Marce to every new home. Fiction would dictate that Giggy was the sole remaining gift Marce had from his now-departed mother, but in real life Marce had many gifts and owned many things that were either from her or reminded him of her. Giggy was simply his good-luck charm.

Marce stuffed all four objects in a small rucksack, and then considered the rucksack. *Not a lot to leave a world with*, he thought. Marce had been doing his best not to think too much about the fact that he was leaving the planet to go to a place where he knew no one and where he would likely spend all the rest of his life. The Flow stream *to* End would last longer than the one going out from it; it might be open for years yet. Theoretically it was possible at this point that he could make it back. It was just deeply unlikely. Marce's way of dealing with the fact he'd never see his father or sister or any of the people he'd ever known in his lifetime was to think about the practical issues of leaving the planet.

Which he had attended to; the day before he'd met with Gazson Magnut, the chief purser of a ship called *Yes, Sir, That's My Baby*, and arranged passage. It hadn't been cheap—it had in fact cost more money than Marce figured he'd ever spent on everything else he'd ever bought in his life up to that point—and Magnut had tried to upsell him on several other things, including a faked set of travel documents. Marce noted Magnut seemed mildly disappointed when he pointed out his travel documents were in order. With that taken care of, all that remained was to set up resignation and farewell letters, all of which would be sent after the *Yes, Sir* was in the Flow.

And this, the collecting of important objects. Everything else in the apartment could be collected by Claremont staff later.

Marce swung the rucksack over his shoulder, took a last look at the apartment, and decided that he would not miss it at all. It was, like nearly every academic institutional residence, entirely forgettable in every way. Then he headed down the stairs and out of the dormitory, down a street that was almost entirely empty except for a couple of people far down the road, and the van, which drove up to where Marce was, and opened up to reveal a couple of very large men.

The van then took off again, Marce in it, because the very large men had jumped out and dragged him into it before he really knew what was going on. The rucksack with all the sentimental objects stayed behind on the sidewalk, because sometimes that happens when you get kidnapped.

• • •

Ghreni Nohamapetan smiled at Marce Claremont across a small table. "Lord Marce. So good to see you again. I'm glad we could have this meeting on short notice."

"Lord Ghreni," Marce said. "Since you had me kidnapped to be here, I don't think it was something I could really refuse."

The two of them were sitting in a windowless room that looked like it had been made out of a storage container—which meant it probably was a storage container, repurposed. Marce had no idea of its location. He'd been in the room all of ten minutes, placed there by the thugs who had grabbed him, before Ghreni arrived.

"I don't like the word 'kidnapped,'" Ghreni said.

"With all due respect, Lord Ghreni, at the moment I don't really give a damn what you like."

"Fair enough." Ghreni leaned back in his chair and considered Marce. "Rumor is that you're planning to leave End behind."

"If I were, I don't see how it's any of your business."

"Well, see. There's a war on, and the duke has noticed that several of his nobles—or their children, adult or otherwise—are now suddenly trying to book passage off the planet."

"That will happen when there's a war."

"I suppose it might," Ghreni agreed. "The duke doesn't see it as a vote of confidence in his leadership skills, however, so he's been inviting those who are interested in leaving to stay."

"I don't think you've kidnapped me to extend me this invitation, Lord Ghreni," Marce said.

"No, I suppose that would be going the long way around to do it. You're correct. I've invited you here for other reasons entirely. You'll recall the other day when I asked your father to assist the duke with the release of imperial funds."

"I recall him telling you 'maybe.' "

"He did—which I took to mean 'no, but politely.' And to be clear, if that really was his answer, his reasons were both ethically and legally sound. It was a good choice for him to make, for those reasons."

"I'll tell him you said that."

"I don't doubt that you would," Ghreni said. "Just not yet. The problem with your father's answer, legally and ethically admirable as it might be, is that right now the duke really needs that money, because he really needs those weapons. And even 'maybe' doesn't work with the time frame we're under. So where persuasion didn't work, compulsion might."

"You're holding me for ransom."

"Yes. And I do apologize for that. Your father isn't susceptible to other . . . blandishments that I or the duke might offer. He doesn't seem interested in money or power or anything else tangible. And he has no patriotism for End or loyalty to the duke. But there's no doubt that he loves both you and your sister. From there it was just the matter of choosing which of the two of you to pick. We considered your sister . . ."

Marce laughed at this, and Ghreni as gracefully as possible acknowledged the laugh.

". . . but she presented problems in terms of acquisition."

"You mean that she would have gutted the thugs you sent after her, and then would have come after you next, after they gave you up."

"That's exactly what I mean. You were, and I mean this with no disrespect whatsoever, the softer target."

Marce nodded at this. It was true enough. He was a scientist, and Vrenna was a soldier, or had been before she had taken over Claremont's constabulary. Of the two of them, he was much more likely to be taken by surprise, and rather less likely to snap anyone's neck.

"There is also the matter that you are intended to leave the planet, and she's not."

"So?"

"You've never left End before. You've never even gone to the imperial station, even when your sister was in the marines. Your leaving now is interesting."

"You mentioned there was a war going on."

"Yes, but I don't think that's why you're leaving. If you were leaving because of the war, it wouldn't just be you. Your sister and father would be leaving as well, or at least trying to. But it's just you." Ghreni reached into his pocket and pulled out a data crypt, laid it on the table. "And by this, at least, you're not leaving with the family inheritance."

Marce stared at the data crypt. It had been taken from him when he'd been kidnapped, along with the other personal items that were on his body rather than in the now-missing rucksack.

Ghreni pushed it over to him. "Take it."

Marce took it, put it in his pocket. "Is it empty?"

"No. I don't need your pictures and music, and I'm afraid the duke needs more than a hundred thousand marks from your family. Until and unless your father helps us, it's not as if you're going anywhere anyway. And because I think he wants you to go, now, I think we'll get what we want from him."

"And if you don't?"

Ghreni shrugged. "For starters, you're not leaving the planet."

"'For starters.'"

"The duke really needs access to that money."

"Enough to kill me?"

"He wouldn't be killing you himself. But now that you mention it, at the moment, hundreds and possibly thousands of people are dying daily in this stupid rebellion. If placing one life in the balance—yours—means thousands more will live, isn't that a risk worth taking?"

"You really just attempted to morally justify kidnapping me."

Ghreni shrugged again. "It's certainly an argument I can see the duke making to ease his conscience. Whether it holds water is not something I think he'll trouble himself with. The duke is many things, but a great thinker is not one of them."

"This isn't going to work."

"We'll see. Either way, war excuses many lapses, especially if the duke gets his weapons and quashes the rebellion. In the meantime, Lord Marce, you get to find out how much you are worth to your father. If not for yourself, then for whatever reason he has for sending you off the planet. You don't want to tell me what that is, do you?"

"It's not any of your business."

"I know you believe that. But you might be surprised at the scope of my business."

"Since the scope of your business clearly involves kidnapping, I don't think anything you'd do at this point would surprise me much."

"Again, fair point. I'm willing to listen if you want to tell me why you're really planning to leave End."

Marce stayed silent, staring at Ghreni.

"That's fine," Ghreni said, after a minute. "If your father doesn't move quickly enough, we'll be torturing you a bit to motivate him. Video and all of that. While we're doing that I'll have them ask you about this again."

"Torture doesn't get truthful answers."

"That's what they say. Again, we'll see." Ghreni stood up and pointed to the far end of the container. "In the meantime, there's a toilet in that far corner, and over here there's a cooler with water and a few snacks." He pointed toward the near end. "The door is here. If you get within five feet of it, an electric current goes through it. If you touch it, you probably won't die, but you'll wish you had. If you still somehow manage to open it anyway, my people on the other side will make you wish you hadn't. You understand?"

Marce nodded.

"Good." Ghreni considered Marce. "I do apologize about this. This wasn't how I would have done it. And I realize this will make things awkward between us from here on out."

"For starters," Marce said, echoing Ghreni's comments from earlier. Ghreni smiled and exited.

Marce went to the cooler, took out a bottle of water, and drank from it, looking at his surroundings again. Table lamp, chairs, toilet, cooler. No cot. A cold metal floor and cold metal walls. He walked to the front of the room, not too close to the wide doors, and heard voices on the other side, low, masculine. He couldn't make out what they were saying.

This is lovely, he thought. The only good news in any of this was that Ghreni gave back his data crypt, which was rather more valuable than he knew. Otherwise, this was a mess. By now his father would probably have been contacted by Ghreni Nohamapetan. Marce didn't know how his father would react. On one hand this was exactly the sort of thing he'd push back against. On the other hand, Ghreni was right that the only things Dad really cared about in this life were his children.

There was also the matter that somewhere between a week and a month from now, Interdependency marks were going to be worth less, pound for pound, than dirt. That being the case, Dad might hand the money over simply because it wouldn't matter in the long run, or even the slightly-longer-than-short run.

But then this uprising, which was beginning to look like it might sort itself out, and not in the duke's favor, might get a new burst of life from those additional weapons. More death, more destruction, more people displaced from their homes—at a time when everyone on End's life was going to be turned upside down anyway, because of the Flow stream out from the planet closing up.

Marce took another swallow from his water. He was afraid, and deeply concerned for his individual well-being—Ghreni Nohamapetan struck him as just the sort of smug sociopath that would in fact have him tortured just for fun—but he also felt strangely detached. Whether that was shock at his current state of being, or just awareness that human civilization was close to the end, so relatively speaking this was nothing, or both, was something he couldn't parse. He was scared, but he was also tired. At the moment, at least, being tired was something he could actually do something about.

So Marce Claremont went back to his chair, sat in it, put his feet up on the table, crossed his arms, closed his eyes, and tried to take a nap.

Some indefinite time later he felt himself being shaken awake. "Look who's here to see you," said a familiar voice.

Marce opened his eyes, blinking, and tried to focus on the thing directly in front of him. It was Giggy, his stuffed pig. The person behind Giggy, waving him in Marce's face, was his sister Vrenna.

"You found me," Marce said, groggy.

"That's what I do," Vrenna replied, handing Giggy over to her brother.

"Why weren't you electrified?"

"What?" Vrenna looked puzzled.

"Never mind. *How* did you find me?"

"I had help. I'll explain later. Are you okay to walk?"

"I'm fine."

"Then let's get moving before the two chunks I stunned wake up."

Vrenna led Marce out of the room, which was, as suspected, a repurposed cargo container, located inside a tumbledown warehouse. Marce's container was not the only one; two more, presumably currently unoccupied, were lined up next to his. One of them had a long streak of blood curving away from it, as if a body had been dragged away. Outside Marce's container two men lay on the floor of the warehouse, the same two who had grabbed him and pulled him into the van. They were breathing, which was more than Marce really wanted for them at the moment.

"What is this place?"

"It looks like an extracurricular detention center," Vrenna said.

"For the duke?"

"Maybe. Come on." Vrenna led her brother out of the warehouse, and pushed him toward a nondescript groundcar. Marce got in and buckled up while Vrenna put the thing into manual drive.

"Where are the others?" Marce asked, looking around.

"What others?" Vrenna asked.

"You came to get me alone?"

"I didn't have a lot of time to make a project out of it." Vrenna checked her surroundings and began driving off.

"What if I had been injured? What if I hadn't been able to walk? What if there had been more than two of them?"

"I would have figured something out."

"I have notes on this rescue."

"I can put you back if you like."

Marce giggled and clutched his stuffed pig tighter. "Don't mind me, sis," he said. "I'm just having a little post-kidnapping freakout."

Vrenna reached over and took her brother's hand. "I know," she said. "Go ahead and freak out a little. I don't mind."

After a couple of minutes of relatively restrained freakout, Marce held up Giggy and looked at him. "You brought Giggy with you."

"I did. I thought it might distract you from thinking too much while I got you out of there."

"It worked, but I'm wondering how you got him in the first place."

"He was given to me. Along with the rest of the stuff you had in a rucksack when you were kidnapped."

"Okay, but how did you get any of *that*?"

"It was given to me by the people who were watching you."

"People were watching me?"

"Yes."

"Who?"

The call from Ghreni Nohamapetan after he lost Marce Claremont had to be one of the most satisfying calls Kiva had ever gotten in her life.

"Marce Claremont is gone," he said.

"Who?" Kiva replied.

"Don't fuck with me, Kiva. I want to know where he is."

"I couldn't tell you where he is. It's not my job to keep track of him. My job, as I understood it, was to tell you if he tried to book passage on my ship. He did, and I told you. You were supposed to wait until he was about to board to snatch him, if I remember correctly. You decided not to wait. So it looks like this one is on you."

"The people I had with Claremont tell me they were attacked by a woman."

"It wasn't me."

"It was Vrenna Claremont."

"You mean the sister who had years of training to murder people for the state, and then became a cop? Yes, that would be my logical guess too."

"I want to know how she came to find out we were targeting her brother."

"So ask her."

"Kiva."

"*I* didn't tell her, if that's what you were asking. Why would I tell her? I had three million marks riding on you snatching him."

"Someone in your crew told them."

"Or, and here's just a *theory*, when you tried to extort the Count of Claremont in front of his adult children and you didn't immediately get what you wanted, maybe they figured an asshole like you would try to force his hand with something like kidnapping, so they made preparations, particularly the one of them who was a fucking soldier and is now a goddamned *cop*, Ghreni."

There was silence on the other end of the call for a moment. Then, "I'd like to know how you heard about that."

"Because Marce Claremont fucking *told* us," Kiva said. "He told my chief purser about it when he was booking passage, and then my purser told me, because his job is to tell me things that will affect my ship's bottom line. Are you really such a smug asshole that you didn't think the Claremont kids wouldn't talk about that? If there wasn't a fucking war going on and the rule of law wasn't basically *suspended* while the duke thrashes about for a few more days before the end, your ass would already be in jail for extortion, with the duke letting you be the fall guy. For fuck's sake, Ghreni. You tried to extort an imperial official in front of a fucking cop. You have to be spectacularly dense to try to pull a stunt like that."

There was another silence, and Kiva merrily counted off the seconds before Ghreni spoke again. She got to six.

"Have you heard from Marce or Vrenna Claremont?"

Kiva snorted. "Why the fuck would I hear from them? I'm not the one they were dealing with. It's doubtful they have the first clue who I am. If they were going to contact anyone, it would be my chief purser. And before you ask, they haven't contacted *him* since you pulled your stupid stunt. If I were going to guess, I'd suspect they're probably trying to book passage on another ship leaving End."

"Which ones are leaving in the same time frame as yours?"

"Do I look like a fucking traffic controller to you, Ghreni? I don't know, and I don't really care."

"I'd like you to delay your departure."

"Why would I do that? Even if I wanted to, which I don't, our spot at Imperial Station is already scheduled to be taken over by another ship. We've got nowhere to stay."

"Your ship could stay within system."

"Or we could leave when we're supposed to, because we've got a fucking schedule and you don't make it."

"I would owe you a favor," Ghreni said.

Kiva laughed out loud at this. Then, "Say that again, Ghreni. I want to see if I'll laugh as much a second time."

"We used to be friends."

"We used to fuck each other. It's not the same thing. Which you of all people know."

More silence. Then, "I'd like to talk about the three million marks."

"I'm sure you would."

"I don't have Claremont. I'm not sure why you should have my three million marks."

"I should have them because the deal was I let you know if he booked passage. He did. The rest was up to you. It's not my fault you hire incompetents."

"Kiva, if I find out that you were behind him escaping, you won't like it."

"Well, I have two responses to that. One, fuck you, you shitty little example of a human. Two, if I *were* behind it, what the fuck could you do to me? I'm leaving End, you asshole. I'll be back home within the year and I'll be taking a job at corporate. I've done my time on a ship. You, meanwhile, will still be here, a pimple on the ass end of space. So threaten all you want, you amoral fuck. It doesn't mean anything."

Ghreni sighed. "Kiva. Despite everything I still like you a little bit."

"I'm touched, Ghreni. Really, I am."

"This is why I'm telling you now that you have no idea what's coming, and why in the end it wouldn't be a bad thing to stay on my good side."

"I'm perfectly happy to stay on your good side, Ghreni. What I'm not perfectly happy to do is give you back three fucking million marks because you didn't think through the terms of the deal. Or to pretend to be intimidated by you huffing and puffing at me about how you'll make me regret crossing you. Grow the fuck up, Ghreni."

"I'd like you to tell me if the Claremonts contact you. And by 'you,' I mean any member of your crew."

"I'll be happy to do that for another half million marks."

"Kiva."

"'Kiva' what, Ghreni? We're doing business here. You want information. You were willing to pay for that information before. I'm letting you have more information. At a substantial discount from before."

"You know I'll still have people at Imperial Station looking for him to board your ship."

"Of course. I would too, in your shoes. But I don't think you're going to find him. If he has any brains at all he'll find someone else to get him off this fucking rock. Which I will note is fine with me. I already have his half million marks for passage, nonrefundable. Which I will note was the amount that finally pushed this whole fucking shitbag of a trip into the black. Well, that and your three million marks."

"Congratulations."

"Thank you."

"Where are you now? On the station or on the planet?"

"I'm on the planet having meetings with our people here before we head out. Tell your fucking duke we'll expect our money back with interest. That is, if he manages to keep his head for the next week, which I'm officially doubting and which would not bother me at all."

"Would you like to have dinner?"

"What?" Kiva said.

"Would you like to have dinner before you go?"

"You know of a restaurant that's open during a civil war?"

"We could have it at my place."

Kiva laughed. "You're actually literally still trying to fuck me."

"I'm not going to lie. I wouldn't mind. We did it pretty well, before everything."

"Yes, we did," Kiva admitted. "The actual fucking was good, Ghreni. It's the metaphorical fucking I'm not in the mood to forgive. Now or ever."

"Fair enough. Let me know if the Claremonts contact you."

"You know the fee."

"Fine."

"Good doing business with you, Ghreni."

Ghreni snorted and broke the connection.

"You know that he would have tried to kill you if you went to dinner with him," Vrenna Claremont said. She and Marce were sitting with Kiva in a conference room at the House of Lagos's local offices.

"I would have broken his goddamned spine," Kiva said. Vrenna smiled at this.

"I'd like to go back to the part where you told Ghreni Noham-apetan that I booked passage from you," Marce said.

"What about it?"

"You told him?"

"You already know I did."

"Why?"

"Because I needed the three million marks he offered for the information."

"Yeah, but then he grabbed me and held me hostage and planned to torture and maybe kill me."

Kiva shrugged. "We told your sister immediately after they grabbed you, because I had people watching you. And then we gave her all the information she needed to find you and get you. Hell, we even gave her your rucksack with the adorable little stuffed pig in it as proof we weren't fucking around."

"I still could have been hurt. Or I could have died."

"You weren't and didn't."

"But—"

Kiva held up a hand. "Can I just wrap up this whole line of conversation by saying I really don't give a shit whether you're upset? If you were actually hurt, or dead, then I'd say sorry. But you're not, so suck it up. The way I see it, if Ghreni wanted you bad enough to give me three million fucking marks for you, then sooner or later he would have just tried to grab you any-way, whether or not I told him anything. Since that was the case, I decided to get paid. This trip was in the red, now it's not. And we *did* give your sister information to save your ass. Stop whining about it, for fuck's sake."

"I . . . I literally don't know what to say to that," Marce said.

"You could say 'thank you,'" Kiva said, and noticed Vrenna smiling.

"I don't think I will," Marce said.

"Okay. But either way, let's table this and move on, shall we?"

Marce lapsed into silence, next to his still grinning sister, and Kiva noted that both of them were attractive, Marce in a nerdy, probably attentive and considerate way, and Vrenna in a way that suggested that it was fifty/fifty whether your bedframe would be a pile of kindling at the end of a fuck date. Whether Kiva had wanted to admit it or not, Ghreni's totally insincere attempt at a rendezvous had reminded her it'd been a week since her last attempt at an orgasm, with that assistant purser, and in the time since she was either too busy or too pissed off even to rock herself off.

This qualified as an absolute fucking tragedy, no pun intended, which Kiva would need to attend to one way or another. She idly wondered whether either of the Claremont twins would be the sort to assist her in this regard. She decided that Marce probably wouldn't, at least not at the moment—he still seemed put out at the idea that Kiva was fine letting him be snatched for three million marks, and honestly, that was totally fair—but maybe Vrenna might. Kiva regretted that time, necessity, and circumstances made following up on that an impossibility.

"Lady Kiva?" Vrenna prompted.

"I'm sorry," Kiva said. "I got distracted thinking about sex."

Vrenna smiled. "We still have the problem of getting Marce onto your ship," she said. "Ghreni Nohamapetan still plans to have people on hand at Imperial Station in order to grab him."

"Ghreni is looking at the front door," Kiva said. "He's not looking at the servants' entrance."

"What does that mean?" Marce asked.

Kiva looked at him. "That means you're not coming onto the *Yes, Sir* as Marce Claremont, you're coming on as Kristian Jansen, crew member."

"How am I going to do that?"

"I imagine that when you booked passage Gazson Magnut tried to sell you some forged travel documents."

"He did. I didn't need to get them."

"Well, now you do. More accurately, they've been gotten for you."

"For which you'll no doubt charge me," Marce said.

"I'm charging you at cost, not the ridiculous fucking markup we're charging everyone else."

"Travel documents aren't going to be enough," Vrenna said. "Crew on trade ships have to have biometrics as well. With all due respect, if Nohamapetan is willing to pay three million marks to get Marce, he's going to be checking the servant entrance as well, and that includes getting into Imperial Station's biometric database."

"You act like this is our first time smuggling someone on as a crew member," Kiva said. She turned back to Marce. "Shave your head, you're getting a dermal wig with cultivated hair. Scalp and beard. If anyone plucks a hair out of your head, the DNA would match Kristian, not you. You'll get contacts to fake iris and retinal patterns, and you'll get a thumb pad with the correct thumbprint and DNA. We'll put lifts in your shoes. You won't look like you. Unless they take a blood sample you'll be fine."

"And if they take a blood sample?" Marce asked.

"Well, then, I guess you're fucked, aren't you? But they don't do that."

"No one will notice you've manufactured a human out of thin air," Vrenna said.

"'Kristian' has worked for us before," Kiva said. "We have one or two of these for every system we work. So does every other house."

"Why?" Marce asked.

"Because sometimes someone important fucks up and has to leave town in a hurry before someone like her," Kiva jerked a thumb at Vrenna, "catches up with them and sends them into a hole. It's entirely possible Ghreni will be using one of these himself soon, at the rate he's going."

"So I'll have to be 'Kristian' this entire trip."

"That'll be your name, yes. Once we get into the Flow you can ditch the fake parts. We'll update you in the system. One catch: You're going to have to be an actual crew member the entire trip."

"Why does he have to do that?" Vrenna asked.

"Because 'Kristian' is taking the place of an actual crew member. You take up crew space, you take up crew responsibilities. That's the deal."

"I don't suppose I'll get paid."

"Sure you'll get paid. Standard rates. Not that you'll be able to spend them anywhere, it's a straight shot to Hub."

"And a refund on the passage fee we gave you?"

"Don't be stupid."

Marce smiled. "Just checking."

"I'll be charging you for the new identity too, by the way. Also at cost. Not cheap."

"How do we get out of here, now?" Vrenna asked. "You know Nohamapetan will have people watching this building if he doesn't have them doing that already."

"Neither of you leaves yet." Kiva pointed to Marce. "He stays here and we'll bring in our people to work on him. Then he can walk out as Kristian." She pointed at Vrenna. "You'll have to wait until we're gone. Sorry."

Vrenna shrugged. "It's not the worst place I've been holed up."

Kiva nodded, and then stood up. "I'm heading back to the ship." She nodded to Vrenna. "I'll never see you again, which I figure is a tragedy." Vrenna smiled at this. Kiva turned her attention to Marce. "You I'll see on the ship, but we won't exactly be socializing. So, nice to meet you, welcome to the *Yes, Sir,* and thank you for allowing me to screw Ghreni Nohamapetan one more time before I never have to fucking see him again."

Marce smiled and nodded, and then Kiva was out of the conference room. Her local staff had already been briefed on what to do with the Claremont siblings and were warned that if their identity or location were leaked to anyone that the House of Lagos would make it a priority to fuck with the lives of everyone in their family for six generations at least. She was reasonably confident that no one would talk.

As she got into her fortified groundcar to head back to port, taking a circuitous route to avoid the neighborhoods where the fighting was still going on, or that had been reduced to rubble, Kiva reflected on two things.

The first was that the civil war on End both took and gave away—it fucked her and the House of Lagos with regard to the haverfruit and their monopolies, but sent enough rich people scurrying her way that her trip ended up making a profit. When that profit was added to the licensing and other fees that would eventually be recouped here on End, the House of Lagos would be in a very good position, with regard to other houses, and its ability to exercise power among them. Kiva had pulled out a save, and that was something she could use at home.

The second was that while she let the Claremont twins listen along to her conversation with Ghreni Nohamapetan, they didn't know one important piece of information that Kiva did, discovered through the graces of the investigators that Magnut paid a frankly rapacious amount of money to in order to discover:

The Duke of End never told Ghreni Nohamapetan to ask the Count of Claremont to release imperial funds. And he certainly never authorized Ghreni to fucking *kidnap* one of the count's children and hold him for ransom. He did both of those things on his own.

What the fuck are you up to, Ghreni? Kiva asked herself, as her groundcar lumbered off to port. *What are you planning?*

And while we're at it, what is the rest of your fucking family planning, too?

"The forensics from the scene are confused, Your Majesty," said Imperial Guard head Sir Hibert Limbar. The Guard was responsible for the emperox's security. Sir Hibert was pretty sure that he would soon be out of a job. "Some witnesses said they saw something launch from the crowd outside the cathedral and strike the balcony, but there is no conclusive video of that. Even if there was something launched from the crowd, the balcony is intentionally designed to withstand anything short of an artillery attack. We figured whatever was exploded there was planted there some time before. But we don't know. It will be a bit of time before we have it sorted out."

Cardenia nodded. She was in her private apartments at the palace, ears still ringing and on a medical watch due to concussion, but otherwise unharmed. At least physically. Where her heart was, there was a Naffa-shaped hole. She was attended by Limbar, by Archbishop Korbijn, and by Gell Deng, who was at least temporarily acting in the role Naffa held. Also in the room, Amit Nohamapetan, for reasons Cardenia did not understand yet but assumed she would soon learn.

"Reports are additionally complicated by the bombs that went off in the crowd near-simultaneous to the explosion on the balcony. It added chaos to an already chaotic scene," Limbar concluded.

"How many dead in the crowd?" Cardenia asked.

"Ma'am, you shouldn't worry about that right now—"

"Why not?" Cardenia said, and slipped into imperial mode, which gave her just enough emotional distance to deal with these people in her space, telling her horrible things. "Are we not emperox? Are those not our citizens? How many?"

"At least eighty, ma'am. Another hundred wounded, many critically."

"And in the cathedral? How many dead?"

"Two, ma'am. Naffa Dolg and a member of the guard. Another guard member is critically injured."

"And who was responsible?"

"We don't know for sure. No one has come forward." Limbar nodded to Amit Nohamapetan. "But Lord Nohamapetan has some information you may find relevant."

Cardenia turned to Amit, regarding him tiredly. "What is it, Lord Nohamapetan?"

"Your Majesty, as you may know, a few years ago my younger brother Ghreni went to End to represent our interests there. In the time since, he has become a confidant and advisor to the Duke of End, who has been fending off a well-organized and well-funded rebellion. Your father and parliament authorized further funding and equipping of the duke and his forces, if not the direct, overt involvement of the marines at End's Imperial Station. My brother wrote in his confidential reports that when news of that vote reached End, the rebels there vowed to retaliate."

"You're saying this is the work of End rebels?" Cardenia asked.

"My brother's reports are of course delayed by a substantial amount of time, ma'am," Amit said. "This is one of the problems with a far-flung empire. News is slow if it comes at all. But, yes. My brother was emphatic on the point that they were planning something."

"When was this report from your brother?"

"We received it roughly three standard months ago, ma'am, which means he filed it nine months earlier."

"And you did not think to inform our father?"

"The House of Nohamapetan did not presume to trouble your father on the matter without further investigation, especially during his illness. We have confidential reports from all our system representatives, which outline all sorts of local unrest, wherever our interests are. This proclamation was not in itself that noteworthy. Also, our analysts presumed that any retaliation would be focused on imperial interests on End, not here. You may be assured that Ghreni, my brother, would have informed local imperial authorities so they could take precautions. In retrospect, of course, we should have shared the information further. I apologize, ma'am."

"No one thought they would have this far a reach," Archbishop Korbijn said.

"You represent the executive committee here," Cardenia said, to her. "Tell us what their thinking is."

"Their thinking is livid," Korbijn said. "An attempted assassination on the day of your coronation. The damage at one of the church's holiest places. And scores murdered in a cowardly attack on innocents. The committee is ready to support you whatever you decide to do, ma'am. As will the guilds, the parliament and, I most strenuously assure you, the church."

"We all stand ready," Amit said.

Cardenia nodded. "We thank you." She turned to Limbar. "Your thoughts on this End theory?"

"We need to investigate further, but the information Lord Nohamapetan has already shared with us is compelling. We're looking for any End nationals here on Xi'an and Hub and digging into their histories to see what comes up. If there's a connection here, we will find it."

"Find it soon," Cardenia said.

"Yes, ma'am."

"What will you do now, ma'am?" Korbijn asked. "This is an indelicate question, but many thousands are still here, waiting to hear how you want to proceed with respect to your coronation. The rest of the Hub system is also anxious to know. It's already been a day."

"How long were the coronation celebrations going to last?"

"Five days, ma'am," Gell Deng said.

"We're in a period of mourning for five days, then," Cardenia said. "From the moment of the coronation forward. See to it that the victims are honored." She turned to Korbijn. "You will hold a service for them tonight in the cathedral." Korbijn nodded. "At the end of the mourning period we will address the entire system, and the Interdependency."

"The parliament will not want to wait to address this," Korbijn said.

"We did not suggest work or investigations stop during this period."

"Yes, ma'am."

"In the interim, publicly at least, we will be in seclusion." She nodded to Deng. "Gell here will be your point of contact for the next several days." She looked back at Korbijn. "We trust the executive committee will not protest handling administrative issues a short while longer."

"No, of course not."

"I will send updated reports when I have them and be available if you have questions," Limbar said.

"We thank you," Cardenia said, and rose. Everyone else rose with her, taking the hint they were dismissed. Only Deng remained sitting; he knew he was still needed.

"Your Majesty, a private word, if I may," Amit Nohamapetan said, as the others exited.

"Yes, Lord Nohamapetan," Cardenia said. She was still standing and did not offer to have him sit, and she assumed that he would take the hint that any word he wanted to have would be brief.

Amit picked up the hint, and his eyes flicked to Deng, still seated, registering that the word would not be all that private, either. He approached Cardenia instead, stopping at a still respectful distance, and spoke in low tones. "I wanted to personally convey my condolences to you in this moment of loss," he said. "I know you and Naffa Dolg were close. It is hard to lose anyone we love, as my own sister learned with the loss of your brother."

Oh, nice, Cardenia thought. Even in attempting to express a moment of condolence, Amit Nohamapetan couldn't help but remind her that his family still considered the position of the emperox's spouse their own property. She looked at him and saw the unremarkable face and unremarkable body and behind both, the reportedly unremarkable mind happiest in the pursuit of unremarkable pleasures. The sister and the younger brother were apparently the brains of the Nohamapetan outfit. This one was a lump. His appearance in this meeting was obviously an attempt to ingratiate him toward Cardenia by offering up useful information, followed by the humanizing moment that was happening right now. All delightfully scripted for her consumption.

Cardenia thought about the prospect of being married to, and having children with, this lump, and barely suppressed an impolite shudder. "We thank you, Lord Nohamapetan, and are gratified for your concern."

If Amit picked up on the fact that Cardenia was still using the imperial address, he didn't let it stop him. "I hope, after an appropriate time, that we can meet again in happier and friendlier circumstances."

"It is to be hoped," Cardenia said. *Those circumstances being you no less than thirty meters away,* she thought.

Amit, however, was not a mind reader and chose to interpret the carefully ambiguous words in a manner that was positive toward him, which was exactly how Cardenia had planned it, as much as she hated the necessity of it at the moment. He smiled, bowed, and exited. Cardenia waited until he was out of the room before she sagged a bit.

"Are you all right, ma'am?" Deng asked.

"No," Cardenia said. "My friend is dead and this creep is still trying to arrange a marriage with me." She stopped suddenly and turned to Deng. "I apologize, Gell," she said. "I didn't mean to speak like that. I'm . . . I'm used to Naffa being here. And speaking freely to her when we're alone."

The old secretary smiled at his emperox. "Your Majesty, I was loyal to, and silent for, your father for nearly forty years. It's in the nature of the position. I would not presume to be in the place of your dear friend. But I promise you that you may always speak freely near me, if you choose. My loyalty is to you now."

"You don't even know me," Cardenia said.

"With respect, ma'am, I disagree. I've known you for years. First through your father and his peculiar but fond relationship with you. And for the last year, I've seen enough of you to get a sense of you. If I know nothing else, ma'am, I know that you are worth being loyal to."

Cardenia's eyes suddenly welled up. "That's one of you, at least. That's a start."

"What may I do for you now?" Deng asked.

"Can you bring back Naffa?"

"No, ma'am."

Cardenia jerked a thumb back in the direction of Nohamapetan. "Can you tell this creep to take a hike?"

"If you wish it, ma'am."

"But you don't advise it."

"I don't consider it my place to give advice to emperoxs, ma'am."

"I need someone to give me advice right now. I don't have anyone else."

"Rather than my own advice, let me tell you what your father thought of the Nohamapetans, to help you make your own decisions," Deng said. "I'm sure he wouldn't mind me telling you now."

"Please."

"He thought their ambition was admirable. He didn't consider them particularly wise, however. He thought that left unchecked they would eventually cause him, as emperox, to, as he called it, 'make a mess to get them back into line.' Which is why he eventually manipulated the Nohamapetans into suggesting that Nadashe Nohamapetan should marry your brother. He believed that as a couple their ambitions were in accord, and that then the Nohamapetans would have a reason to act with less stupidity. That was his word, not mine."

"So you think my father would want me to marry Amit Nohamapetan. To keep them in line."

Deng looked slightly pained.

"What?" Cardenia asked.

"This will not be kind," Deng said.

"Say it anyway."

"Your father believed the marriage of your brother and Na-dashe would work because they were complementary to each other. Complementary with an 'e,' not 'i.' He didn't believe you and Amit were complementary. He considered you passive, and Amit unintelligent. And the marriage of the two of you would leave Nadashe, who is the power of her generation of Noham-apetans, unfulfilled in terms of ambition. And that would spell trouble for you. And for the throne."

"Maybe he would have preferred I marry Nadashe," Carde-nia said.

"Oh, no," Deng said. "She would have rolled right over you. Uh, or so your father believed," he added, quickly.

"My father didn't think much of me."

"On the contrary, he thought very well of you, ma'am. He just wished your brother had lived to be emperox."

"Well, Gell. So do I. But he didn't. So here we are."

"Yes, ma'am. And what are the emperox's wishes?"

"When is Naffa's funeral?"

"It is two days from now."

"I will attend." Deng looked pained again. "What is it?"

"I have a note from a Dolg family representative, ma'am. It arrived earlier and I've waited to speak to you about it. The family notes that your presence at the funeral would be a disruption, because the security around you would be immense, especially now. Also, Naffa's parents are republicans, as will be many of the people at the service, and your presence might pro-voke some of those friends to do or say something improper."

"They don't want me to start a riot."

"That's the gist of it, I'm afraid."

"I want to talk to her parents, then."

"The letter also suggests that you wait on that, too. My understanding is that the parents have said they don't blame you. But there's a difference between not blaming you, and being reminded their daughter is dead because she worked for you. It would be . . . difficult for them right now."

Cardenia hitched in her breath at that and sat silently with it for a few moments.

"I'm sorry, ma'am," Deng said, eventually.

Cardenia waved him off. "At the very least, I don't want them to pay for anything."

"Her parents?" Deng asked. Cardenia nodded. "You mean regarding funeral expenses."

"I mean for anything, ever again. Their daughter's dead. She was my friend. If I can't do anything else right now, at least I can do this. Yes?"

"You are the emperox," Deng said. "This is something you may do."

"Then do it, please."

"Yes, ma'am." Deng stood. "Will there be anything else?"

Cardenia shook her head. Deng bowed, collected his materials, and moved to leave.

"Where will you be?" Cardenia asked. "In case I need you?"

Deng turned and smiled. "I am always nearby, ma'am. All you have to do is call."

"Thank you, Gell."

"Ma'am." He left.

Cardenia waited until he was well out of the room before she had a good long cry, maybe the seventh or eighth she'd had since Naffa's death.

Then she remembered where she last saw Naffa, and what Naffa had said to her. Not in real life, but in her dream.

Cardenia looked over to the door to the Memory Room, sat there for a couple of minutes thinking. Then got up and let herself into it.

Jiyi appeared the moment she entered. "Hello, Emperox Grayland II. How are you?"

"I am alone," Cardenia said, and immediately hated the adolescent drama of the statement, but it was true, and there it was.

"You are always alone in the Memory Room," Jiyi said. "And in another sense, you are never alone in it."

"Did you think that up yourself?"

"I do not think," Jiyi said. "It was programmed into me years ago."

"Why?"

"Because eventually every emperox tells me they are alone."

"*Every* emperox?"

"Yes."

"That . . . weirdly makes me feel better."

"That is a frequent reaction."

"The Prophet is in here, yes? Rachela I."

"Yes."

"I would like to speak to her, please."

Jiyi nodded and shimmered out, replaced by a woman. She was small and in this image nondescriptively middle-aged, which was different from the usual depictions of the Prophet, which showed her young and with flowing hair and striking cheekbones. The image did not look anything like this.

It also did not look anything like Naffa. Cardenia felt a momentary spasm of disappointment about this, then inwardly chastised herself for it. There was no reason she should have expected the Prophet to be Naffa outside of her dream.

"You are Rachela I," Cardenia asked the image.

"I am."

"The founder of the Interdependency, and the Interdependent Church."

"Basically."

"Basically?"

"It's a little more complicated than that, in both cases. But we decided that having me be the founder of both would serve the mythology the best, so that's what we said."

"Were you an actual prophet?"

"Yes."

"So you knew the things you were saying about the Interdependency and the principles of interdependency would come true."

"No, of course not."

"But you just said you were a prophet."

"Anyone can be a prophet. You just have to say that what you're talking about is a reflection of God. Or of the gods. Or of some divine spirit. However you want to put it. Whether those things come true isn't one way or another about it."

"But what you said did come true. You preached for interdependency and it happened."

"Yes, it was good for me that it turned out that way."

"So you didn't know they would."

"I already told you that I didn't. But we certainly worked hard to *make* them happen, and to give it the appearance of inevitability. And of course the whole mystical angle helped too."

Cardenia furrowed her brow. "You're a founder of a church."

"Yes."

"But listening to you, you don't seem to be particularly religious."

"Not really, no."

"Or to believe in God. Or gods."

"I really don't. And when we designed the church, we intentionally made the divine aspect of it as ambiguous as possible. People don't mind having the mystical aspect of a church being poorly defined as long as you make the rules of the church clear. We did that. We modeled a bit off of Confucianism, which strictly speaking wasn't a religion, and added bits we thought would be useful from other religions."

"So you don't believe in your own church!"

"Of course I do," Rachela said. "We created a set of moral precepts to bind the various human systems together. We did it because we thought it was desirable and to some extent necessary. Since I believe in those precepts, I believe in the mission of the church. At least, the mission of the church when we founded it. Human institutions tend to drift from their creators' intent over time. Another reason to have clear rules."

"But the divine element is fake."

"We decided that it was no more fake than the divine aspect of any other religion. As far as the evidence goes, in any event."

Cardenia felt a little light-headed. It was one thing to believe the predominant church of the Interdependency was bunk, which was a thing Cardenia had believed for as long as she could remember thinking about it. It was inconvenient when, strictly speaking, you were now head of that church, but she could at least keep that to herself. It was another thing to have the founder of the church, or at least the core of memories that comprised her, confirm it was bunk.

"Naffa was right," Cardenia said. "The Interdependency is a scam."

"I don't know who Naffa is," Rachela I said.

"She was a friend of mine," Cardenia said. "I had a dream

where she appeared to me, as you, telling me the Interdependency was a scam."

"If I were telling this story, I would have said that I had had a mystical vision of the Prophet," Rachela I said.

"It was just a dream."

"In our line of business there is no such thing. Emperoxs never just dream. They have visions. That's what we do. Or what we were supposed to do, when I became the first emperox."

"Well, I had the thing, and it wasn't a vision. It was a dream."

"It was a dream that made you think. A dream that caused you to search for wisdom. A dream that made you consult me, the Prophet. Sounds like a vision to me."

Cardenia gawked at Rachela I. "You're unbelievable."

"I worked in marketing," Rachela I said. "Before I was a prophet. After, too, but we didn't call it that after that point."

"I'm having a hard time believing what you're telling me."

Rachela I nodded. "That's not unusual. Sooner or later every emperox activates me to have a conversation like this. Most of them respond like you do."

"Most of them? What about the others?"

"They feel happy they guessed it correctly."

"How do you feel about that?"

"I don't feel anything about it. I'm not alive. Strictly speaking, I'm not here."

"'You're always alone in the Memory Room, and never alone in the Memory Room.'"

Rachela I nodded again. "I said that. Or something close enough to it, anyway."

"Is the Interdependency a scam?" Cardenia asked, directly.

"The answer to that is complicated."

"Give me the short version."

"The short version is 'Yes, but.' The slightly longer version is 'No, and.' Which version would you like?"

Cardenia stared at Rachela I for a moment. Then she went to the bench in the Memory Room and sat.

"Tell me everything," she said.

"I have an itch," Marce Claremont said to his sister.

"Where?" Vrenna asked.

"My entire head," Marce replied.

As required, Marce had shaved his entire head short of eyebrows and eyelashes, and had been fitted with cultivated hair and a beard, each embedded in an epidermis-thin substrate of actual skin, which had been secured to his own with the use of a glue made from, or so the person applying it to his face told him, real human collagens. Next came the thumb pad, which made Marce feel like he had tape on his hand, against which he had to mightily fight the urge to pick it off. Then the contacts which changed his eye color and iris pattern, and which included holographic fake corneas that would give the illusion of depth to the fake retinal pattern.

"I can barely see out of these contacts, either."

"It's not a bad eye color for you, though," Vrenna observed. "Maybe keep those in after you get on the ship."

"You're funny."

The two of them were waiting on the elevator that would take Marce down to the lobby. The newly hired crew for the *Yes, Sir* were told to collect there in order for their papers to be processed and then to be bussed to port, to head to the ship. That was convenient for Marce, who could blend in with the rest of the new crew.

But it also meant that these were literally the last moments he would spend with his sister, possibly in his entire life.

"Tell Dad I'm sorry I didn't get to say good-bye," he said, to Vrenna.

"I will. He'll understand. He won't be happy, but he'll understand. He'll be okay."

"And how about you? Are you going to be okay?"

Vrenna smiled. "I'm pretty good at being okay. If nothing else, I'm good at keeping busy. And the thing is, rumor has it that no matter what, everyone on End is going to be really busy soon. I have an agenda, anyway."

"What's on the agenda?"

"The first thing is to dangle Ghreni Nohamapetan off a building for kidnapping my brother."

Marce laughed at this, and then the elevator bell dinged and the door opened.

Vrenna grabbed her brother in a fierce hug, gave him a peck on the cheek, and then pushed him, gently, into the elevator. "Go on," she said. "Go tell the emperox everything. Save everyone if you can. And then come back."

"I'll try."

"Love you, Marce," Vrenna said, as the door started to close.

"Love you, Vrenna," Marce said, just before it did.

Marce had twenty floors to get his emotions in check.

The elevator opened up to a couple dozen people milling about and three people in official House of Lagos crew uniforms. One of them looked over to Marce as the elevator opened up. "What the hell are you doing in the elevator?" she asked.

"I was looking for a bathroom," Marce said.

"Well, there's not one in there. Get out of that."

Marce got out. The crew member held out her hand for his papers; he handed them over.

"Kristian Jansen," she said, looking at them.

"That's me."

"Any relation to Knud Jansen?"

"I don't think so."

"I shipped with him once. He was from End, too."

"There's a lot of Jansens."

The crew member nodded, and then held up her tablet. "Thumb." Marce pressed his fake thumb on the tablet, which scanned the print on it. The crew member then held up the tablet close to Marce's eyes. "Don't blink." The camera on the back of the tablet scanned Marce's contacts.

"Well, you really are Kristian Jansen, and you don't have any outstanding warrants or debts, your guild union dues are paid up, and your personnel ratings are good," the crew member said. "Welcome aboard."

"Thank you, uh . . ."

"Ndan. Petty Officer Gtan Ndan."

"Thank you, ma'am."

"You're welcome, crewman." Ndan looked at Marce's rucksack. "You're traveling light."

"My other bag got boosted."

Ndan nodded. "Sucks. When you get squared away go to the quartermaster and get new kit. You'll be charged extortionate rates but that's your problem. You got marks?"

"A few."

"If you're short, come find me. I can lend."

"That's very kind."

"No it's not. It's business. My interest rates are also extortionate." Ndan pointed out of the lobby to a bus waiting outside.

"Get on that. We leave in about five minutes. Do you still need a head?"

It took a second for it to register that Ndan was talking about a bathroom. "I'm fine."

"Off you go, then." She turned to see who else she needed to process.

It took five seconds for Marce to get from the lobby door to the bus and he felt exposed the entire way. But he managed to get on the bus without incident, find a seat, and wait. He looked up through the window at the House of Lagos building and wondered if Vrenna was looking down. He felt briefly sorry for Ghreni Nohamapetan, whom Vrenna was likely to thump the crap out of sometime soon. Then in the distance there was a brief thump that sounded like a shell hitting a building, and Marce remembered there were other things Vrenna and their father might still have to worry about first.

From the bus to the port he went, through another paper check and thumb scan at imperial customs, then up the beanstalk, which was disappointing to Marce because there were no windows and the video screen in the cramped passenger cabin showed nothing but informational customs videos and ads.

At a certain point in the trip up the beanstalk, Marce was aware that his (fake) hair felt like it was being pressed down onto his scalp. He mentioned this to his seatmate, who nodded but didn't look up from whatever he was reading on his tablet. "Push field," he said, then went back to his reading.

Marce nodded to himself. Push fields were humanity's best approximation for artificial gravity, in which objects were pushed on from "above"—whatever "above" was in any particular scenario—rather than pulled on from below, as gravity was generally understood to work. The physics of push fields were discovered accidentally. Researchers back on Earth had tried to work out the problem of shaping a small bubble of local space-time around a starship in order to take advantage of the then newly discovered Flow, and ended up taking a lot of side detours in the math. Most of these detours offered nothing of any benefit, but one of them did, and it was pressing on Marce's hair.

Marce looked up and found the push field generator tubes, running down the length of the passenger compartment like fluorescent lighting. He of course understood the physics of the push field, since it was a consonant subset of the Flow physics. But he'd never been off End. He'd never experienced one. As he was experiencing it now, he found it slightly unsettling. He didn't like what basically felt like a giant hand pressing down on his head and shoulders, and he didn't like how it made his fake hair lay on his scalp. He looked around the compartment and noted there was a reason why most of the experienced crew kept their hair either very short or in tightly wrapped braids and queues.

From the beanstalk now to Imperial Station, which featured a rotating ring section for the marines and imperial staff who stayed at the station long term, and a separate merchant section managed by push fields, where visiting ships unloaded and managed their cargo. Marce and the other crew got out in the merchant area, and he immediately understood why long-term residents would prefer to live in the ring. The push fields here, set to a standard G, were almost intolerably pushy.

As Marce and the rest of the crew were led to the crew muster area for the *Yes, Sir,* he saw a collection of people in the cargo hold, waiting. Those would be the *Yes, Sir'*s passengers, he knew, with whom he would have been, if Ghreni Nohamapetan hadn't kidnapped him and marked him. The passengers certainly didn't look like refugees. They looked like what they were—wealthy people. They were milling with their children and their stacks of cargo at a thousand marks a kilo as if they were about to have an adventure, rather than flee a planet forever.

Despite the fact that he fully intended to be one of them, Marce managed to feel resentment toward them, toward the people who could, in fact, leave their problems behind through the simple application of money.

Well, you're *a hypocrite*, his brain told him. Well, maybe he was. But then again he wasn't leaving to escape. He was leaving because someone needed to tell the emperox, and then explain to the parliament and everyone else, how the end was coming. That person just happened to be Marce.

Nope, still a hypocrite, his brain said. Then they were out of the cargo area and into a tunnel, funneling them toward the muster area and a shuttle.

A final check of papers and thumbprint and the shuttle detached from Imperial Station to the *Yes, Sir.* Again there were no windows—windows were a positive hazard in the blank vacuum of space—but this time Marce could access a camera feed from his tablet. He did so and saw the *Yes, Sir* hone into view, a long tube with two rotating rings, an ungainly but strangely beautiful object. His home for the next nine months.

"What a fucking hole," his seatmate said, looking at Marce's tablet screen.

"I think it's beautiful," Marce said.

"Looks pretty from a distance. But I've friends who have crewed Lagos ships before. They all have problems. House of Lagos is cheap. They run their ships until they fall apart and only repair them when the alternative is exploding. They scare me."

"And yet you're here, about to crew a Lagos ship."

"I was going to crew on the *Tell Me Another One*, but it's been impounded. Captain let pirates take her cargo, I heard. Switched over. Last-minute add. Worth it. Things are going to hell on End."

"The rebels."

The man nodded. "That and the other thing. About the Flow streams."

"What?" Marce said. He set down the tablet and gave his full attention to his seatmate.

"A friend of mine who crews on the *Tell Me*—the one who was getting me the gig on it—said they dropped out of the goddamn Flow stream halfway here and only barely made back in before they were stranded forever. He's got another friend who told him this wasn't the first time. Flow streams are getting spotty all over the goddamn place. It's only a matter of time before the shit really drops. I sure as hell don't want to be on End when it does. I'm from Kealakekua. I'm going home."

"This is the first I've heard about this," Marce said.

"You haven't shipped in the last few years, then. Everyone who crews has heard the rumors."

"Just rumors."

"Sure, just rumors, but what the hell else are they going to be?" the man said, irritably. "It can take five years for a piece of news to go from one end of space to the other, and the story's going to change in the telling. So you don't listen to the story. You listen to the pattern. And right now, the pattern is, weird fucking shit going on with the Flow."

"The guilds know about this, then."

The man looked at Marce like he was an idiot. "They don't want to know. A ship goes in the Flow and doesn't come out and they say, oh, pirates got them before they could report in. Or there was some problem shaping the bubble inside the Flow and they just disappeared in it. There's always an explanation that doesn't mean the Flow is the problem. They don't *want* to believe it. And if they don't believe it, then who is going to tell the Interdependency? You? Me? Like they're fucking going to believe *us*."

"They might."

"Well, *you* try it and let me know. What *I'm* going to do is go home. I got kids. I want to see them again."

There was a thump and the shuttle landed in the *Yes, Sir*'s bay.

"You're not worried that something might happen to this ship on the way out," Marce said, while they waited for the air to be pumped back into the bay.

"I figure this ship is safe. I didn't want to hang around after that."

"Why not?"

"My friend on the *Tell Me*'s heard that this stream—the one out of End—is getting shaky."

"How so?"

"How do I know? It's a rumor, man. They don't come up with a science report. But my friend is anxious about it. He even considered jumping ship and coming with us. But the *Tell Me*'s whole crew is grounded for legal depositions and he didn't know where to get reliable forged IDs. It's hard to fool the biometrics."

"I've heard."

The man nodded. "So he's stuck. And he's worried he's going to be stuck here forever."

"There are worse places to be stuck than End," Marce said.

The man snorted at this. "An open planet is no place for humans. Give me a decent ring habitat any day."

"Earth was an open planet."

"And we left it." The door to the shuttle opened and the new crew began to file out.

"What's your friend's name?" Marce asked the man. "The one on the *Tell Me*."

"Why? You going to send him a condolence note?"

"I might."

The man shrugged. "Sjo Tinnuin. And I'm Yared Brenn, in case you're at all curious."

"Kristian."

"No, I'm with the Interdependent Church. Mostly." Brenn shuffled off before Marce could correct the confusion.

An hour later Marce had what passed for an orientation and was assigned his quarters, a tiny, sealable bunk in a room with fifteen other crew members. Each crew member had their own bunk and locker, with a common lavatory and living space, the latter of which couldn't possibly fit all sixteen of them at the same time. As the newest crew member, he got the worst bunk, the highest of four nearest the lavatory, at the same altitude where the lavatory fumes gathered.

Marce slipped into his bunk area, which had barely enough room to sit up, and connected his tablet to the ship's system. There was already a message waiting for him, informing him where to report to his new superior, and when, the latter being a half hour from then.

Marce opened up an app that would allow him to text anonymously and securely and pinged Vrenna. *This is your friend Kristian*, he texted.

I already said good-bye to you. Now you're ruining the moment, Vrenna responded.

Marce smiled at that. *I need you to look up someone. A man named Sjo Tinnuin. He crews on the* Tell Me Another One. *I need you to do it before the* Yes, Sir *hits the Flow shoal.*

All right. Why?

Because he's heard a rumor about that thing that I'm interested in.

I love it when you're vague.

Particularly the thing I'm about to deal with. Vague enough?

Perfectly.

Good. It would be helpful to know where he heard the rumor. It's a very weirdly specific thing to have a rumor about.

I'm on it. How is the ship?

I'm in a bunk the size of a dresser drawer.

Jealous. All I have is my massive bed back at the palace, in a room the size of a small village.

I hate you.

Hate you too, Kristian. Be safe. I'll ping the ship with a message when I get news.

Thanks— and here Marce almost typed "sis" but stopped and just added a period instead. Then he turned off his tablet, sealed up his bunk, and spent a few minutes in the uncomfortably close dark, having the first twinges of homesickness.

"You said you wanted to be informed if something unusual happened on our way out from End," Captain Tomi Blinnikka said, to Kiva. They were two days out from End, and another day out from the Flow shoal that would have them heading toward Hub. Kiva and Blinnikka were in the captain's private room, off the bridge of the *Yes, Sir*, along with Chief of Security Nubt Pinton. The room could comfortably fit two people tops, and Pinton was exceedingly large. Kiva felt like she could actually taste his sweat particles.

"What is it?" she asked.

Blinnikka activated a tablet and showed it to Kiva. It featured a live feed of the *Yes, Sir*'s position in space, along with the logarithmically mapped position of other objects and ships within a light-minute of distance. "We've got a ship coming toward us."

"Toward us? Or toward the shoal?"

"Us. We plotted its course and it's going to intercept us in about fourteen hours. When we first saw it and saw its course, I made the assumption it was also running to the shoal and just wasn't paying attention to our position. I boosted our velocity by half a percent, to get us clear of each other. They didn't respond immediately, but over the last couple of hours they've boosted their own velocity to match ours. We're definitely the targets."

"So, pirates."

"Yes."

"*Stupid* pirates." The best time to nab a ship was when it was exiting the Flow, not trying to get to it; inertia would send a target ship into the Flow shoal regardless. Pirate ships were usually relatively small, relatively fast, and almost always local—which is to say, with no equipment to shape a time-space bubble around their ships. If they entered the Flow, they'd die. A pirate attacking an outgoing ship would likely have only a very small window of time to attack successfully, board, unload cargo, and disengage.

"Stupid or they have a plan we don't understand."

"We can handle them, right?" The *Yes, Sir* came with a full complement of defensive weapons, and a small contingent of offensive weapons as well. The offensive weapons were technically illegal for a trade ship to have, but fuck that, when you're in space, sometimes you have to shoot first and lie about it to a guild inquiry later.

"The ship is too far away to get a good look at its true capabilities, but if the thrust signature is correct, it's a Winston-class freighter. It's probably modified all to hell but no matter what they're still small, which limits their offensive capabilities. We can probably handle them. *If* their intention is to pirate the ship."

"What other intention would they have? They want to invite us to tea?"

"We don't know. Right now our posture is to watch and monitor."

"You can outrun them to the shoal. Power up now."

Blinnikka shook his head. "The second we boost velocity more than trivially we give away that we know we're being tracked. They'll boost as well, probably to intercept earlier. If we plan to outrun them, we do it as late as possible, and when they're close enough for us to target with those missiles we're not supposed to have. But again, that's if they are attempting the usual piracy."

Kiva found herself getting irritated. "What the fuck would unusual piracy be in this case?"

"We don't know, and that's the point. They're coming at us from the wrong direction and they wouldn't have enough time to fully unload even if they didn't have to burn time fighting us. But they should also know that we don't have anything worth stealing right now. Pirates have spies at stations, who give them information about ships and their cargo manifests. It's how they decide who to target. But they wouldn't even have to be crafty to know that the only cargo we took on at End was people, since we didn't make a secret of that. And unless they really want haverfruit concentrate, we have nothing of value."

"They know we have nothing they want or can use and they're coming at us anyway."

"Yes. This is what worries me."

Kiva nodded. "Fine. What's the second thing?"

"One of our passengers is acting strangely," Nubt Pinton said.

"All our passengers are rich assholes," Kiva said. "Acting strangely is part of their so-called charm."

Pinton smiled slightly at that. "I will take the lady's word for that," he said. "However, in this case, the problem is not the passenger being eccentric, but the passenger methodically casing the ship." Pinton picked up his own tablet and sent video to the one Kiva was holding. In the video, a man was walking through the ship corridors, looking around.

"Oh my God, this man is walking, let's kill him," Kiva said.

"It's not that he's walking, it's *where* he's walking. He's not wandering the ship randomly or generally. He's going into areas relating to engineering, propulsion, and life support management."

"So, only to those places?"

"No," Pinton said. "He goes other places as well. But these are the places he's come back to. He doesn't come in far and he never stays long. But he comes back."

"Why don't you have the passengers on a fucking lockdown?" Kiva asked, setting down the tablet. "We don't need these assholes wandering the ship anyway."

"That was our original plan, and in fact our passengers have already been given a list of areas they are absolutely not allowed to go into."

"Which this guy ignores."

"No, but he's come close. But he's not focused, say, on Engineering directly. He's focused on places on the ship where it might be easy to disrupt engineering systems."

"Which brings me back to my first fucking question, Pinton."

Pinton waggled the tablet he held in his hand. "We didn't lock them down entirely because one of our crew recognizes this man, and we wanted to see what he might be up to."

"Which rich asshole is he?"

"That's just it. The crew person says he's not a rich asshole. He's someone who *works* for a rich asshole."

"Which crew member said this?"

"A new purser named Kristian Jensen. I understand you know him."

"And who does he say this dude worked for?"

"Ghreni Nohamapetan."

"Get him in here now," Kiva said.

● ● ●

"So, I used to work for the family of the Count of Claremont," Jensen began.

"Oh, for fuck's sake," Kiva said, exasperatedly. "Lord Marce, everyone in this room knows you're you."

"I wasn't sure," Marce said.

"Well, now you are, so get on with it."

Marce nodded. "I didn't have a lot of contact with Lord Ghreni, but I'd see him sometimes at court functions at the duke's, and other events and parties where the presence of a noble was considered a plus. Ghreni was one of those nobles who would travel with an entourage of friends and employees." He pointed at Pinton's tablet. "This was one of the employees. Former military, working for Ghreni as a bodyguard."

"You're sure about that," Blinnikka asked Marce.

"I'm sure," Marce said. "Vrenna pointed him out to me once. He and she were in the same unit for a while. Said he was a competent solider but a shit human being and that at one point she nearly fed him his testicles because he kept propositioning her in the barracks. Every time I saw him since I imagined his own balls in his mouth."

"That's a lovely image," Kiva said.

"When I saw him in the passenger ring section, I checked in with security." Marce nodded to Pinton.

"I assume this asshole is traveling on fake documents," Kiva said, to Pinton.

"Yes," Pinton confirmed. "For our records he's Tysu Gouko. Bear in mind we gave him that particular fake identity, so we can't really hold it against him. But he presented himself as a franchisee of the House of Sykes, when he came to us. Name of Frinn Klimta."

"Is there a real Frinn Klimta?"

"Maybe? We didn't check. We didn't believe you cared, ma'am, as long as their money was real, and it was."

Kiva turned to Marce. "What's this asshole's real name?"

"His personal name is Chat. His family name I think is Ubdal. Or Uttal. One of the two."

"Any idea why he's here?"

"I have no idea," Marce said. "But if he came to you with an already fake identity, I think that's enough for you to be suspicious."

"When did he book passage?" Kiva asked Pinton.

"Just before we left. He was one of the last people we booked. Magnut charged him a late fee of a quarter million marks."

Kiva pointed at Marce. "So that would have been after you were kidnapped."

Marce nodded. "Yes."

"He one of the guys who grabbed you?"

"No. I definitely would have remembered that."

"So he doesn't know who you are right now."

"I don't know. Probably not. He hasn't responded to me yet."

"But he would recognize you out of this disguise."

"Yes."

Kiva reached over to Marce, grabbed his hair, and tugged. Marce yelped in pain and surprise. "Stop it! It doesn't just come off. You have to dissolve the glue."

"Where is this asshole now?" Kiva asked Pinton.

"He's in the passenger ring section," Pinton replied. "What do you want to do?"

"I want to find out what he's up to."

"The *Yes, Sir* is underway," Blinnikka reminded Kiva. "Whatever you plan to do, I have to approve. I don't want this asshole damaging the ship."

"It'll be fine," Kiva promised. She turned back to Marce. "So this asshole is a marine."

"Was a marine, yes. Is now a bodyguard."

"You think you could take him?"

"What? No."

"Does this asshole know that?"

"Yeah."

"Okay, good."

•   •   •

They waited until Chat went on a walk and then positioned a couple of security crew at the end of a corridor they knew he was casing, giving every appearance of just having a conversation with each other. Chat saw them, decided to consult his tablet about something, and then headed back in the direction which he had come from, to find two other security crew there. He stopped and appeared to be calculating his odds when Marce stepped into the corridor, his Kristian Jansen disguise removed, and walked toward him.

"Hello, Chat," Marce said, and that was as far as he got before Chat materialized a blade out of fucking nowhere and rushed directly for him.

And then was on the floor half a second later, twitching, three stun bolts in him.

"Did you pee yourself?" Kiva asked Marce ten seconds later, when the all clear had been given. She and Pinton had been waiting a bit down the corridor and had been watching through the corridor camera, feed piped into a tablet.

"Maybe a little," Marce admitted, looking at the downed Chat, who was now being bundled up by security.

"There's no shame in pissing yourself like a goddamned fire hydrant when a trained killer is about to knife you in the throat."

"Can we change the subject?" Marce asked, plaintively.

"Why don't you take the rest of your shift off and shiver in your bunk," Kiva suggested. "In your shoes that's what I'd do."

Marce motioned toward Chat. "What are you going to do with him?"

"I'm going to encourage him to talk."

"That's not going to work."

"You know nothing of my methods."

"He's trained not to talk."

"He was also trained to kill, and look how he fucked that up."

"I want to be there when you question him."

"No you don't."

"I really do."

"Let me put it another way, Lord Marce. Fuck you, go away."

"He almost killed me. I think I deserve to know why."

"And maybe I'll tell you, later. But for now, if you don't fuck off, right this second, I'm going to stab you myself. And none of these security guys are going to put a bolt into me, I guarantee you that."

Marce looked like he was going to say something else, then shook his head and walked off.

"Your people skills are admirable," Pinton said to Kiva.

"Fuck you, too," Kiva said.

Pinton smiled at that and pointed at Chat, secured and ready for transport. "He's right, you know. This one's not going to talk. They're trained to resist aggressive questioning."

" 'Aggressive questioning'?"

"That's the euphemism we used for torture in the imperial service, ma'am."

"Just fucking call it torture, then."

"My point is he's been trained to deal with whatever humans can do to him."

"We can do better than humans," Kiva said.

• • •

"He's coming to," Pinton said, some time later.

"Turn on the speaker," Kiva said. Pinton pressed the button to open a channel. "Good morning, fuckface," she said, to Chat.

Chat looked at his surroundings. "Where am I?" he asked.

"You're in a service airlock, in an EVA suit," Kiva said. "Well, most of one, anyway. You might have noticed you're missing a helmet."

"I noticed," Chat said.

"Good. So, this is the deal. You tell us everything we ask you questions about, and don't give us any shit about it, and I don't purge you out the airlock without that fucking helmet."

Chat looked exasperated, confused, and tired. "Look, I don't even know what's going o—"

Kiva pressed the "Emergency Purge" command. The airlock door burst open and Chat was sucked out into space.

"Well, that was quick," Pinton said.

"I told you I don't fuck around," Kiva replied. She pressed the "Emergency Retrieve" button. The winch that held the cord attached to the EVA suit slammed into overdrive, reeling the suit back in, triple-time. "Anyway. So how long can a human live in hard vacuum?"

"Maybe a minute, if he didn't hold his breath."

"He was talking," Kiva said. "He didn't have time to hold his breath."

Less than a minute later Chat was back inside the airlock, which was fully pressurized with an oxygen-rich mixture. A minute after that Chat was awake, coughing and vomiting. He looked up at the airlock camera with hemorrhaged eyeballs. Pinton opened the communication circuit again.

"So, here's the deal," Kiva repeated. "You tell us everything we ask you questions about, and you don't give us any shit about it, and I don't purge you out of the airlock without that fucking helmet. I'm not going to repeat myself again. You fuck with me and you die. Got it?"

Chat croaked and nodded.

"Can you talk yet?"

Chat held up a gloved finger as if to say *Give me a second*.

"How about now?" Kiva asked, ten seconds later.

Chat looked up through bloodshot eyes with an expression that said *You have to be fucking kidding me*, but nodded.

"You're Chat Ubdal."

Nod.

"You came onto this ship under false pretenses."

Nod.

"You work for Ghreni Nohamapetan."

Nod.

"Who sent you out on this ship."

Nod.

"To kill Marce Claremont."

Chat held up a hand and made a wiggling motion. *Sorta*.

"What the fuck does that mean?"

Chat tried to make words, stopped, swallowed, and tried again. "Not primary goal," he managed to croak.

"What was your primary goal?"

"Take him alive."

"How the fuck were you going to take him alive? You can't leave the fucking ship!"

Chat looked at the airlock door and then back at the camera, as if to say, *Oh, really.*

"You can't leave the ship *alive*, then, you enormous asshole."

"Pirates," Chat croaked.

"Oh, shit," Kiva said, looking over at Pinton.

"The pirates aren't coming for our cargo," Pinton said. "They're a shuttle service."

"But we could get away from the pirates," Kiva said, back to Chat. "Maybe."

Chat shook his head. "Bomb," he said.

"A bomb?" Kiva was incredulous. "You were going to put a fucking bomb on this ship?" Chat nodded. "How does blowing up the fucking ship serve your purpose?"

Chat shook his head and tried talking but he was trying to make too many words and choked to a stop.

"Let me try," Pinton said, and leaned over so Chat could hear him. "You weren't going to blow up the ship, were you? You were just going to disrupt the ship's systems enough that it couldn't get into the Flow."

Chat nodded and pointed to the camera, as if to say, *You got it.*

"That's why he was touring those particular corridors," Pinton said, to Kiva. "He was looking for the right place to put the thing."

"And he didn't think we would notice? Blinnikka would space him the second he did that."

"We'd have to deal with the explosion and damage first, and then there would be pirates and we'd be too busy to worry about him for a while. I suspect he intended to leave on the pirate ship, along with Claremont."

"And how would he get a bomb on the fucking ship anyway? Don't we fucking *screen* for that?"

"It's probably not a big bomb," Pinton said. "He could probably make it on the ship." Pinton leaned back over. "If we go through your personal effects, we're going to find bomb components disguised as toiletries and sundries, yes?"

Chat nodded.

"There you go," Pinton said.

"This motherfucker," Kiva said. "I want to space him just on principle."

"Microphone," Pinton said, pointing.

Kiva realized she was close enough to the open circuit that Chat heard that last comment. She looked at the screen to see him with a concerned expression on his face. She rolled her eyes and leaned in again. "I'm not going to kill you, you miserable shitfuck. Unless you stop talking. Or croaking. Or whatever the fuck it is you're doing at the moment. Just keep doing it." Chat nodded. Kiva turned to Pinton. "Turn that thing off for a second."

Pinton slapped closed the communication circuit. "What is it?"

"Something's not right about this," Kiva said.

"None of it is right," Pinton said. "This is all highly fucked up, ma'am."

"No, I mean—" Kiva pointed at Chat, who was waiting, looking up at the camera. "He wants to bring Claremont back, and he's willing to damage the ship to do it. Ghreni is willing to deal with fucking *pirates* to bring him back."

"You said that Lord Ghreni tried holding him hostage to get those imperial funds released. Maybe he just really needs them."

"Yeah, okay, but shithole here," Kiva motioned again toward Chat, "tried to kill him once he realized he was trapped and found out. If he couldn't bring him back, he needed to kill him.

But if he killed him, then he couldn't use him as a fucking hostage, now, could he? So what was the fucking point? Why did Ghreni go through all this effort? What's the reason?"

"You got me," Pinton said.

"Yeah. Open that circuit." Pinton turned it back on. "Important question, Chat. If I don't believe you, your lungs are coming out through your nose. You got it?"

Chat nodded.

"Why does your boss want Marce Claremont so fucking bad?"

"Don't know," Chat croaked.

"Your fucking *lungs*, Chat."

"I. Don't. *Know*," Chat said again, so emphatically the last word came out as a wheeze. "I thought ransom. But makes no sense."

"Because you were told to kill him if you couldn't bring him back alive."

Chat nodded.

"Well, can't you fucking *guess*?" Kiva asked. "You work directly with Ghreni. You have to have heard something. You have to be able to *speculate*."

Chat shook his head. "Doesn't talk. Unless involved, nothing."

"You're *involved*, Chat."

"To *do*. Not for *why*."

Kiva nodded to Pinton again, and he closed the circuit. "Well?" she asked him.

"I think he's telling the truth."

"I *know* the fucker is telling the truth," Kiva said. "I want to know what you think we do now."

"Well, we don't space him," Pinton pointed at Chat. "He's been cooperative."

"Hard vacuum will do that."

"So he's not a problem anymore. But we still have the pirates on their way. And if Lord Ghreni was willing to go this far to get Claremont back, then you have to figure he has a plan for if Chat here failed."

"You mean the pirates are going to either come away with their prize or make sure he's dead."

"Yes."

"And if we all happen to die too, then that's just the way it goes."

"Yes."

"Well, then, shit, Pinton," Kiva said. She looked back to Chat. "I guess we better give them what they want."

12

Marce's tablet pinged with the command for him to report to Nubt Pinton, the *Yes, Sir*'s head of security. He briefly considered not responding to the order, but then did anyway, moving through the ship with a gradually increasing awareness of and comfort with his surroundings. Because the ship was under acceleration at the moment, the ship's artificial gravity was more push fields than ring rotation, and Marce felt pressed down. But he noticed that it was bothering him less even a couple of days in. A body could get used to it, it seemed.

Nubt Pinton was in the *Yes, Sir*'s brig, a small and unhappy room with even smaller and more unhappy cells, inside one of which was Chat Ubdal. Marce looked in at Chat, who looked back, balefully.

"He's a mess," Marce said.

"Yes, well. Lady Kiva tossed him out an airlock," Pinton answered.

"You threw him into *space*?"

"Yup."

"And he didn't die?"

"We only threw him out a little bit."

Marce looked again at Chat, whose eyeballs looked spray-painted red. "I almost feel sorry for him."

"Don't get too broken up, Lord Marce. He'd still murder you if he had a chance."

"You asked to see me, sir," Marce said, turning away from Chat.

"I did. I needed to get a good look at you."

"All right. Why?"

"We're being tailed by pirates. Your would-be assassin here tells us that their plan is to take you off the ship. We suspect that if they can't manage that they'd rather destroy the *Yes, Sir* than let you escape. We could fight them but if their goal is to blow us up rather than board us then our options are limited."

"Are you planning to turn me over?"

"If I were planning that I wouldn't be talking to you. I would have had you stunned when you weren't looking and then prepped you for delivery."

"Good to know."

Pinton nodded. "What I need from you is your willingness to help us save ourselves, and save you, and in the process maybe cause a little pain to these pirates, and the people behind them."

"You mean Ghreni Nohamapetan."

"Yes, that's the one."

"I'm in."

"It won't be entirely risk free for you."

"I don't care. I'm in."

"Good."

"How do we do this?"

Pinton pointed to Chat. "The first thing we do is make it look like this one was successful."

"In killing me?"

"In planting a bomb that was meant to keep us from entering the Flow. Once we do that we're pretty sure the pirates are going to hail us and discuss their terms."

"What's the second thing?" Marce asked.

"Well," Pinton said. "Have you noticed that you and Chat here are roughly the same size and coloration?"

"Not really, no."

"Well, I have."

• • •

The fake bomb "went off" a half hour later, and the *Yes, Sir* sent a general unencrypted distress call toward Imperial Station to let it know of its predicament. The idea would be to make the station aware an event happened and that the station should prep rescue and retrieval efforts, to be deployed if and when the *Yes, Sir* followed up with an even more dire distress call. The drawback was that even the fastest imperial cutters would be more than a day out. The *Yes, Sir* was alone, save for the one small ship trailing it, now only a few hours out from intercept.

Which hailed the *Yes, Sir*, as expected, shortly after the distress call went out.

"Free freighter *Red Rose*, hailing *Yes, Sir, That's My Baby*," the hail said. Marce heard it on the bridge, where he and Kiva Lagos stood in a corner, staying out of the way but needing to hear what happened next.

"Lagos fiver *Yes, Sir, That's My Baby*, responding," said Drean Musann, *Yes, Sir*'s communications officer.

"We understand you're experiencing an event. Permission to come aside and assist."

"The captain thanks you for your willingness to assist but says no assistance is required at this time. Please maintain current distance."

"We are concerned that should a further event occur we would not be able to properly assist. Moving to come alongside."

"*Red Rose*, the captain once again thanks you but wishes to inform you that our concern for the well-being of your ship in the event of a further incident compels us to again request you maintain your current distance."

"We thank your captain for the concern, but feel the risk is worth taking. Moving to assist."

"That's enough foreplay," Blinnikka said to Musann.

"Yes, sir," Musann said, then turned back to her console. "*Red Rose*, Captain Blinnikka formally requests we cut the shit and just get to it."

There was a pause. "Copy that," came the response, a moment later. "Please stand by."

Blinnikka turned to Kiva Lagos. "How are we on preparations?"

"Busy as the proverbial fucking bee," Kiva said.

Blinnikka nodded, glanced at Marce, and then turned his attention back to his command screen.

In spite of everything, Marce was thrilled. It was his first time on a command deck of any sort, and the calm professionalism of the *Yes, Sir* bridge crew in the face of what could reasonably be considered enemy action was inspiring. These were good people, Marce decided. Except possibly for Kiva Lagos. He hadn't quite gotten a bead on her yet.

He looked over at Lady Kiva, whose current expression could be read as intent, or condescending smugness, depending on one's own personal inclinations. Every experience Marce had of her was of someone one did not want to mess with. She reminded him of Vrenna that way, albeit with less of an actual conscience.

"What are you smirking about?" Kiva asked him. She'd caught him glancing at her.

"I was just thinking about you spacing Chat," Marce replied, lying.

"What about it?"

"I was wondering if you would have spaced him for good if he hadn't talked."

"Hell, yes. Motherfucker was going to set off a bomb on my ship," Kiva said. "You don't fuck with my ship. You don't fuck with my people."

"I'm a crew member now," Marce said. "That means I'm one of your people, too."

"And we're not going to give you up, now, are we?"

"Hopefully not."

Kiva nodded. "So there you go. Don't be a dick about it, Claremont."

Marce grinned at this.

The communication channel between ships crackled open again. "This is Captain Wimson of the *Red Rose*, asking for direct parley with Captain Blinnikka of the *Yes, Sir*."

Blinnikka slapped open his personal circuit. "Blinnikka here."

"I understand you wish to cut the shit, Captain."

"If that's all right with you, Captain."

"It certainly is. Why not be civilized about it. By now you've figured out what we are."

"You're pirates. You've been tracking us for most of a day."

"Correct. And by now you realize that one of our associates has disabled your ability to enter the Flow."

"Affirmative."

"However, today is your lucky day, Captain. We are willing to leave you your cargo and stay out of your way while you either repair your ship or turn back to Imperial Station. All we need from you is to deliver two people to us."

"Who are those people?"

"The first is our associate, the one who planted the bomb, who I'm sure you probably now have sitting in the brig. The second is a passenger. Lord Marce Claremont."

"Captain, we can't turn over your associate."

" 'Can't' is a very strong word, Captain."

"Let me amend. We can turn him over, just in very small pieces. He appears to have mistimed his bomb. He went up with it."

"That's unfortunate."

"If you want we can scrape the walls and hand him over in a bag."

"Thank you, no. His retrieval was optional. Lord Marce's, however, is not."

"Our passenger manifest has no Marce Claremont, lord or otherwise."

"I thought we agreed to cut the shit, Captain. Marce Claremont is currently on your ship under the name of Kristian Jansen, which is an identity the House of Lagos uses when it wants to smuggle someone off-system. You might want to inform your employers that they should change up their house identities more often than they do. You do have a Kristian Jansen on board, yes?"

"Yes, we do."

"Good."

"But there's a problem."

"Captain Blinnikka, I regret to inform you that if the 'problem' is Claremont is also in small pieces, I'm going to be required to do the same to your ship."

"What does that mean?"

"That means that I either get Claremont alive, or make the *Yes, Sir* dead. Those are your options."

"We would take you with us," Blinnikka said.

"No, you wouldn't. Now, what is the problem with Claremont?"

"He's not dead. But he is currently in a medically induced coma."

"Why?"

"Because he was in the corridor with your 'associate' when the bomb went off. He and several other crew members were trying to interrupt your friend. He survived. Two other crew members didn't."

"Condolences, Captain."

"You just threatened to destroy my ship and kill my entire crew, Captain. Your condolences are hollow."

"Understood. Can Claremont travel?"

"We can hand him off to you alive and stable. Everything else is up to you."

"Agreed. We will come alongside in three and a half hours. We'll have a shuttle ready to transfer him."

"No. We'll send a shuttle to you."

"Captain—"

"None of you are setting foot on my ship. You want him, fine. I'll give him to you. But we're coming to you."

"Then I want you on the shuttle for the handoff. As assurance you're not sending a shuttle-sized bomb."

"Not me," Blinnikka said. "I'll send the owner's representative instead. That will suit your purpose. And a medical staffer. They stay on the shuttle, you send in your own people to take Claremont out of it. Everything done in ten minutes maximum. Any longer and we're going down together, whether you believe it or not."

"Done. We'll inform you when we're ready to receive you. *Red Rose* out." The connection was cut.

"Thanks for volunteering me, asshole," Kiva said, as soon as the connection was wiped.

"The ship is underway," Blinnikka said. "I'm in command now, Lady Kiva. And I need you to do this thing. So shut up and do it, ma'am."

"Fine." She pointed at Marce. "And you're coming with me. Congratulations, you just got promoted to the medical staff." She looked over at Blinnikka. "Okay?" Blinnikka nodded.

"I don't think this is a good idea," Marce said.

"You don't get a vote. And you also told Pinton you were willing to help. Stop whining like a fucking child."

"You could have just said, 'I need your help.'"

"All right. I need your help. Stop whining like a fucking child."

"That's not better."

"Where is your Kristian costume?"

"I threw it away."

"Well, go dig it out. And then go to the medical bay. We have things to do."

• • •

"Hold out your thumb," the *Red Rose* medical technician said to Kiva.

"The fuck you say," Kiva replied.

The technician sighed, turned away, and called out the open ramp of the shuttle. A *Red Rose* crew member with a bolt thrower strode on the shuttle ramp.

"Hold out your thumb, or Sax here will blow your head off," the medical technician said.

Kiva held out her thumb; the technician jabbed it. Then she did a retinal scan. "You're Lady Kiva Lagos," she said.

"How the fuck did you get our personnel database?" Kiva asked the technician.

The technician ignored her and went over to Marce. "Thumb," she said. Marce offered it.

"Gusteen Obrecht," she said. She went over to the body on the medical gurney. For that one, she checked the thumb, and the retina, and drew blood from a vein in the right arm. Marce watched that final test, and waited for the result.

"Marce Claremont," she confirmed, and then Sax called to another *Red Rose* crewperson, who came on board and whisked the gurney away. The medical technician nodded to Kiva and Marce, and turned.

"Hey," Kiva said. The technician turned back, and Kiva reached over and grabbed a small rucksack—the rucksack Marce brought on to the *Yes, Sir*, in fact—and held it out to the technician.

"What is that?" the technician asked.

"What he brought onto the ship with him. Some toiletries and sundries."

"He might want to shave once he regains consciousness," Marce added.

The technician took the rucksack, nodded to the two of them, and then walked out of the shuttle.

"Let's button this thing up and get the fuck out of here," Kiva said.

"Agreed," Marce said. Kiva pounded on the door of the pilot compartment to signal the transfer had been made.

"Were you nervous?" Marce asked Kiva, as the shuttle headed back to the *Yes, Sir*.

"About what?"

"About the transfer. About them checking Chat's body for my genetics."

"No," Kiva said. "The thumb pad and the contacts we made from your scrapings are the same quality as we get for our fake identities. Our medical facilities are top notch like that."

Marce nodded and then winced a little bit, remembering the corneal scraping he endured to get the seed material for the contacts overlaid onto Chat's eyes. The contacts were fast-grown, as was the thumb pad, which ran the risk of genetic anomalies that would give them away. They got lucky. "I was thinking of the blood draw."

Kiva shrugged. "It was your blood. Sucked it out of you, clipped off the major vessels in his arms, drained that blood, put yours in. It's not complicated."

"I didn't know if the shunts would hold."

"They'll dissolve soon and his normal blood flow will come back. If he's lucky his muscles won't be necrotic and he'll be able to keep his arms."

"And if he's not lucky?"

"If he's not lucky, then fuck him, he tried to put a bomb in my ship."

"And kill me," Marce reminded her.

"Right," Kiva said.

"What if it hadn't worked?"

"You mean, what if they figured out that was Chat on the gurney while we were still there?"

"Yes."

"I had a backup plan."

"What? Run?"

"No. I'd give them you."

"What?" Marce looked at Kiva, shocked.

Kiva looked back. "Don't look at me like that. Why do you think I had you go? Because I like your company?"

"I thought I was one of your people now."

"Yeah, but you're *new*," Kiva said. "And there were a whole lot of other people to think about."

Marce didn't say anything else to Kiva for the short remainder of the journey.

As they exited the shuttle on the *Yes, Sir* and the ship accelerated away from the *Red Rose*, Marce received a ping on his tablet: a forwarded message from Vrenna.

Tracked down that thing you asked. Sjo Tinnuin heard the rumor from a friend who works for the House of Nohamapetan. Says the Nohamapetans have been paying for navigational data from ships for the last couple of years.

It sounds like maybe they're seeing some of the same things we see. I don't know what that means for us, but I don't think it means anything good.

Be careful out there. Miss you already.

—V

Kiva tapped Marce on the shoulder. He looked up from his tablet. "Come with me," she said.

"I'm tired," Marce said, putting his tablet away.

"Do you honestly think you're going to sleep until we're in the Flow and these pirates are well fucking behind us? Come on." She walked out of the shuttle bay. Marce stared after her and followed.

Presently they came to Kiva's cabin. Marce entered and was immediately jealous. "You have a room the size of a room," he said to Kiva, who had entered the room behind him. He stared at the immense expanse of the wall in front of him, which featured schedules, notes, and personal photos.

"Of course I do," Kiva said. "My family owns the ship. I'm the owner's representative. You think they're going to put me in a fucking bunk?"

"No, I suppose not. It's just funny."

"It's not that funny."

"Says the woman who doesn't sleep in a bunk the size of a coffin."

"Well, you won't be sleeping there tonight, anyway."

"What?" Marce turned and Kiva was entirely undressed.

"Let's get laid," she said, to Marce.

"Uh, okay," Marce said, and then paused. "No, hold on. I'm confused."

"You've had sex before, yes?" Marce nodded. "With women?" He nodded again. "And you *liked* it."

"Yes—"

"Then what's to be confused about?" she asked, coming up to him.

"I don't think you actually *like* me," Marce said.

"I like you just fine." She grabbed his waistband, and worked the uniform tab there.

"You were willing to give me up to the pirates if you had to. Ten minutes ago."

"Yes. And?"

"You tell me to shut the fuck up nearly every time we talk."

"I tell everyone that."

"I mean—"

"Look, we've both had a stressful day," Kiva said, and pulled down his uniform trousers. "Now, you could stand around trying to talk to me about all the things that *didn't* happen, in which case I toss your ass out and you go back to your tiny bunk and smell your own farts until you fall asleep, or you can shut the fuck up, get naked with me, and then we bang each other until we collapse from exhaustion. It's your choice, but if I were you I know what I would rather do. So, are we going to fuck or what?"

"This is your idea of romance, isn't it?" Marce asked Kiva.

"Basically," Kiva said, and then dragged him onto the bed.

A few hours later, as Marce dozed with Kiva nestled up against him, a long mellow ping reverberated throughout the ship.

"Hmmmm," Kiva said and opened up her eyes.

"What was that?" Marce asked.

"It's the signal that we've entered the Flow."

"So we're safe."

"Nothing is safe in the Flow. If our bubble collapses, we cease to exist."

"I mean we don't have to worry about pirates or Ghreni No-hamapetan," Marce said. He was aware of Kiva's body next to his and felt an erection pop up almost instantly.

Kiva felt it too and shifted her body on top of his, reached down to position Marce where she wanted him, and then pushed herself onto him. "No, you don't have to worry about pirates, or the fucking Nohamapetans," she said, working herself on him. "You might have to worry about *me*, though."

Marce smiled at this. "If this is what I have to worry about, I think I can handle it."

"This isn't what you have to worry about."

"Then what are you talking about?"

"I'm talking about whatever it is that Ghreni Nohamapetan was fucking willing to kill you over, Marce."

"Wait," Marce said. "Are we having an actual conversation? Now?" He started to prop himself up.

Kiva pushed him back down. "Yes, we're having an actual conversation right now," she said, increasing her pace. "I can fucking do both. Here's the thing. You're going to tell me whatever it is you're not telling me. You're going to tell me why you're on the ship. You're going to tell me why you're going to Hub. You're going to tell me why Ghreni Nohamapetan wants you dead. You're going to tell me, or I'm going to rip out your fucking heart."

"When did you want me to tell you?" Marce asked.

"Give me just a minute," Kiva said.

INTERLUDE

Ghreni Nohamapetan was not having a very good day.

Point one: The *Yes, Sir, That's My Baby* had managed to make it into the Flow, despite reporting damage to its engineering systems from the bomb Chat Ubdal had by all reports successfully planted, also allegedly blowing himself up in the process. Reports of Chat's demise had given Ghreni a slight twinge. Chat had been one of his more useful people, which is why Ghreni had used him for this particular and delicate mission. On the other hand, now Ghreni wouldn't have to pay out Chat's completion bonus, which would have been considerable. So that was the one silver lining on this particular mess.

Point two: Not that Chat would have gotten that bonus anyway, come to think of it, because he failed to do what he was supposed to: deliver or kill Marce Claremont. Ghreni had thought he'd managed the latter, despite blowing himself up, when the *Red Rose* messaged that they had taken delivery of Claremont, albeit in a damaged state, and that various tests confirmed Claremont's identity.

But then, more than an hour later, a message from the *Red Rose*:

Claremont out of coma and screaming that he is not Claremont but your lieutenant Chat Ubdal. Is in considerable pain, particularly in his limbs

Followed by

Confirmed Claremont is in fact not Claremont but Ubdal. Tricked our scans with contacts and thumb pad and blood replacement in arms. Last serious, may cause permanent damage

Followed by

Ubdal mostly not coherent but says did not plant the bomb and Yes, Sir is fully operational. Moving to intercept and destroy per agreement

Followed by

fucking hell those assholes took your fucking bomb and got it on our fucking ship what the actual fuck

Followed, rather some time later, by

Bomb Ubdal was to plant on Yes, Sir exploded on our ship, causing operational damage. Could not move to intercept and destroy. Captain Wimson unhappy Ubdal's bomb came onto our ship. Sent Ubdal out the airlock in his medical gurney. Specific message for you from captain: You owe us double for damages and triple for guns now. You pay off damages first. Also says fuck you and your incompetent fucking minions

Point three: Ghreni now didn't have the weapons he wanted, which annoyed him.

The weapons were part of a shipment authorized by the parliament and the emperox, to help the duke fight his little rebellion. The House of Nohamapetan had been instrumental in helping get the resolution for the weapons passed in parliament; Ghreni had been instrumental in arranging for the weapons to be pirated. That part at least went to plan.

But then Captain Wimson decided to hold on to the weapons, and told Ghreni to pay more to take delivery. This was upsetting to Ghreni, as aside from the *principle* of the thing, he'd already funded their acquisition out of House of Nohamapetan funds and found himself rather unfortunately illiquid. His plan to fund their reacquisition out of imperial funds hit a snag when the Count of Claremont decided to have ethics, then hit another snag when Marce Claremont's kidnapping also failed to produce results.

The new plan had been to reacquire Marce Claremont or destroy the *Yes, Sir*. The former would optimally yield the Count of Claremont's cooperation; the latter, while far less optimal because it would exacerbate the already-bad blood between the houses of Nohamapetan and Lagos if his hand in it ever came to light, would allow Ghreni to convince the duke to acquire the substantial funds the local Lagos offices would receive from local offices of the House of Aiello, who held the monopoly on insurance. From there he'd skim enough to cover the weapons.

But now the *Yes, Sir* was gone, and Marce Claremont with it, and the price of the weapons had not only gone up but now there was another debt in front of it he'd have to deal with.

Point four: And while at one point maybe Ghreni could have stiffed the *Red Rose* on the weapons—they were the ones who reneged on the original deal, that was their risk—there was no way he couldn't repay the damages to the pirate ship. They'd fucking kill him, and slowly. Neither his noble title nor his proximity to the duke, nor his own security people, would keep them from coming to get him. So he'd at least need to get the money for that, soon.

Ghreni briefly considered trying to track down Vrenna Claremont for her hostage value but then just as quickly dismissed it out of his mind because

Point five: Vrenna Claremont was utterly impossible to find. She'd gone to ground—but not before sending Ghreni a note from her personal address, which read, in its entirety:

Don't sleep in the same bed twice.

Ghreni had read Vrenna Claremont's service history. He was aware this was not at all an idle threat.

Which brought him to

Point six: The call he'd gotten from Sir Ontain Mount, operations chief of End's Imperial Station, which started, without preamble, "What the hell is this I'm hearing about you kidnapping Marce Claremont?"

"I don't know what you're talking about, sir," Ghreni said.

"Really."

"Of course. That's a very serious allegation. I'd like to know who is slandering me."

"Reputable sources, Lord Ghreni."

"It's ludicrous. For one thing, as I understand it Marce Claremont has left End. On the *Yes, Sir, That's My Baby.*"

"This would be the ship my marines tell me was tracked and almost attacked by a privateer just a few hours ago," Mount said.

"I couldn't say," Ghreni replied. "I have no knowledge of these things. We're rather busy enough down here, sir."

"Your duke's not doing very well at the moment, is he?"

"We've had setbacks, but nothing we can't handle."

"You're not making a convincing case for the last part, Lord Ghreni," Mount said.

"The assistance of the emperox's marines would be appreciated," Ghreni suggested.

"I'll repeat what I tell you every time you hint, which is that the Interdependency considers this an entirely local matter."

"Excepting the arms parliament authorized."

"For use by the duke's troops, not mine."

"A distinction perhaps without a difference."

"There's a difference to me, which is what matters. Either your duke will take care of this problem, or soon some rebel or another will petition me to be the new duke when all your nonsense is over."

"And what will you do then?"

"I suppose that might depend on whether the current duke's head is still on his shoulders. Until then, a friendly admonition, Lord Ghreni. The Count of Claremont and his family and his lands are under the emperox's protection. Which means they are under *my* protection. If I hear any more rumors of you interfering with them, either at the behest of the duke, or under your initiative, I promise that you will see what imperial intervention looks like, and you will not be happy about it. Are we clear?"

They were clear.

And then there was **point seven**, which was the coded note Ghreni had received from General Livy Onjsten, leader of the rebellion, which read:

Where are those weapons? You said you would have them to us by now. We undertook this last offensive on the basis of you getting those to us. We have our asses hanging out here. If we don't get them soon—or if the duke's troops get them instead of us—we're in real trouble.

Remember what I told you when we started this on your behalf. You're in this with us. We rise, you rise. We fall, you fall.

If we fall because of you, you will fall so much harder.

—LO

Why is everyone threatening me today? Ghreni asked himself.

Well, and the answer to *that* was because he'd overleveraged himself—and his house, and all their assets on End—in order to topple the current duke and install himself as the Duke of End. He'd overleveraged himself, and now all his precisely timed, precisely laid plans were on the verge of teetering over and collapsing.

This is what happens when you risk it all, Ghreni thought. *It's never going to run smoothly.*

True enough. But it shouldn't be *this* rough. Not now. Not all of a sudden.

At least the Duke of End wasn't yelling at him.

His tablet pinged. It was the duke calling. "You're kidnapping nobles now?" he yelled.

Ghreni smiled grimly in spite of himself. "That's not quite how it happened, Your Grace."

"Don't 'Your Grace' me, Ghreni. I just got an earload from Sir Ontain about it. Says you grabbed young Lord Marce Claremont right off the street in front of his apartment."

"That's a bit of an exaggeration. I asked Lord Marce to meet with me in order to see if I could get him to convince his father to be more active in defending End."

"What did he say?"

"He said he was leaving the planet within hours and was not in a position to plead our case."

"How did Sir Ontain get kidnapping out of *that*?"

"I may have been slightly overzealous in trying to convince Lord Marce to assist us. The conversation became heated. The rest of it is our enemies exaggerating and that exaggeration getting back to the Count of Claremont, and, I imagine, him complaining to Sir Ontain, and then him complaining to you. He did the same to me, sir, just a few moments ago."

"What did you tell him?"

"What I just told you, in slightly less detail with slightly fewer affirmations."

"We can't be going about antagonizing the nobles, Ghreni. Not now. And especially not *Claremont*. Ontain and his marines are practically the count's bodyguards. And if word gets around to the other nobles that we're trying to strong-arm the count, or threatening his children . . . well. We need their support right now, is what I'm saying."

"I understand entirely, sir. But as I said, this is just misunderstanding and rumor."

"Then you won't mind apologizing to the Count of Claremont personally."

"Excuse me, sir?"

"I've invited the count this morning to a small meeting. More of drinks and a chat, really, at Weatherfair." That would be the duke's "getaway" palace, not far outside the city. "You and me and him. There you'll explain the entire situation to him, and apologize to him."

"Sir, for what? As I said, this is entirely a misunderstanding."

"Then you'll apologize for the misunderstanding. Ghreni, it doesn't matter whether you actually have anything to apologize *for*. The act of apologizing is the thing. You should know that already. That's basic diplomacy."

"The meeting will be just the three of us?"

"Yes. I think that's best. No need to make a spectacle about it. The word will get out anyway."

"The Lady Vrenna will not be there?"

"The count's daughter? No. Why?"

"Just checking."

"We could invite her if you like."

"I'd rather not."

"Then I'll see you in a few hours. Dress casually. Practice groveling." The duke disconnected.

And that was **point eight**.

So, to recap: People wanted Ghreni dead or at least seriously injured, his plans to maneuver himself to a dukedom through fomenting a revolution were falling apart at a rapidly accelerating rate, and in a few hours he'd have to feign regret for an incident he'd have to maintain never happened, even though it had and Ghreni had absolutely no regrets doing it, save that it didn't go to plan. Unless something miraculous happened in short order, Ghreni would be dead or in jail and the House of Nohamapetan legally on the hook of his actions.

The worst of it was, none of this was originally *his* idea.

• • •

By the time they were all in their teenage years, it was clear to anyone who cared to look that each of the Nohamapetan scions had a certain leading characteristic. Amit was the conventional one—unoriginal, unthreatening, but always ready to be out front for family and house, a tractable figurehead who would one day publicly take the reins of the House of Nohamapetan. Ghreni was the useful one, the one good with people, the "salesman"—or the confidence man—the one who could intrigue you with an idea and get you to sign your name on the line, whether or not you really understood what you were buying.

But it was Nadashe, the sister, who was the brains of the operation. She was the one who told the figurehead what to say, and pointed the salesman at the mark, and set into motion the plans that would take years, or even decades, to come to their fruition.

As she did that first night, when the siblings were all gathered in Xi'an to celebrate the birthday of Rennered Wu, the crown prince, whom Nadashe had so recently begun negotiations with, in regards to a marriage.

"He's a prick," Ghreni had said, to his sister, after the three of them had departed the festivities and decamped to the Nohamapetan apartments, not too far from the imperial palace.

"I kind of like him," Amit replied. Amit was lounged on a chaise, a glass of Nohamapetan shiraz in his hand. The shiraz was contraband, or would be if anyone other than the Nohamapetans themselves were to drink it; the House of Patric owned the monopoly on grapes and all their products. But when the Interdependency was formed, and the monopolies parceled out, the existing Nohamapetan grape stock was grandfathered in, for the family's private use only. The house's famous shiraz, acknowledged to be one of the finest outside the now-lost environs of Earth, was now accessible only if one was a Nohamapetan. Or one of their guests, for a small private party or perhaps even something more intimate. It was not unheard of for especially fervent oenophiles to proposition Nohamapetans on the chance there might be a particularly vintage bottle in the offing.

"You would," Ghreni said. From his point of view, Rennered Wu and his brother were cut out of the same boring, playboy-ish cloth. Ghreni didn't dislike Amit, nor did Amit dislike Ghreni, but in their adult years they didn't spend all that much time with each other. They both had friends who were more suitably interesting to each of them.

Ghreni didn't spend that much time with his sister, either, although not for lack of interest. It's just that Nadashe had *plans*. When they involved Ghreni, he saw her. When they didn't, he didn't. The fact that she had dragged them both back to her apartments, minus their escorts for the evening, meant that her plans involved them in some way.

But she wasn't telling them what they were yet, so Ghreni decided to needle her, just for fun. "And what's your excuse, Nada? Why are you consorting with that stiff Rennered?"

Nadashe, standing behind Amit's chaise, reached over and took her brother's wineglass from him and took a swig. Amit protested mildly but shut up when it was returned to him. "You mean, aside from the fact that one day he will be emperox and that allying with the imperial house will give our family an unassailable position among the guilds, and that one of my children will be the next emperox, forever embedding our interests into the fabric of the Interdependency?"

"Yes," Ghreni said. "Besides that."

"He's an acceptable dancer."

"Well," Ghreni said, looking over to his brother, who rolled his eyes. "That's something."

"There's also another reason, which is why I brought the two of you here tonight." She took the glass from Amit again.

"Stop that," Amit said.

"No," Nadashe said, and walked the glass over to the bar. "I need you sober for this part. You'll get the glass back when I'm done."

"I already don't like whatever this is," Amit said.

"What's going on, Nada?" Ghreni asked.

"Just the future," Nadashe replied, and then told the house computer to dim the lights and bring a presentation on a monitor. The presentation contained a map of the Interdependency, with the major Flow streams highlighted, all centering on Hub.

"This is the future?" Amit asked.

"This is the present," Nadashe said. Then she snapped her fingers and the map changed—not the star systems of the Interdependency but the Flow streams, which rearranged themselves, drastically in some cases. Most notably, the space around Hub, previously crowded with the inward and outgoing vectors of the Flow, was now populated by only three streams, two incoming and one outgoing. A different system was now the hub of the majority of Flow streams, its space crowded with the representations of the traffic going in and going out.

It was End.

"*This* is the future," Nadashe said.

Ghreni got up and walked closer to the monitor, studying the new map. "Where did you get this?"

"I have a friend from university who grew up to be a Flow physicist," she said. "My friend was casting about for something to do her doctoral thesis on and she came across a monograph about a potential long-term shift in the Flow. The person who wrote the monograph never did anything with it. She tracked down his information and he'd become a tax collector for the Interdependency. So she followed up, worked the data, and came to the conclusion that after more than a thousand years of relative stability, the Flow streams are about to shift, probably to this map."

"When?" Amit asked.

"She says the data indicate it's already starting. First slowly but then quicker and quicker. It'll probably start in the next decade." Nadashe pointed at the monitor. "This map is likely to be what the Interdependency looks like in thirty years, she says."

Ghreni furrowed his brow. "'Likely'? What does that mean?"

"She's modeling what she sees as the most probable pattern of collapses and shifts, based on her data set. She says this pattern has an eighty-five percent probability of being what things will be once the pattern stabilizes. And when it stabilizes, it'll likely hold for another thousand years."

Ghreni pointed. "And she's sure End is going to be the place all those streams are going to focus on."

Nadashe nodded. "She says that's actually the most predictable part of the shift. It's happened before, apparently. The shift of the Flow streams. Her data suggests the locus of the Flow activity switches off between Hub and End every thousand or two thousand years. There's a less than one chance in a hundred thousand that some other system will be the focus of the Flow streams."

"All right, but so what?" Amit said.

"So whoever controls the system the Flow streams are focused in controls the Interdependency," Ghreni said.

"At least one brother is paying attention," Nadashe said, smiling.

"But we don't control that system," Amit pointed out. "We're in the Terhathum system."

"That's the present," Nadashe said, and then pointed again at the monitor. "This is the future."

"There's already a Duke of End," Ghreni told his sister.

"There is one," Nadashe agreed. "But historically they don't stick around very long. They get deposed often enough that when there's yet another rebellion, the Interdependency's policy is to let them fight it out and then pass on the dukedom to whoever's left standing."

"You want to depose the current duke?"

"No, I want *you* to depose him, Ghreni."

"What? Why me?"

"Because Amit's busy preparing to take over the family business, and I'm busy trying to merge our line with the emperox's. You're the only one not currently busy."

"I'm busy," Ghreni said, and he was. He was a vice president of marketing for the house, which was a suitable position for him, given his age and work experience. After a certain point in time he'd leave that position to become part of the house board of directors and he'd have the option of coasting, just as third children of all the major houses did.

"You're not *that* busy. And besides if we put you in charge of our interests on End, that would be a promotion. Which would look good for you, and is a natural progression in your career."

"But it's on End."

"And?"

"There's nothing on End. That's why it's *called* End."

"The future is on End, Ghreni. We're going to need you there so we can be ready when it happens."

"You're already planning to marry into the imperial house, Nada," Amit said. "If you're going to do that, then why do we even need Ghreni on End?"

"You want to answer that one?" Nadashe asked Ghreni.

"Because whoever is running End will be in a good position to challenge the emperox for power," Ghreni said, to his brother.

"The whole reason the House of Wu is the imperial house is because they control the space around Hub. You can't dip a toe into it without paying tolls and tariffs and taxes. If that all shifts to End, one of the emperox's biggest revenue sources dries up."

"We marry into the House of Wu to get power now," Nadashe continued. "We secure End to stay in power when things shift. And if our families hold both Hub and End, we'll keep the Interdependency from falling apart in a civil war."

"Which would be bad for business," Amit concluded. "Everyone's, including ours."

Ghreni looked at the monitor again. "You want to risk a lot on a doctoral thesis, sis."

Nadashe shrugged. "Worse-case scenario, we're wrong about the shift. The result is you're Duke of End and I'm the imperial consort."

"Actually the worst-case scenario is you don't marry Rennered and Ghreni is arrested for treason, and the shift happens anyway," Amit pointed out.

"You're not helping," Ghreni said, to his brother.

"I'm just making sure we're clear on what the failure states are," Amit replied. "I know you two think I'm not as smart as either of you, and you're right. I'm not. But I'm smart enough to know this plan of yours, Nadashe, has a lot of risk and a more than minor chance of failure. If this is going to work, you're going to need me to keep feathers unruffled with the house board."

"Only if we tell them," Nadashe said.

Amit snorted. "You want to run a planetary coup clandestinely, out of the House of Nohamapetan?"

"Why not? Use local funds. It's End, we can keep the expenditures off the books for years if we have to. If we're smart about it, we don't have to tell the board until after it's done."

"Oh, dear," Amit said, and got up from the chaise. "I actually *am* going to need a drink for this." He went to the bar.

"We keep it quiet. Just between us."

"Even with local funds we won't be able to keep this quiet," Ghreni said. "Especially if we are running the rebellion."

"This is a place where some or another group revolts against the sitting duke a couple of times a decade," Nadashe pointed out. "You don't have to *run* it. You find one that's already running."

"And you think the current duke will somehow sit still for this."

"Depends on whether he figures out you're involved. If you make yourself useful to him, he might not."

"Lots of moving parts on this one," Amit said, from the bar.

"He's not wrong," Ghreni agreed. He pointed to the monitor, with the map still open. "And there's no guarantee your physicist friend isn't a complete fraud. Why isn't this actual news, Nadashe? You'd think this would be something people might be concerned about. The fact I've never heard of this before suggests to me there's less here than meets the eye."

"She came to me with it exclusively," Nadashe said.

"Why did she do that?"

"She needed money and she thought this would be something she could trade for it. I paid her way through the rest of her doctoral thesis—not on this—and she worked on this for me."

"Who is she?"

"She's a friend of mine from university. I told you this already."

"Does she have a name?"

"Hatide Roynold."

"Did I meet her?"

Nadashe snorted at this. "No. As difficult as it may be for you to accept this, Ghreni, you didn't manage to meet and have sex with *all* of my university friends."

"This data she has for you isn't peer reviewed?" Amit asked. His glass was full of shiraz again.

"No. Obviously we didn't want it leaked. I think she may have at some point tried to correspond with the tax collector whose work she was following up on, but I don't think anything came of that."

"So except for a minor imperial bureaucrat who may or may not know anything but clearly doesn't care, literally no one else knows anything about this?" Nadashe nodded. "Well," Amit said. "If nothing else, no one will see this coming."

"So now you want to do this?" Ghreni asked his brother.

"I didn't say I *want* to do this," Amit said. "This is a high-risk, high-reward investment, which is the most polite way I can think of to describe this crackpot scheme. I don't like risk. And we already have a monopoly franchise, so we already *have* a reward." He motioned toward the monitor. "But if *this* has any chance of being true, then there's also a risk of the Interdependency collapsing in on itself if we do nothing. And that's a some-risk, high-penalty scenario. I have to decide whether I want *that* less than I want *this*."

"We can make it work," Nadashe said.

"By which you mean *I* will have to make it work," Ghreni said. "I'll be months away from you."

"We can plan it out before you leave."

"All those plans will mean nothing when they hit the real world."

"Then improvise. Gain people's confidence. Keep them in the dark about your true intentions. You're good at that."

"Yes," Ghreni agreed. "But that'll only get me so far."

"You'll figure out the rest." Nadashe walked over and patted her brother on the cheek. "And when you don't know what to do next, just come out firing. It couldn't hurt."

"Actually it could hurt a lot," Amit said. He poured himself some more shiraz.

"Be bold," Nadashe said, ignoring Amit. "Be bold, Ghreni. And then, be Duke of End."

Nadashe didn't convince either Amit or Ghreni that night. Too many questions and too many ways the three of them would end up in very small prison cells for the rest of their lives for treason, fraud, and terrorism. But the question was when, not if, Nadashe would bring them around, with her plans and her persuasions. Within a month she had her brothers agreeing in principle with the idea. A month after that Ghreni, still not entirely believing he was signing on to this harebrained scheme, was on the Nohamapetan fiver *Some Nerve!*, heading toward End.

In retrospect, his part of the scheme had gone surprisingly well. There was indeed an affronted group ready to take on the Duke of End that he could funnel money and weapons to, in exchange for their doing all the work of the rebellion. He'd quickly ingratiated himself into the inner circle of the Duke of End, who despite the proud title was a provincial rube whose own father came to power by overthrowing the former duke, and who was deeply impressed with Ghreni, whose family could trace its noble origins back to before the founding of the Interdependency.

In a few short months, the rebellion went into overdrive and he was the duke's confidant and political hatchet man—and in a position to undermine his patron quietly while preparing the way for his own inevitable ascendance when the duke's head rolled into the dust. Certainly he was doing better on his end of the plan than Nadashe was doing on hers, although that wasn't entirely her fault. As far as Ghreni knew she had nothing to do with Rennered smashing into that wall. At least, if she *had*, she'd kept him out of it.

But now it was all crashing down, and Ghreni sensed he was within days if not hours of disgrace and discovery, which was not only a danger to him but to the entire House of Nohamapetan. It was one thing to fuck up on your own time. It was another to sideswipe the house while you did it.

Be bold, Nadashe had said to him. *And then be Duke of End.* Ghreni smiled at this memory and tried to imagine what his sister would do in his shoes. Then, with less than two hours left before he had to present himself to the Duke of End and the Count of Claremont, he set about doing that.

• • •

The duke and the count and Ghreni spent an hour having a high tea on Weatherfair's eastern outside gallery, the one with a spectacular view of the city, talking about utterly inconsequential things. Ghreni could see this took some effort on the part of the count, because he clearly thought Ghreni had kidnapped, and intended to torture, his son. Then the three went into the duke's private office to be alone while they talked about consequential things *not* relating to Ghreni kidnapping and intending to torture the count's son, and that took another hour or so.

Then the duke signaled it was time to do the apology thing. Ghreni nodded, stood up, positioned himself between the count in his chair and the duke behind his desk. He took a deep breath that seemed to hint at the difficulty he was going to have saying the words that would follow. He then reached into his right interior jacket pocket, where he'd secreted a small bolt

thrower, and shot the count with it, stunning him into uncon-
sciousness.

"Ghreni, what the hell are you do—" the duke began, and
then stopped because one of his lungs had a hole in it, put there
by the small pistol that Ghreni had produced from his left interior jacket pocket and fired at him, after dropping the bolt
thrower to the floor to free his hands for the new weapon. The
duke barely had time to look at the entry wound and then back
up at Ghreni in confusion before he died from the bullet Ghreni
shot into his face. The bullet entered just below the duke's right
eye and then scored through his brain, settling, its velocity
spent, into the rear interior of the duke's skull.

Ghreni very quickly pulled out a handkerchief, rubbed his
prints off the pistol, and placed it into the hand of the unconscious count. He made sure to get the count's prints on the grip
and trigger. Then he picked up the bolt thrower, rubbed it off
as well, and got the duke's prints on it, then let it drop to the
floor where it naturally would have. He opened the drawer on
the duke's desk where it would be logical for the noble to have
placed a bolt thrower for personal protection.

Then Ghreni ran for the door of the office and opened it just
as the duke's staff and security people, having heard the shots,
reached the other side of it.

"They shot each other!" is all Ghreni said before the staff and
security people barreled through the entrance. Ghreni collapsed
by the door, feigning shock, and faked hyperventilating. It
didn't matter; no one was paying attention to him because there
was the far more serious issue of a dead duke in the room.

Which was fine with Ghreni. He didn't want anyone paying
attention to him. He wanted all their attention on the duke and
the count. He wanted everyone in the room to see the obvious:
The count had pulled a small pistol, the duke had pulled the

bolt thrower set to stun, and then someone shot first and everything went to hell, and now one was dead and the other was out like a light. The more others saw that—and by now the room was jammed with staff—the more that their eyes would allow their brains to believe the story Ghreni was going to tell.

"The duke had called me to apologize to the count," Ghreni said to Sir Ontain Mount, some time later. The imperial bureaucrat had gotten involved because the assassination of a sitting duke by a sitting count was an imperial problem, even if it was the Duke of End, whom Sir Ontain had previously been content to let hang if the rebels ever got hold of him. The two of them were alone in the hospital morgue, with the body of the duke laid out on a slab before them.

"This would have been for kidnapping his son," Mount said.

"Allegedly kidnapping," Ghreni said. "And I did apologize, although not for kidnapping Marce Claremont, which I did not do. I apologized instead for having a heated conversation with the count's son, from which this misunderstanding arose."

"How did the count take it?"

Ghreni motioned to the mortuary slab. "He was not convinced."

"Why didn't the count shoot *you*, Lord Ghreni?"

"Sir?"

"You are the one he alleges kidnapped his son. *You* are the more logical target for his rage. And you were literally right in his sights."

"The count thought I did it at the behest of the duke. At least that's what he said before the shooting started."

"And he thought that why?"

"Because the duke had sent me to see the count a few days earlier to try to convince the count to illegally divert imperial funds to him, in order to pay for weapons pirates had stolen and were ransoming. The count said no—as he should have—so naturally the count assumed the duke also assigned me to this alleged kidnapping to apply pressure."

"But you *did* speak to the young Claremont on the duke's account."

"Yes." Ghreni noted Mount's apparent acceptance of his spin on the kidnapping, but obviously said nothing about it. "The duke was aware I didn't approve of his plan to 'borrow' the funds, but I still asked because he was my duke."

"Still odd he wouldn't try for you as well."

"Perhaps he planned to. But then there was the duke's bolt thrower. I don't think he was expecting the duke to have that."

"No," Mount agreed. "The head of the duke's security detail was surprised by it, too. Said to me the duke didn't generally like or carry weapons. He left that to his bodyguards."

"The duke was probably being prudent. He knew the count was upset with him."

"Yes, but where did he get the bolt thrower? His security people said they'd never seen it before."

Ghreni allowed himself to look uncomfortable.

"Yes, Lord Ghreni?" Mount pressed.

"It's mine and I lent it to him," Ghreni said. "I bought it a while ago when things started getting bad with the rebellion."

"You have your own security people."

"I don't have them with me all the time. The duke was aware I had it—I never carried it around him, for obvious reasons—so he asked me to bring it for the meeting. For his own safety."

"He could have just had his security attend the meeting. Or have his people frisk the count when he arrived."

"I think he thought either would just enrage the count more. The meeting was supposed to repair the wound between them. That's why he chose to have the meeting at Weatherfair. A private residence rather than the public office. A friendly meeting, not a formal one."

Mount looked back at the slab. "It appears the duke miscalculated."

"What are you going to do about the Count of Claremont?" Ghreni asked.

"For now he's upstairs in a private room with six of my marines around him. He's still out of it. I don't imagine when he wakes up he'll tell me the same story you just did, will he?"

"I couldn't say," Ghreni said. "I know he's still angry with me. I wouldn't be surprised if he tries to suggest I was involved in some way. Other than lending the duke my bolt thrower, I mean. He wouldn't know about that. Is there a recording from the office?"

Mount shook his head. "Security tells me the duke didn't have any of that at Weatherfair. He called it his 'place of refuge,' whatever that means."

Ghreni nodded, as if he didn't know Weatherfair had no real security measures. "The next duke will know better," he said.

"Whoever *that* is." Mount motioned to the slab. "This one has no heirs and no close family, and the duke's prenup with the duchess specifies she cannot inherit. Apparently there were trust issues there."

"Isn't there a protocol? As the emperox's representative you'd have to approve whomever claimed the title, yes?"

"In the absence of a direct heir I'd be the one to appoint an acting duke, yes. My recommendation would still have to be approved by the emperox, of course. My first inclination would simply be to pass it along to the next-highest-ranking noble. Which in this case would be the Count of Claremont."

"That wouldn't be the best idea under the circumstances," Ghreni said.

"No, it would not. There are a few other counts and barons who I would have found acceptable but some of them have fled the planet, and the others are either currently hiding or have allied themselves with the rebels, which makes them untenable. For now, anyway."

"What if the rebel leader presents herself? Livy Onjsten, their general."

Mount snorted. "I'm not going to appoint her just because the duke died and now she doesn't have to *overthrow* him. They are still in rebellion. You don't win a rebellion by default."

Ghreni made himself look thoughtful and silent and waited for Mount to notice. "What is it?" Mount finally said.

"This wasn't something I was supposed to talk about." Ghreni made himself talk haltingly. "For the last few months, the duke has quietly had me treating with the rebels to find out if there's a way out of this mess. Their resources are stretched thin and so are ours. Both our sides are looking for an acceptable way out. But now the duke is dead. The rebels will want the ducal throne. If we don't act quickly the rebellion will fracture into competing factions of leaders claiming the dukedom for themselves, which will make it worse for everyone else on End."

"What do you suggest, then? That I *do* make this Onjsten woman the duke?"

Ghreni shook his head. "Has the duke's death made the news yet?"

"No," Mount said. "For the moment, all anyone knows is that the Count of Claremont is upstairs. They don't know *he*," Mount pointed at the duke, "is down here. That won't last, though."

"I can reach Onjsten as soon as you and I stop talking. Let me offer her an immediate truce, acceptance of several of the rebels' political goals, and a title for her."

"Which title?"

"Countess."

"Of Claremont?" Mount said, sarcastically.

"Possibly, if it becomes vacant after a trial. But you said several counts have fled. Give her one of those vacant titles. Lesser titles for her lieutenants. General amnesty for her fighters. We can end this now, with a single call."

"That's a lot for a single call to do," Mount observed.

"It's not the call, it's the months of work before it," Ghreni said. "Her people and I already have most of this hammered out in principle. This would just be us implementing it."

"And if Onjsten doesn't agree?"

"Then I tell her the Imperial Marines are stepping in."

Mount stiffened. "We have no intention of doing that, Lord Ghreni."

"Of course not! But she doesn't have to know that, and it makes fine leverage. I'll be saying 'Have everything you want or the Interdependency will crush you.' It's motivation to act."

"You're confident you can do this?"

"I think it's the best chance we have right now. And the best chance we'll have for a long time."

Mount nodded. "Do it."

"The thing is, Sir Ontain, I don't have the formal power to do any of this. Yet."

Ghreni waited for Mount to figure out what it was he was saying, which didn't take long, because Mount wasn't stupid. Then Ghreni had to wait while Mount weighed everything that had just happened in his head. He watched as microexpressions flashed across Mount's face—the realization that Ghreni had basically walked him into a trap where Mount would have to give him what he wanted; irritation that he'd been that easily maneuvered; suspicion that Ghreni might have orchestrated the assassination outright for this very purpose; veiled admiration if that was in fact the case; recognition that this rebellion was a goddamned stupid mess and that the sooner it was over, by whatever means, the better off everyone would be; resignation that this sneaky little Nohamapetan was probably the best chance Mount had to get this whole shitshow off his hands quickly.

Ghreni knew Mount was going to offer him the dukedom probably a few hundredths of a second before Mount did.

"All right, Lord Ghreni," Mount said. "Get a cease-fire in the next hour and a truce in the next twenty-four and you're acting duke. I'll start the paperwork for the recommendation to make it stick. But I want to be clear with you about this, my young friend. If I discover that the assassination of the duke is in any way different than how you've related it to me here, your dukedom is going to be a three-meter-by-three-meter cell for the rest of your natural life. And I will make it my personal business to assure you live a very long life indeed. Are we clear?"

"Of course, Sir Ontain."

"Then congratulations, Lord Ghreni, provisional Duke of End. Get to work." Mount strode out of the morgue. Ghreni suppressed the urge to pump his fists in joy.

One hour later he'd secured the cease-fire and dispatched people to get to work on the treaty. He hadn't had to threaten General Onjsten with the Imperial Marines, of course; she was working for him anyway.

Two hours later he'd informed Captain Wimson of the *Red Rose* that payment for the ship damages and the weapons would be forthcoming pending Ghreni's formal installation as acting duke, so please be patient and don't have him murdered.

Three hours later the new acting Duke of End was informed that the Count of Claremont was awake and cognizant. Ghreni decided to pay him a visit, and ordered everyone, including the six Imperial Marines, to wait on the other side of the door. They complied, although not happily. Ghreni took the chair in the corner of the room and sat it next to the hospital bed, so he could talk very quietly to the count.

"I'm the Duke of End now," he said to the count.

"Congratulations," the count said, after a moment. There was a distinct lack of enthusiasm to his voice.

Nevertheless Ghreni nodded. "Thank you. Now, here's the thing. You and I need to get our stories straight. The story is, you assassinated the duke for ordering me to kidnap your son. You two had an argument, you pulled your pistol, he pulled a bolt thrower, you don't remember anything after that because the stun bolt messed with your memory."

"You want me to confess to murder."

"Yes. Yes, I do."

"Not a great plan you have, Lord Ghreni."

Ghreni ignored the count's refusal to upgrade his title. "Here's what I'll give you in return. You'll be sentenced for the murder but I'll allow you to serve your sentence under house arrest at Claremont. You'll abdicate your title and I'll make sure it goes to your daughter rather than it being taken from you in disgrace. You'll give up your job as imperial auditor and I'll install someone of my own choosing in that role. But I'll make sure you keep your pension and I'll add a stipend to it to keep up your residence. You keep your mouth shut about everything to everyone, including your daughter. Oh, also, you tell her not to try to murder me in the night."

The count snorted at this. Ghreni pressed on.

"If you agree to everything, in five years, I'll pardon you. I'll say that the late duke had threatened you and your family to such an extent you felt you had no choice. You were under extreme duress. And since I was there for all of it, I'm in a position to confirm that. So that's it. Confess, five years at home, and then a pardon."

The count laughed, weakly.

"Why are you laughing?" Ghreni demanded.

"Lord Ghreni, you have no idea what's coming in the next five years," the count said.

"On the contrary, Claremont, I do. Changes are coming. End is going to become the heart of the Interdependency. All paths will lead to here."

"No. No paths will lead to here. In five years we'll be alone. It's a physical certainty."

Ghreni began to feel uncomfortable and realized it was the count's last sentence that did it. "What do you mean?"

"Why do you think I sent my son away, Lord Ghreni. At this specific time?"

"To escape the fighting here, and to complain to the emperox about me kidnapping him." The latter was why Ghreni wanted Marce out of the way if he couldn't be retrieved. Ghreni wasn't sure how much pull the Count of Claremont had at the imperial court, but he knew Nadashe and Amit wouldn't appreciate a report from End about his actions making their lives harder.

The count shook his head. "I had him leave now because if he didn't, it would be impossible for him to ever leave."

Ghreni was puzzled. "Are you talking about the Flow stream?" What would an imperial auditor know about Flow streams? The count's specialty was taxes, not phys—

"Oh my God," Ghreni said, and openly stared at the count. "You're *him*."

The Count of Claremont seemed puzzled but amused. "Who am I, Lord Ghreni?"

"You're him! The Flow physicist! The one whose work Hatide Roynold based hers off of."

Claremont continued to look puzzled for a moment, but then Ghreni saw a sort of slow realization come over his face. "I know that name. I remember that name. She sent me some of her work and a list of questions years ago."

"And you didn't respond."

"No, I didn't. I had been ordered by the emperox not to discuss my work with anyone." Another expression popped onto Claremont's face then. Concern. "You think her work is accurate, don't you? You think the Flow streams are moving to End. That's it, isn't it?"

Ghreni's mouth gaped.

Claremont slapped the side of his bed. "That *is* it! That's *actually* it!" Claremont started laughing, a loud, almost agitated noise. One of the marines opened the door and poked a head in to investigate. Ghreni angrily waved him away.

Eventually Claremont got control of himself, wiped a tear away from his eye, and looked at Ghreni. "Oh, you sad, ambitious fool," he said.

"What do you know?" Ghreni asked.

"I know that Hatide Roynold was sloppy with her math. I know if she didn't check some of her base assumptions, she's probably iterating wildly away in a direction that has no basis in reality. Has any of her work you've seen had peer review?"

"No," Ghreni said.

Claremont nodded. "Of course not. She's like me—snapped up by a patron and working alone. Peer review is important, Lord Ghreni. Until Marce was old enough to start checking my work, I was flying blind. Made some stupid mistakes I just didn't see. Roynold was making them too. I know, I saw them. She probably never corrected them." Claremont leaned forward and weakly poked Ghreni in the chest. "And you, you ignorant grasping poltroon. You didn't know any better."

Ghreni actually flinched from the poke. "What are you saying?" he asked.

Claremont smiled and then lay back into his bed. "What I'm saying is nothing, Lord Ghreni. Not until you decide to send a report back to your house, detailing your sudden ascendance to the dukedom. You *are* going to be doing that, yes?"

"I am." The report would go out on a mail drone, a small unmanned craft that floated in space right outside a Flow shoal, onto which electronic communication—personal letters and pictures, business communications, reports, intellectual property that could be digitized—was recorded. Once a day one of these drones headed into the Flow with its stash of information; once a day a drone appeared out of the Flow, with letters, communication, IP, and so on to transmit to End. The mail was always late, because End was far away from everything. But it always arrived.

Claremont nodded again. "File your report. Send it. And then when *it* happens, you come back to me, and I'll tell you *my* terms."

"When *what* happens?"

"You'll know it."

"And what terms do you think you'll be able to dictate?"

"I'd like not to have a murder on my record, for starters. After that, we'll see. But I'll tell you this, Lord Ghreni, you have this all wrong. *I* don't need you. You, on the other hand, might need me. More than you know. So go write your report. I'll stay quiet until you get back."

Claremont actually made shooing motions, dismissing Ghreni. More out of bemusement than anything, he left.

•   •   •

Ghreni went to his office at the House of Nohamapetan building—it would take a while to move his concerns into the ducal palace, a thought that sent a thrill down his spine—and composed his report to Nadashe. The report was both in code and encrypted. Then he sent it on a secure beam to the mail drone, and waited for a receipt that it had been. The receipt came minutes later, along with the timer for the departure of the drone, which would be on its way in under half an hour. Ghreni noted the receipt and then busied himself with other work, primarily fielding reports from the team writing up the truce with the rebels.

This was involved enough that it wasn't until three hours later that he noticed he'd received an additional note from the mail service, informing him that his mail would not be delivered on time. The reason was "drone failure," which meant the drone was defective in some way. The information in the drone, including his report, would be transferred to a different drone (there were dozens parked out near the Flow shoal) and then sent through.

Ghreni noted this and was about to click through when he noticed two other reports of delays due to material failure. As he read the third one a fourth entered into his queue.

Ghreni pinged his assistant. "What's going on with the mail drones?" he said.

"I don't know, sir," was the reply. "Everyone's complaining about it. All the mail is bouncing from one drone to another."

Before Ghreni could respond to this his tablet pinged to let him know Sir Ontain Mount was trying to reach him. He disconnected from his assistant without acknowledgement and hailed Mount.

"We seem to have a problem," Mount said.

"With the treaty discussions?" Ghreni asked.

"No, something else. A fiver named *Because I Said So* just reported in to Imperial Station. It was about to translate into the Flow."

"Is there a problem with the ship?"

"This ship is fine. It's the Flow shoal."

"What about it?"

"It isn't there, Lord Ghreni. It's entirely gone."

Several hours and a number of semi-frantic meetings later Ghreni returned to the hospital and to the Count of Claremont's room.

"Oh good, you're back," Claremont said. He pointed at the Imperial Marines. "I've been told I'm fine and they're going to release me now. They're about to hand me over to the local authorities, which I suppose are your people now. I'm going to jail, apparently."

"I need the room," Ghreni said, to everyone who was not the count. The room cleared out. Ghreni turned his attention back to Claremont. "You knew. About the Flow."

Claremont nodded. "It was possible that it hadn't collapsed yet when you sent along your report, in which case this would be a different conversation. For now, at least. But if it hadn't collapsed today, it would have been tomorrow, or the next day. Within a week, in any event. And we'd be having this conversation then."

"If the Flow stream collapsed then you sent your son to his death."

"No. I predicted this stream is collapsing from the entrance shoal. The exit shoal will be open for months yet. Not that it will matter. Nothing else can get into it, so for all purposes once the stream empties of ships currently in it, it's gone. Everyone who's on End will be here for the duration."

"And how long is that? How long is 'the duration'?"

"Why, Lord Ghreni. That's *forever*, of course."

Ghreni had nothing to say to this.

"There is one thing," Claremont said.

"What is it?"

"The Flow stream out from End is closed. But I predict the Flow stream *to* End will stay open for several years yet. It's already showing some signs of decay. But it should hold for a while. It might even be the last Flow stream in the Interdependency to collapse entirely."

"What does that mean?" Ghreni asked.

"It means we should be getting ready for visitors."

"Visitors."

"Yes."

"How many?"

"As many who can make it here alive, I expect," Claremont said, and then clapped his hands together. "Now, Lord Ghreni. You're a murderer and a usurper, and you tried to hurt my son. In a perfect world you'd be dead or rotting in jail for what you've been doing for the last few years. Either option would be fine by me. But right now, for better or worse, you're the Duke of End. I suppose now that you're duke you've magically found a way to end the rebellion, yes?"

Ghreni nodded.

"Which means you were actively *involved* in the rebellion in some horribly duplicitous way, yes?"

Ghreni gave a full-body shrug to this.

"That's what I thought. Regardless, now we're at peace, which we're going to need for what comes next, and you, alas, are instrumental in keeping it. Which means that getting rid of you at this point would cause even more problems than it would solve. I could try arguing the point—I suppose I could contact Sir Ontain and make a fuss. But now that you know about the Flow stream collapse, you know we have bigger problems on our hands than rebellions and coups. So I'm going to offer you my support."

"Really." Ghreni blinked at this. "With all due respect, sir, I think you're misjudging who needs whose support."

"I'm not. You have some decisions to make that will decide whether humanity—the part of it here now, and the parts of it to come—survive the collapse. You're ambitious and you're greedy and you clearly were part of some larger plan by your house to take control of the Interdependency. Good."

"Good?"

"That last part, yes. It means your ambition and greed are in service for something more than just yourself. It means that you might be something other than just a grasping sociopath. That you might actually *care* about the Interdependency, and the people in it, and what happens to them. If you do, or if at the very least you can learn to, then I'm here to help you. If you don't, you might as well have those marines on the other side of the door shoot me now. At this point, it's all the same to me. But if you *are* going to use me, and you should, I have some terms and requests. Some things I need from you, so I can trust that there is more to you than the shallow, self-centered hustler you've been up to this point. I need to believe you might actually be able to save the world."

For the life of him, Ghreni had nothing to say to any of this. It was literally like his tongue and brain—his two advantages— had simply shriveled up and blown away.

Claremont peered at Ghreni closely. "You didn't think this was how it was going to go, did you? Being duke? Getting everything you planned for?"

Ghreni opened his mouth to respond and croaked. He swallowed, embarrassed, and tried again. "No," he said.

"Well, surprise, then, Lord Ghreni," Claremont said. "And now, tell me: What's it going to be? Are you going to use me, or not?"

PART THREE

13

Less than ten minutes after *Yes, Sir, That's My Baby* emerged out of the Flow in the Hub system and began its thirty-seven-hour real-space trip to Hub's imperial station, a bomb went off in the entertainment district of the city of Chadwick, on Hub. The bomb had been placed in a restaurant and went off just after the lunch rush, killing ten people in the restaurant, two people on the street outside. The restaurant itself was gutted.

The response was quick. Automated fire suppression units sprang from their hidey-holes to minimize that threat; the public air systems in that area switched over to particulate filtering mode to keep the air breathable for the immediate environment. The massive doors to that section of Chadwick, so rarely activated, ground closed in order to seal off the spread of any possible conflagration, the damage of which would be horrifying in that enclosed, underground environment. Transport tubes in and out of Chadwick were shut down and physically sealed off. Until local and imperial authorities reopened the tubes, the only way in or out of Chadwick would be overland, in hard vacuum. But even the access tunnels to the surface were closed off and policed.

Not that it mattered. "They've looked at the security cameras for the week prior to the bombing, both from the restaurant and on the streets around it," said Gjiven Lobland, the imperial investigator at the scene, in video piped into the executive committee's meeting room at the imperial palace, three hours after the bombing. "There's nothing. No drops, nothing left behind by a customer, no suspicious activity. We've identified all the patrons and staff who ate or worked there and we're working through them, starting with the ones with criminal records. So far, all of them have come up clean."

"So how did the bomb get in there?" asked Upeksha Ranatunga, representing parliament.

"We're looking into it. What video we have shows the explosion originating in the back of the restaurant, in the storage areas. We have the forensics people in there now."

"If it went off in the storage areas then it might be something that was delivered," Archbishop Korbijn said. "In which case it could have been something that had been sitting there for days, or weeks."

"Yes, Your Grace," Lobland agreed. "We've got investigators looking through delivery records. We'll find it."

"Has anyone claimed responsibility?" Cardenia asked.

"No, Your Majesty. Not yet. We're monitoring communications planetwide. When we know, you will know."

Cardenia nodded and motioned for the feed to be cut.

"I think we know who this is," a voice said, down the table.

Cardenia looked up and saw Nadashe Nohamapetan, the most recently installed member of the executive committee. She had replaced Samman Temamenan, who unfortunately had to go and die on Cardenia, opening up the slot. Cardenia regretted Temamenan's death, on several levels.

"You're going to say the End separatists," Cardenia said.

"It's the fourth bombing in the last two months on Hub,"

Nadashe said. "All with basically the same modus operandi. We have reports of similar activity in three other systems as well, all of which began after news of your coronation and the bombing of it reached those systems."

"They could be copycats," Ranatunga said. "And we apprehended the coronation bombers."

"We *killed* the coronation bombers," Korbijn amended.

"Alleged coronation bombers," Cardenia added. The two alleged bombers had indeed originated out of End but otherwise very little was known about them, except that they blew themselves up with a small bomb just before imperial forces slammed down their door, and that the apartment they were found in on Hub had physical evidence linking them to the coronation bombing.

"We killed two individuals," Nadashe said. "We don't know if we got rid of their whole cell or network."

"What do you suggest we do, Lady Nadashe?" Korbijn asked. "Other than what we're already doing, which is substantial?"

"Archbishop, I agree that our local and imperial investigators are doing everything they can. The problem isn't here. It's on End. It's time for the Interdependency to step in and take control of the planet and snip out the rebellion there."

"As you've said before, and as you've had your members of parliament suggest," Ranatunga said.

"It's not only the MPs from Terhathum who believe this, Minister Ranatunga."

"When I said 'your members of parliament' I wasn't referring to just the ones from your home system, Lady Nadashe. I was also referring to the ones from other systems that you've purchased for this crusade of yours."

Nadashe appeared to bristle. "I resent the implication that the House of Nohamapetan is acting improperly, or indeed any differently than any other house or guild when it has an interest."

"And what *is* your interest, Lady Nadashe?" Cardenia asked.

"*Our* interest is avoiding the possible disruption of trade, and in the lives of the citizens of the Interdependency. It's also in our interest to make sure that those who attack the emperox are seen to be punished. An emperox who is seen as weak or vulnerable invites chaos."

"You would have us subjugate a constituent system of the Interdependency for the optics," Cardenia said.

"Not only for the optics," Nadashe said. "And not primarily for the optics. But for the optics, *too*? Certainly."

Cardenia turned to Ranatunga. "What is the current temperature of the parliament on this?"

Ranatunga looked over at Nadashe before answering. "The parliament was outraged at the initial attack on your coronation, ma'am. I think it found the deaths of the alleged attackers anticlimactic. With this new raft of attacks, there's considerable support for a more robust response."

"What do the MPs from End say?"

"When I've spoken to them they tell me they've received no intelligence or instruction from their duke. They're dubious that the current rebellion has the reach or means to attack the rest of the Interdependency—"

"Of course they would say that," Nadashe interjected.

"—or the interest," Ranatunga continued. "There have been innumerable rebellions on End before. It's the nature of the place because it's where the Interdependency sends its troublesome people. But it's always kept those rebellions self-contained. So they're skeptical."

"Which is cold comfort to the families of the victims," Nadashe said.

"Despite their skepticism, if a resolution for an imperial take-over of End were sent to the floor, it could expect support. Especially now that the attacks appear to be escalating."

"The guilds would also support it," Nadashe said.

"It would disrupt trade," Cardenia noted.

"It would *temporarily* disrupt trade to End. Which is preferable to attacks indefinitely disrupting trade across the Interdependency. And besides, End is End. It's not a significant income generator for most houses and guilds. It's one percent of my house's gross revenues. I think it's similar for most other houses."

Cardenia turned to Korbijn. "And what of the church?"

"The church would have concerns on humanitarian grounds," Korbijn said, "as we always do in times of conflict. But, remember, ma'am, the coronation bombing wasn't only an attack on you. It was an attack on the church and on our cathedral. And in a larger sense, the church has concern for the safety of every soul in the Interdependency. If these bombings are indeed related to the rebellion on End, then for their sake we need to consider action."

Cardenia looked at the archbishop for a moment, thoughtful. "Thank you."

"What are your thoughts, Your Majesty?" Nadashe asked.

"Our thoughts are that until we know definitively who is behind these bombings and what their goals are, we should not act upon End." Cardenia held up her hand at Nadashe, who was clearly about to respond. "We do not disagree with the assessment that these appear to be the acts of terrorists from End. But to commit to a course of action of this magnitude without proof is folly. We will let the investigations continue."

"Parliament might get ahead of you on this, ma'am," Rana-tunga said. "Especially if the attacks continue."

"There will be pressure from the guilds as well," Nadashe said.

"We understand their urgency," Cardenia said. "The troopship *Prophecies of Rachela* is stationed here at Hub. We can dispatch ten thousand marines to End immediately if necessary. But we would hope the committee would remind parliament and the guilds that *we* were the target of the first of these attacks. *We* were the first to lose people. We were the first to suffer. We suffer still. For all that, we counsel patience. The people of End will suffer, one way or another, if we take their independence. Let us be sure."

"Yes, ma'am," Ranatunga said. Nadashe said nothing. Cardenia nodded to them all, dismissing them.

"Lady Nadashe, we should like a word with you privately," Cardenia said, as the other members of the executive committee dispersed.

"Ma'am," Nadashe said, and stayed.

"I've received a letter of protest about your appointment to the executive committee," Cardenia said, when they were alone, dropping the royal "we." It was a signal to Nadashe that the discussion would be informal and off the record.

"Let me guess," Nadashe said. "From the House of Lagos."

"The House of Lagos is a signatory but not the only one."

"What's the problem?"

"They're concerned that the House of Nohamapetan has too much access to me, between your presence on the committee, your previous association with Rennered, and the fact that your brother Amit is actively trying to get me to marry him."

Nadashe smiled, thinly. "With respect, ma'am, 'active' is not the word I would use to describe it. Or perhaps more accurately, Amit is active. You are less so."

"I made it clear to Amit that I would be in mourning for Naffa Dolg for a year."

"Yes, you did. That is a substantial amount of time for mourning, ma'am."

"She was like a sister, Lady Nohamapetan. And the mourning period includes the other victims of the coronation bombing. To attempt to shorten that period now would be disrespectful to all their memories." The third reason, which was to buy her time before considering Amit Nohamapetan as a husband, was left unsaid, but both Cardenia and Nadashe were aware of it as subtext. "Nevertheless the perception stands among many houses that yours has perhaps too much influence."

"I'd remind them that I was appointed by vote by the guilds. As the houses control their respective guilds, I am the choice of the majority of the houses."

"This is true. The letter reminds me, however, that while the custom is for the emperox to accept the selections of the church, guilds, and parliament for the executive committee, the emperox may reject or dismiss a member if they are not to their suiting. The letter also helpfully offers up several examples of when this has happened before."

"Do you plan to dismiss me, ma'am?" Nadashe asked, and Cardenia caught the undercurrent of tension in her voice.

"I would not disrespect the guilds in that manner without cause," Cardenia said. "But now that it has been pointed out to me, I acknowledge that the House of Nohamapetan is persistently and obviously a feature of my life, and the *appearance* of undue influence is an issue. It might be wise for your house to decide which it would prefer: a seat on the executive committee, or a chance at imperial consort."

"May I speak freely, ma'am?" Nadashe said, after a moment.

"Please."

"You're not really offering me much of a choice, are you? If I stay on the executive committee, you have an excuse to dismiss my brother's suit, and you will still have the option of dismissing me from the committee if I become troublesome. If I abandon the committee, then you still have the option of dismissing my brother's suit, which, to continue to speak freely, I don't believe you've seriously considered, or plan to consider. If you want to dismiss me, or my brother, then do so. It's your right and privilege as emperox. But don't use this nonsense as an excuse."

Cardenia smiled at this and had a very slight twinge of regret that her preferences for sexual and romantic partners swung so heavily toward the opposite sex. Unlike her brother, Nadashe was not boring.

And she would eat you alive, some part of her brain said. And, well, that was probably true. Nadashe would have no interest in being a quiet consort; she would want to rule. Which, if Cardenia was going to be entirely honest with herself, was not necessarily a bad thing. Cardenia never wanted to be emperox. All she wanted was to be the patron of a nice little arts charity or something. The idea of having an ambitious spouse who would be happy to handle the drudge work of running an empire had its appeal.

As long as that spouse was following your agenda, her brain pointed out. Which would be a primary problem with Nadashe Nohamapetan. Whatever her plans were, they were made well in advance of Cardenia arriving on the throne. That would be a disqualifier on Nadashe's part. Plus, Cardenia not really being interested in having sex with her was an issue. In mourning or not, it had been a damn long time since Cardenia had gotten laid.

But you don't want to have sex with Amit, either, her brain reminded her. Which was also true enough. He had the right gender but the wrong personality and was so transparently a puppet for his sister's machinations that the only thing Cardenia could ever think while in his presence was *When can I leave.* It was also clear to Cardenia that Amit found her attractive, or attractive enough, anyway, which meant he would definitely want to have sex with her.

If you don't want to have sex with either of them, then you might as well marry the one who won't want to have sex with you either, her brain reasoned. This was an excellent point, except she didn't know Nadashe's sexuality, aside from "ambitious." Nadashe *would* marry Cardenia, if that was on offer. Would she want everything else that was supposed to come with it? Possibly. But that's not what Cardenia wanted.

Not that you couldn't get sex if you wanted, anyway. Which was also a thing. Political marriages were what they were, and the House of Murn, which controlled the sex work guild, had a thriving presence on Xi'an. She could very easily get as much service as she could stand. Certainly she wouldn't be the first emperox to do so. She knew that from the Memory Room, where she foolishly asked the simulation of her father about his imperial marriage, and Attavio VI revealed the extent of his own extracurricular activity.

This squicked out Cardenia, not for the fact of the sex, but because she, like most people, preferred not to picture a parent going at it. Cardenia wasn't opposed to sex work or getting sex that way, if one were feeling a need and it was the easiest way to deal with it. But she didn't want that as the *default* for her. Or to have lovers on the side doing the job of a spouse. If she was going to be married, she wanted a spouse who would be the focus for all of that. Call her old-fashioned.

And beyond all this nonsense about sex, the issue of children: conventionally solvable with Amit Nohamapetan, technically solvable with Nadashe, but leaving unanswered the question of whether she wanted children with either. She didn't care for the Nohamapetans much. She had no doubt she would love any child she had, but she was worried that she wouldn't *like* them, if the Nohamapetan personality set was the dominant one.

And none of any of *that* changed the fact that when it came right down to it, Cardenia didn't want to marry either Amit or Nadashe Nohamapetan, not only because she didn't find either attractive but because she resented being forced into a political marriage at all. She resented the Nohamapetans for pressing a claim that she had not been party to. She resented the executive committee for tacitly and explicitly promoting their suit. She resented the political realities with the guilds that made a marriage to a Nohamapetan a prudent move, in terms of the emperox retaining and exercising power. She resented her brother for dying, and she resented her father for suggesting that she didn't have to marry a Nohamapetan, after all, when every other person, faction, and reality itself, strongly suggested otherwise.

My life sucks, Cardenia thought to herself. *I am emperox of all humanity, and my life sucks.* She laughed a little bit at that.

"Ma'am?" Nadashe said, bringing her out of her reverie.

"Sorry," Cardenia said. "I was thinking about our predicament."

"May I offer a suggestion?" Nadashe asked.

"You may."

"For my house and for my brother I would be willing to give up my seat on the council, but *only* if it were because you agreed to marriage. So let me suggest this. While you are in mourning, spend significant time with Amit. Not merely formal settings but situations where the two of you could be yourselves with each other, if you were together. Where you might learn to see him as a partner. A consort. A spouse. On the anniversary of your coronation, tell him whether you accept him. If you do, I'll resign from the executive committee. But if not, I'll stay on, and at least Amit and my house have an answer. But I would need your promise that you wouldn't then attempt to dismiss me from the committee. Is that acceptable?"

Cardenia thought about it. "I think so," she said.

"Good," Nadashe said. "In that case, I have an invitation for you, from Amit. Your construction yards have just completed the House of Nohamapetan's latest tenner, the *If You Want to Sing Out, Sing Out*. He invites you to a private tour of the ship, with him."

"When?"

"In two days."

"And your brother issued this invitation when?"

"Yesterday. He would have sent it directly but I'm on the committee and he knew I'd see you."

"And you anticipated us having this conversation, Nadashe?"

Nadashe smiled. "No, ma'am. I wouldn't have imagined that the House of Lagos would convince other houses to try to have me removed, although I'm not surprised now that I know. Or could know that you and I would make a deal because of it. No, the thing is, ma'am, Amit actually seems to *like* you. So he asked me to intercede on his behalf."

"You're a good sister."

"I'm an adequate sister," Nadashe said. "I mean, I was going to see you *anyway*. It wasn't any extra effort."

They both had a laugh at that.

Shortly thereafter Cardenia was back in her private wing, with Gell Deng. "I'd like you to keep me updated on the latest about the bombing today," she said. "Not just from the news feeds."

"Of course, ma'am," Deng said.

"Also, I've agreed to tour a new ship with Amit Nohamapetan two days from now. Please contact his people and make the arrangements. Allow for two hours, plus travel. Late afternoon."

Deng raised his eyebrows slightly at this but otherwise said nothing on it directly. Instead he said, "The Imperial Guard will want blueprints and a proposed tour path."

"I don't think there is a proposed tour path. It's meant to be informal."

"The Imperial Guard will be very unhappy about that."

"Then have them inform Nohamapetan's people that there needs to be a tour path, but don't tell *me*. I want to be surprised."

"Yes, ma'am. Also, you asked to be told if there was ever news from the Count of Claremont on End."

"Yes?" In the first week of her reign, Cardenia had sent a letter to the count informing him of Attavio VI's passing and requesting the latest on his research. It would still be far too early for the count to respond directly to that letter.

"It's not the Count of Claremont himself, but his son, Lord Marce Claremont. He just now arrived on a Lagos fiver and will be at Imperial Station in roughly thirty hours. He requests an audience with you."

"His son?"

"Yes, ma'am."

"We're sure about that relationship?"

"The note came with the same security cipher the Count of Claremont used on all his correspondence. It's legitimate."

"Did something happen to the count?"

"The request doesn't say. Would you like to schedule him, or should I shunt him off?" The Office of the Emperox had more than three dozen protocol officers to meet with low-level officials, apparatchiks, and flunkeys. If any of them were important enough to escalate, Deng would get a report and decide whether to bring it to the emperox's attention.

"Schedule him."

"I can give him fifteen minutes prior to your walkabout with Amit Nohamapetan, whatever time that is. That should be enough time for Lord Claremont to disembark and catch a shuttle to Xi'an."

"Have someone meet him. It's probably his first time off End. I don't want him to get lost."

"Yes, ma'am."

"Do I have anything else for the rest of the day?"

"Only a few minor things. Nothing that won't keep."

Cardenia nodded. "Then I'm going to speak to my ancestors for a while. About political marriages."

"They would know all about those, ma'am."

"Yes they would." Cardenia nodded and headed off to the Memory Room.

"We have two very real problems," Kiva said to Countess Huma Lagos, her mother and the sitting matriarch of the House of Lagos. "One is bigger than the other."

"Let's start with the smaller one," Huma suggested.

"The fucking Nohamapetans," Kiva said.

Huma laughed.

The two were in the Hub offices for the House of Lagos in the Guild House, the single largest commercial building on Hub. The Guild House was seven hundred years old and populated by some of the oldest and most influential houses in the Interdependency, with smaller buildings holding lesser houses clustered around it like supplicants. The proximity of a house's headquarters on Hub to the Guild House was a rough map of the political influence it wielded. Lagos was in the Guild House, on three low-level floors. The House of Nohamapetan was a few stories up but held only one floor and a half interest on another. The House of Wu, the imperial house, held the twelve stories at the top, including the roof, high up enough that one could practically reach up and touch the top of the Hubfall habitat dome the Guild House resided in.

Countess Lagos wasn't typically at Guild House. She ran the

house from the Lagos home system of Ikoyi, and let a cousin serve as the director at Hub and at Xi'an. But the countess had arrived at Hub a week earlier to sit in on the final negotiations for a cross-licensing agreement with the House of Jemisin. Count Jemisin was scheduled to arrive in two days; in the meantime Kiva preferred presenting her issues to her mother rather than Lord Pretar, the Lagos senior director at Hub, whom Kiva had always considered an officious cockwomble.

"What are our problems with the Nohamapetans?" Huma asked. "Aside from the usual ones?"

"One, I'm certain the Nohamapetans sabotaged our product on End by introducing a virus and causing the duke there to embargo us and escrow our money. Two, I'm also certain it was Ghreni Nohamapetan, their director on End, who *convinced* the duke to escrow our money and then use it to fund his current civil war against rebels. Third, pretty sure the Nohamapetans, and specifically Ghreni Nohamapetan, are actually behind the rebellion on End, but I can't prove that. Fourth and most importantly, motherfucking Ghreni Nohamapetan tried to put a bomb on our ship and then sent fucking *pirates* after us."

Huma Lagos silently considered what her daughter was saying to her. Then, "Just out of curiosity, if this is the smaller problem, what is the bigger problem?"

"The complete collapse of the Flow, the end of the Interdependency, and the possible extinction of the human race."

Huma blinked at this. "When?"

"Over the next several years."

"Where did you get this information?"

"From one of the passengers on the *Yes, Sir,* who happens to be a Flow physicist."

"He told you this why?"

"I fucked it out of him."

"And you believe him?"

"Yeah, I do. I don't *understand* it all. But I don't doubt at least some of it is true. We're all magnificently screwed, Mom."

"Where is this passenger now?"

"He's on his way to talk to the emperox about it."

"Huh," Huma said, and then was quiet again, thinking. "Well, is there anything we're going to be able to do about any of the 'end of the Interdependency' shit *before* I sign our deal with the House of Jemisin two days from now?"

"Not really, no."

Huma nodded. "Then let's just focus on the Nohamapetans for the moment. Now. Tell me everything."

Kiva went on at length about the *Yes, Sir*'s entire sojourn at End, loudly and at length, with considerable editorial comment. At one point, the two of them were interrupted as Lord Pretar entered the room, which as it happened was his actual office. Countess Lagos dismissed him without even looking at him; he hastily retreated and sat in his own waiting area. After an hour of waiting he eventually got up to get himself coffee.

"You'd be willing to get up in front of the Guild Court of Grievances and testify that Ghreni Nohamapetan ordered a bomb planted on the *Yes, Sir* and was behind the pirate attack," Huma asked, after Kiva was finished.

"Of course."

"And you think the House of Nohamapetan was behind this. *Not* Ghreni Nohamapetan freelancing for his own personal goals, but acting under orders of his house."

"I know Ghreni Nohamapetan, Mom. We went a few rounds when I was at university and he'd visit Nadashe. He's not the most ambitious one in that family. I don't know what the official House of Nohamapetan position is on the crap he's pulling on End, but I know he's not the brains of this operation."

"You're talking about Nadashe, then."

Kiva nodded. "She's the one I actually went to university with."

"Are you friends with her?"

"'Friends' is stretching it. She tolerated me when I was banging her brother and otherwise we sort of mutually agreed that staying out of each other's hair would be the best thing for everyone. But I respect her. She's smart as fuck and if she pushed you down a hole, she'd make it look like you jumped. If there's anything doing, she's the one doing it."

Another pause from Huma and then, "You know that for the past several months, End rebels have been bombing the shit out of things, here and in other systems, yes?"

"No. How would I know that? I've been away for more than two years, Mom."

"They started—or are presumed to have started—by bombing the new emperox's coronation ceremony. Blew up Grayland's best friend and almost got her too. And since then, every time there's a new attack, it's Nadashe who's agitating for a military response to the guilds and parliament. And it's working. They've got a troop carrier ready to head down the Flow stream to End. They're just waiting for an excuse to send it."

"That fits," Kiva said. "If she wants it to be sent then she has a plan for it when it gets there."

"If they go they'd be meant to support the duke, and you said you think Ghreni Nohamapetan is secretly supporting the rebels."

"Yeah. So? Either he's got a plan to make the extra military work for him or there's something going on we're missing. Or both. Probably both."

Huma nodded, stood up, and then clapped her hands together. "Well, let's go find out, shall we?" She exited the office and headed toward the common elevator bank. Kiva got up and followed her.

Two minutes later the two of them were in the lobby of the House of Nohamapetan. "I need to see Amit Nohamapetan," Huma said to the receptionist.

"Do you have an appointment?" the receptionist asked. Kiva smiled at this and immediately felt pity for the receptionist.

"I am the Countess Huma Lagos, my dear. I don't need an appointment."

"I'm sorry, but unless you have an appoint—"

"Child, I want to be very clear about something." She pointed to the glass door, no doubt with a magnetic lock on it, that separated the reception area from the rest of the floor. "I am about to try that door, and once I'm through it I'm going to Amit Nohamapetan's office, and I'm going to try the door there. If both doors don't open for me, I am going to do two things. One, I am going to file suit in the Guild Court of Grievances against the House of Nohamapetan for obstruction of investigation, which as you probably don't know is a very serious charge and will cost the House of Nohamapetan hundreds of thousands of marks to defend against. And then they'll lose, at which point millions of marks will flow from their accounts into mine, and you'll be fired for having caused an easily avoidable interhouse argument. Two, I'll sue *you* as well, and let the House of Nohamapetan know I'll be happy to drop my suit against them if they fire you. And then, between our two houses, we'll make sure that you never work in any capacity ever again, and that the rest of your life is spent never earning more than the Interdependency minimum benefit, or if you do, that everything you earn above the IMB is garnished and sent to me. And I will spend it on champagne, toasting your misery. Are we *entirely* clear on this?"

The receptionist gaped and then buzzed the door.

"Thank you," Huma said, and swept through. Kiva once again followed.

Amit's office was on a far corner of the floor and large, with impeccable furniture and wide windows that looked out on the Hubfall business district. He and two other people sat in gorgeously comfortable chairs at a table, and all of them seemed surprised when Huma and Kiva appeared in their midst.

Huma pointed at the two who were not Amit. "You and you. Fuck off right now," she said.

They turned to Amit, who nodded. They fucked off. Huma and Kiva sat in their vacated seats.

Amit looked at them, and then reached over to the table and picked up a tablet, which was flashing a message alert on it. He read it. "Apparently you threatened my receptionist, Countess Lagos," he said. "Also, that's not how an obstruction of investigation charge works and you know it." He tossed the tablet back on the table and considered his two guests. "Now, to what do I owe the genuinely unexpected pleasure of your presence?"

"One, your family sabotaged our product on End," Huma said.

"I don't know anything about that," Amit said.

"Well, I do, and our lawyers will be speaking to yours about that. Two, your family has interfered in my daughter's ability to conduct business on End by influencing the duke there to illegally escrow and use our revenues."

Amit glanced at Kiva. "Ah, Lady Kiva. I thought I recognized you. I believe you were friendly with both my sister and brother at one time."

" 'Friendly' isn't the word I'd use," Kiva said.

"Perhaps not," Amit said, agreeably, and then turned his attention back to Huma. "Interference of trade is a serious charge, ma'am, so I assume our lawyers will be discussing that as well. I do not need to remind you that the Court of Grievances is very sensitive to being used as a way for one house to intimidate another. So if you bring a suit and lose, the House of Nohamapetan will get lawyers' fees and treble that in damages. And our lawyers are very good and thus very expensive."

"We won't lose. We're also bringing charges against your brother Ghreni for attempted murder, attempted kidnapping, conspiracy to both, sabotage of a guild vessel, piracy, and extortion."

"What?" Amit said, less genially.

"The little fucker planted a bomb on my ship and sent pirates after one of my passengers," Kiva said.

"And yes, Amit, we have all the evidence we need to make those charges stick," Huma said. "We have Kiva, and the victim of the attempted kidnapping and murder, and the crew of the *Yes, Sir* all willing to testify."

"Plus the security recordings of the attempted murder, and the confession of the hit man, and the recordings of the communications between the *Yes, Sir* and the pirate vessel," Kiva added, helpfully.

Huma nodded. "There is that slight complication that Ghreni is at least a year and a half away, which makes it difficult for him to be recalled to stand trial. But with the evidence we have, I think we can convince both the guild and parliament to issue a bill of attainder."

"And since the little shit was the authorized representative of the House of Nohamapetan on End, we'll make sure the bill attaches to your house," Kiva said. She was freestyling off of what her mother was saying, but she was pretty sure she knew what her mother was up to and that this was where she was going with it. So why the fuck not.

"I can guarantee you that the House of Nohamapetan is not engaged in any plan to destroy one of your ships," Amit said.

"Don't even try that, Lord Amit," Huma said. "We all know your brother doesn't have that much initiative. Neither do you, for that matter. If Ghreni is doing anything, he's doing it under direction. If not from the House of Nohamapetan, then from someone *in* the House of Nohamapetan, which from our point of view is the same thing. We have no problem asking the guild and Interdependency courts to widen the scope of the conspiracy charge and investigate you, your sister, and indeed the entire fucking House of Nohamapetan."

"That might be more difficult than you expect," Amit said.

Huma snorted. "Just because you're trying to land the emperox for your spouse doesn't mean you or your house is immune to justice, Lord Amit. How is that going, by the way? Rumor is she's notably resistant to your charms. She might even be *relieved* to find out you and your whole fucking family are being investigated."

"The attempted murder victim is the son of a very good friend of her father, the former emperox," Kiva noted, helpfully.

"Oh, well, all the more reason for her not to want to be seen anywhere near your felonious ass," Huma said, to Amit.

"As a matter of fact I'm seeing her later today," Amit said, only a little peevishly. "She's touring our new tenner with me."

"That's *adorable*," Huma remarked, and clapped her hands together. "Maybe I'll have one of our people at Xi'an run over a précis of our complaint to her. You know, give you two lovebirds something to talk about while you tour your pretty new toy."

Kiva was now looking at her mother in open admiration. Huma Lagos had always been someone with whom one would not wish to fuck, and Kiva had years of watching her mother argue and negotiate to draw from for her own skills with both. But it was always a joy to watch her mother deftly and profanely shove assholes like Amit Nohamapetan up against a wall, then reach down and squeeze (or reach in and twist, as the case might be). It was nice when you could look up to your parent, even as an adult, and think, *This is who I fucking want to be when I grow up.*

Amit sighed, brought his hand to his face, and rubbed it. "All right, Countess Lagos. What do you want?"

"Why, Lord Amit, whatever do you mean?"

"I mean that if you really wanted to bring a suit to the Court of Grievances or to the Interdependency courts, you would have just done it and surprised us with it. The fact you're here in my office means you want this resolved another way. Fine. Tell me what you want."

"I want to give the House of Nohamapetan a haircut."

"I don't even know what that means," Amit said.

"It means that I have three things I want from you, and all of them are going to hurt."

"What are they?"

"First, you fucked with our business. We can fight about it in the court, but you're not going to like how it turns out." Huma turned to Kiva. "How much revenue were we expecting from your trip?"

"A hundred million marks," Kiva said.

"So you want a hundred million marks from us," Amit said.

"I want two hundred million marks."

"That's ridiculous."

"You fucked with our product, which was bad enough. But you also fucked with our reputation. This is the cost of fucking with our reputation. So two hundred million marks, in our accounts, in three days."

Amit looked like he was going to say something else but then thought better of it. "Number two," he prompted.

"You might be aware we signed a letter protesting your sister's seat on the executive committee," Huma said.

"She mentioned something about that."

"Then it won't be a surprise that we want her to resign her seat."

"To be replaced by a Lagos, no doubt."

Huma shook her head. "No. But literally anyone else would be better than your sister."

"I'll tell her you said that."

"Please do. Three, you tell Emperox Grayland you've had a change of heart about the marriage."

"Come on," Amit protested. "You're already claiming my sister's head. Let me keep mine."

"This isn't a negotiation," Huma and Kiva said, simultaneously, and then looked at each other and grinned. Huma turned her attention back to Amit. "Let's not pretend that once you're the consort you won't still be your sister's hand puppet."

"That's right," Amit said, sarcastically. "I have no will of my own."

"No, you don't," Huma agreed, not sarcastic at all. "You can work that out with a therapist if you want. But in the meantime, you give up marrying into the imperial family."

"What if Grayland wants to marry me?"

Huma laughed. "You poor dear. Just, no."

Amit seemed to deflate a little at that. "And what do *we* get out of these demands?"

"Nothing," Huma said. "As in, we say nothing about what you did at End. And we say nothing for what you have *planned* at End."

"Really," Amit said, and Kiva felt a rush of blood to her head.

If she had any remaining doubts that the Nohamapetans were up to no good on End, they ended right there. She felt a hand on her hand and recognized her mother was warning her off the outburst she was about to have. She held it in.

"Really," Huma said.

"And what assurance do we have of that?"

"You want a fucking written contract on that, Amit? Are you that stupid? Understand something here. You hold no cards. Thanks to your appallingly careless brother we have more than enough to bury you, your sister, and your entire fucking house. At the very least you'll spend the next decade fighting off lawsuits and investigations. At worst, you'll be in prison and your house will see its monopoly auctioned off. No matter what, it'll be bad for your business, Amit. And your sister will lose her seat on the committee, and you won't marry the emperox anyway. This way *all* you lose is money, and take a gut punch to your ego. And you'll survive both, I'm sure."

Amit considered this. "I'll give you an answer tomorrow."

"Or, you could give me an answer now," Huma said.

"Countess Lagos, please," Amit said. "As you've so humiliatingly pointed out to me more than once in this conversation, it's not entirely my call to make. And I do have a meeting with the emperox on my schedule today. I can't exactly put it off."

"Then how about this. In exactly twenty-four hours and one minute from now, unless I hear from you, a sworn affidavit goes to the secretary of the executive committee and to the emperox herself. And I'll let you and your sister sort it out from there. Fair enough?"

"'Fair' is not the word I would use, Countess."

"You might have thought of that before you began all this nonsense, Lord Amit," Huma Lagos said, rising. Kiva rose with her. "And before you decided to drag our house into it." She nodded and left without otherwise saying good-bye. Kiva followed. Her last image of Amit Nohamapetan was of him reaching for his tablet and jabbing in a call code.

"I fucking love you," Kiva said to her mother as they passed by the receptionist on their way out. The receptionist resolutely did not look their way as they walked by.

"Mm-hmm." Huma said nothing more while they waited for the elevator.

"Do you think Nadashe will agree?" Kiva said, when they were in the elevator, alone.

"It doesn't matter," Huma said.

"Two hundred million marks seems like it would matter."

"The point of the discussion wasn't to blackmail the Nohamapetans. That was just a fringe benefit. The point of it was to find out what they're up to, and to unsettle their plans. Now we know what they're up to. They're planning to take over End."

"Right," Kiva said. "But why?"

The elevator opened. "Because they know something they think everyone else doesn't," Huma said, stepping out.

Kiva processed this while they walked. "You think they know," she said, to her mother. "About what's going on with the Flow."

"They know, or they think they know something else equally big," Huma said. "They're risking a lot to position themselves at the ass-end of space, and I think they're willing to give up a lot to keep it quiet."

"So you *do* think they'll give us the money."

Huma nodded. They reached the door of Lord Pretar's office. As they went inside, Pretar stood up and started to welcome them.

"Get out," Huma said. Pretar swallowed his welcome and

marched himself out. Kiva closed the door. "The money is another confirmation," she continued, to her daughter.

"What if they don't give us the money?"

"Then I think you and I had better not step out anywhere there's a direct line of sight between us and a tall roof. But no matter what, we've just thrown a spanner into their plans and schedule. It's going to be interesting to see what they do in the next few days." Huma settled herself at Pretar's desk. "This friend of yours. The Flow physicist."

"Marce Claremont," Kiva said.

"You still have tolerable relations with him?"

"You could say that." Kiva thought back to a recent fuck session and smiled at it.

"I want to meet him. I know *you* believe him, but *I* need to believe him too. If I believe him I need to know how much time we have before everything really turns to shit. Then we need to find out exactly how the Nohamapetans benefit from it—and how it fucks the rest of us. I want to know before everyone else does."

Kiva shook her head. "He's meeting with the emperox today," she said. "I don't think she's going to keep it to herself."

"It's not whether she tells everyone," Huma said. "It's whether they believe her."

"It's the truth."

"Oh, my daughter," Huma said, and smiled. "Don't tell me you don't know how little that actually means."

Marce Claremont didn't realize how much of a country bump-kin he was until he arrived at Hub.

It was one thing to know intellectually that Hub, which in-cluded the namesake planet of Hub, its immense imperial sta-tion, the equally immense autonomous habitat of Xi'an, and dozens of other associated habitats, was the most populated and advanced human nation in the Interdependency. It was an-other thing for Marce to disembark from the *Yes, Sir* at Hub's imperial station, several times the size of End's station, and to take in the bustle and rush of so many humans arriving and departing and doing their business—and knowing that the planet below held even more people in even more crowded hab-itats, pressed together in underground domes or technologi-cally advanced kilometers-long spinning cylinders, living their lives oblivious to, or simply unconcerned about, how close they were to the hard vacuum or cold rock or searing radiation that could kill them in minutes.

These people are nuts, Marce thought, and grinned to himself. It was breathtaking the situations that humans put themselves into, and still managed to thrive. In the Interdependency, with its religious and social ethos of interconnectedness combined with a guild-centered, monopolistic economy, they'd created possibly the most ridiculously complex method of ensuring the survival of the species they could have devised. Bolting on a formal caste system of nobles intertwined with a merchant class, and common workers underneath, complicated proceedings even further.

And yet it worked. It worked because on a social level, apparently enough people wanted it to, and because at the heart of it, billions of humans living in fragile habitats prone to mechanical and environmental breakdowns and degradation, and with limited natural resources, were better off relying on each other than trying to go it alone. Even without the Interdependency, being interdependent was the best way for humanity to survive.

Except now we will all have to find a new way to survive, Marce said to himself. He looked up and around at Hub's imperial station, with all the humans moving in it, and remembered that in less than a decade, all of them might be dead, or on their way to it. Including him.

"Lord Marce?" Marce looked up to see a young man in dark green imperial livery, looking at him, with a sign reading "Lord Marce Claremont" in his hand.

"Yes, that's me," Marce said.

"I'm to take you to Xi'an." The young man looked around. "Do you have any luggage? I understand you are disembarking from a Lagos fiver. Do you have lodgings?"

"My luggage is being sent to the Moreland Hotel, here on the station."

"Excellent choice, sir."

"Thank you." The Moreland had been recommended to him by Kiva, "assuming you can afford it." Marce, currently in possession of eighty million marks in his data crypt, allowed that he might be able to scrape by.

The young man motioned. "This way, sir."

Marce followed the young man, whose name was Verson Sohne, to an area of the imperial station used as a terminal for travel to Xi'an. Marce had his documents checked, rechecked, and his body scanned, also twice, and was asked his business in Xi'an, again twice, by two separate inquisitors. Each time Marce noted he had an appointment with the emperox and presented his tablet with the official appointment notice and security hash displayed. They did not ask him what specifically his meeting was about, for which Marce was thankful. He assumed "about the end of the Interdependency and the possible extinction of the human race" might raise some flags.

Verson apologized for the security measures. "They've been more stringent since those horrible End rebels bombed the coronation," he said, and then suddenly shut up, aware that his charge, in fact, was from End. "I didn't mean to imply anything about you, my lord," he said, after a moment.

Marce smiled at this. He'd only in the past few hours caught up on the death of Attavio VI, the succession to his daughter Cardenia, now Grayland II, and the attempted assassination on the day of her coronation. He personally doubted anyone from End was at all involved. "It's all right," he said, to Verson, who looked visibly relieved.

The shuttle trip from Imperial Station to Xi'an was uneventful but Marce watched via his tablet anyway, looking at the surface of Hub as the shuttle zipped up the termination line from Imperial Station at the equator to where Xi'an hovered, ten degrees north. Marce watched Xi'an grow larger and larger in his tablet, making out the stream of specks that represented the traffic moving to and from the habitat. Farther up and down the terminator line of Hub were other, smaller habitats, which served as homes for the workers who built starships in nearby floating docks. Marce did not see any of those in his tablet.

The shuttle landed and Marce and Verson made their way to the train which traversed the whole of Xi'an, and Marce again found himself plastered to the view, looking at how the landscape went out, above and around him as the interior surface of the cylindrical station looped around to meet up with the train on the other side.

"Your first time at Xi'an, sir?" Verson asked.

"First time in a habitat like this," Marce replied. "I've lived my whole life on End. On the surface of a planet. It's nothing like this."

"What's it like, sir?"

"Flat." Marce kept looking at the ground rising up at him. "Even our foothills are flat compared to this. I don't know how anyone here looks up without wondering why they don't fall right down to the other side of the station."

"Well, it's because Xi'an rotates," Verson began.

Marce laughed at this. "I understand the physics of it. That's not what I mean. But there's a difference between knowing something intellectually and the animal portion of your brain telling you to grab hold of something." He looked at Verson, who had a polite smile on his face. "You grew up in a habitat like this?"

Verson nodded. "I'm from Ancona. It's an associated nation here in the Hub system."

"Right. So you're used to this." Marce looked back out the window. "I'm . . . not."

"Do you think you'll ever get used to it, sir?"

"I hope I will," Marce said. "And I kind of hope I don't, too."

They left the train at the palace station and Verson led Marce to a landing for people who had business at the imperial palace.

Because Marce had an actual appointment with the emperox, Verson led him to the front of the line, annoying everyone who was waiting. Marce mouthed his apologies as Verson directed him forward. Another presentation of documents, another scan, another brief questioning, and then they were through, and Marce was handed off to a young woman, Obelees Atek, who worked at the palace proper. She gave Marce a pass to affix to his blouse, and then started walking, inviting Marce to follow. Marce waved good-bye to Verson and walked after Obelees.

Ten minutes later Marce sat in the anteroom of Emperox Grayland II's office, having passed through a few public areas that displayed more opulence than Marce had ever seen in his life. Until this moment he'd thought the ducal palace on End was the standard for obnoxious opulence, but the imperial palace made it look like the loft of an arriviste, and made his own home, a mansion by any definition, look like a hovel. The imperial palace was stuffed with a millennium of gilded baubles, a testament to the self-interest of a family and the political system that supported it. The anteroom was likewise tastefully stuffed with treasure, including the statue of Prophet-Emperox Rachela I by the sculptor Meis Fujimoro. It was famous throughout the Interdependency and probably worth more than the incomes of some entire human habitats.

Marce looked around and wondered how an emperox, someone so intimately invested in the preservation of a system like the Interdependency, could ever be able to act on the news he had to give her.

You're a lord yourself, Marce's brain reminded him. *You're invested. And yet here you are.*

Yes, but I'm not the emperox. I benefit from the system. She *is* the system.

An emperox sent your father to End to study this.

That emperox is dead.

"Lord Marce." Marce looked up to see Obelees motioning to him. It was time to meet the emperox. Marce got up and walked into the office.

When you first meet the emperox, a bow is sufficient, Obelees had said to him as they had walked to her office. *Some like to kneel, and you may if you like. But you will have only a limited time with her and that will cut into your time. After your introduction it is expected that the emperox will initiate and lead the conversation. Speak when spoken to; answer any questions. When your appointment time is up or if the emperox dismisses you early, bow and exit the room. Always be respectful and reserved. Your emperox deserves no less.*

Marce entered the office of the emperox, took one look at the surroundings, and laughed out loud. Obelees Atek frowned at him.

"Is something funny, Lord Marce?" asked a young woman, standing in front of a desk. She was wearing imperial green. This was clearly the emperox, and equally clearly he'd just blown his entrance.

He bowed. "I'm sorry, Your Majesty," he said. "I was surprised by your office."

"How so?"

"I . . . well. Ma'am. It looks like a museum exploded inside of it."

Obelees Atek sucked in her breath and apparently was now waiting for the emperox to sentence him to a beheading.

Instead she laughed, openly, loudly. "*Thank you,*" she said, with emphasis. "This has been exactly my thought for the last nine months. Sometimes I'm scared to walk around in here. I'm worried I'm going to bump into something and break a priceless historical artifact. I'm terrified of my own workspace, Lord Marce. I'm working up the courage to redecorate."

"You're the emperox, ma'am. I'm pretty sure they'll let you."

"It's not whether I can. It's whether I should." The emperox nodded to Obelees, dismissing her. Obelees bowed, shot Marce one last visual warning to behave, and left. As she did Marce noted that he was alone in the room with the emperox; she had no assistants or ministers or secretaries with her.

"Tell me the thought you just had, Lord Marce," the emperox said, and motioned for him to sit in a chair in front of her desk.

"I was thinking that you have less staff than I expected, ma'am." Marce sat in the chair. She remained standing, leaning on her desk.

"I have even more staff than I imagine you expect," she said. "And usually I will have them sit in on my meetings. I have a lot of meetings, Lord Marce. You might not believe how many. I couldn't possibly keep them all straight without help. So they're with me," the emperox motioned to her desk, "and I sit behind this and I use the imperial 'we' and everyone is very respectful and polite, and no one ever laughs at this absolutely ridiculous office when they come in the room. But you did."

"Yes, ma'am. Sorry."

"I'm not. On the contrary I'm glad you did. But I'd like to know *why* you did, if you don't mind, Lord Marce."

"I suppose because I'm overstimulated, ma'am."

"You make yourself sound like an eight-year-old given too much sugar," the emperox said, smiling.

Marce smiled back. "It's not a bad metaphor," he admitted. "My entire life has been on End, ma'am. It's not exactly the backwater everyone makes it out to be, but it's not . . . *this*. Hub. And Xi'an. And this palace."

The emperox wrinkled her nose and Marce was suddenly aware that whatever he had been expecting from this meeting, this was not it. "It's awful, isn't it?"

"Uh," Marce said.

The emperox laughed again. "I'm sorry, Lord Marce. I didn't mean to make you feel like I was trying to trap you into a faux pas. But you have to understand. I wasn't meant to be emperox. I didn't grow up with all of . . . *this*, as you say. It's as alien to me as I imagine it is to you."

"I am nobility, ma'am. It's not alien. It's just a lot."

"Yes. Yes. Again, thank you. You've perfectly encapsulated what I've been feeling about my life for the last year."

"I aim to please, ma'am."

"You have," the emperox assured him. "So far, this may be my favorite confidential meeting I've had to date." She smiled again, and cocked her head. "And this is why I'm sad that now we have to ruin it by talking about the end of civilization."

Marce nodded. "So, you know."

"You didn't assume that I granted you this audience because I am in the habit of welcoming minor nobility, did you, Lord Marce? I mean, no offense."

"None taken," Marce said. "I just didn't know what you knew and how much I would have to explain to you."

"You may assume that I know as much as my father did about what your father was up to on End, why he was sent, and what the implications of his research are."

"All right."

"So now that we have that out of the way, my first question: Are the Flow streams going to collapse?"

"Yes."

The emperox let out a heavy breath. "When?"

"It's already begun. We estimate the Flow stream from End to Hub has already collapsed. The *Yes, Sir*, the ship I was on, was probably the last ship to make it through."

"How will we know if that's correct?"

"When other ships scheduled to arrive at Hub don't arrive, you'll know."

"Ships are often delayed in their departures and therefore their arrivals."

Marce nodded. "It'll be a couple of weeks at least before people begin to notice that ships are missing. Even then they're likely to blame it on something else."

"Like that civil war of yours."

"It's not *my* civil war," Marce snorted, and then remembered who he was talking to. "Ma'am."

The emperox ignored it. "Is there any way to use the collapse of this Flow stream? The one from End to here?"

"I can present the work and show the math behind it," Marce said. "But I'm going to warn you ahead of time that anyone who isn't already a Flow physicist isn't going to follow it at all, and even then they will argue what it means. It will take time for them to go through my father's work and his prediction model. But by then it won't matter."

"Because more Flow streams will have collapsed, and that will be the evidence."

Marce nodded again. "Right."

"You said you knew that the Flow stream from End to Hub has already collapsed."

"It's very likely, yes."

"So you can predict the collapses."

"We can give you probabilities on which ones are going to collapse and when. It's not predicting. It's looking at the data and offering the most probable outcomes."

"Do you know which one is going to collapse next? I mean, which one is likeliest?"

"Yes. It's likely to be the Flow stream from here to Terhathum. The model predicts it will collapse within the next six weeks."

"Are you sure?"

"No. But it's probable."

"How probable? Give me a percentage."

"I'd say about eighty percent chance you'll have the Hub–Terhathum collapse within six weeks. After that it's hazy but there's an almost one hundred percent chance within a year."

"That's the streams to Terhathum and back?"

Marce shook his head. "No. The Flow streams to a system and from a system are not actually related." He caught the emperox's look at this. "I know, that's not a fact anyone's brain is comfortable with, but it's true. Our model has a prediction from the stream from Terhathum to Hub, but it's very fuzzy because it's further out in time. It could happen in as soon as thirty-eight months and as late as eighty-seven months from now. The second of those dates is when we expect the final streams to close."

"What will be the last stream to close?"

"Right now our prediction models have the stream to End closing sometime between eighty and eighty-seven months from now."

"You carry all these numbers in your head?" the emperox asked.

"Not all of them," Marce confessed. "Just the ones I thought you would ask me about. I have fifteen minutes with you, ma'am. I wanted to be efficient."

"Do you find it at all ironic that End has the first Flow stream to collapse, and also might have the last?"

"It's not ironic, ma'am, it's coincidental. But I'm happy it's likely to be the case. I want to be able to go home."

The emperox gave Marce a look. "You traveled for the better part of a year without knowing whether or not you'd get a meeting with me."

"Begging your pardon, but I wasn't expecting to have a meeting with you at all. I was expecting your father. My condolences to you, also, ma'am."

"Thank you. What would you have done if I hadn't decided to see you?"

"I imagine I would have presented our data to the physicists at the University of Hubfall and told them it was their problem to get the information out to whomever wanted to listen. Then I might have taken a couple of days to sightsee and then headed out on the first ship going to End."

"Is that your plan now? To return to End immediately?"

"My *plan* is done, ma'am. I've spoken to you. I am ready to give you the full report from my father, checked by me, which your father commissioned. You may pass it along to whomever you wish for verification and you may do with it whatever you like, in terms of policy. It doesn't seem like I need to convince you of the reality of the data. I'm confident you will use it wisely, although whether everyone else will follow your lead is an open question."

The door opened and Obelees Atek entered the room. Marce rose.

"Lord Marce, your plan is done, but I still may need you. Will you stay?"

"Ma'am, you are the emperox," Marce said.

"No," the emperox said, and for the first time, Marce heard exasperation in her voice. "Lord Marce, you're not an office to redecorate. I am asking you to stay, to explain this to me further, and to assist me in explaining it to others. I am asking you to stay knowing right now there's a risk involved for you, and that risk gets larger the longer this takes. I *can* command your assistance. But I am *asking* for your help."

Marce looked at the emperox and was reminded again that

whatever he was expecting from this meeting, this wasn't it. "Ma'am, it would be my honor to assist you however I can," he said.

The emperox broke into a grin. "Thank you, Lord Marce. I am off now to tour a new tenner but will be returning late this evening. Will you have a late supper with me? I have more questions."

"Of course," Marce said, and then hesitated.

The emperox caught it. "What is it?"

"I'm trying to figure out my personal logistics. I'm staying at a hotel on Imperial Station. My dinner clothes are there."

"One, I'm going to be exhausted after touring this damn ship, so dinner will be very informal. Two, you're on staff now." The emperox turned to Obelees. "I've hired Lord Marce as a special assistant for science policy. Have someone retrieve his effects from Imperial Station. Please find him quarters in the staff wing suitable to his station." She glanced over to Marce. "Make sure they don't look like a museum exploded in them. And have someone give him an orientation."

"Yes, ma'am," Obelees said.

"See you soon," the emperox said to Marce.

"Ma'am," Marce said, and bowed. The emperox left her office. As soon as she crossed the threshold of the office door, three assistants and a bodyguard attached themselves to her and paced her as she walked through the anteroom.

Marce watched her go and then turned to Obelees. "I have no idea what just happened here," he said.

Obelees smiled. "It seems you had a successful meeting, Lord Marce. Now, come with me and let's see what we can find for you, apartment-wise."

Cardenia felt almost ashamed at how exhilarated she felt after her meeting with Marce Claremont.

Ashamed because, after all, the discussion, as brief as it was, confirmed what her father had worried about, a worry she had inherited: that the human species was threatened with extinction, not in an abstract way or over a long period of time, but in a concrete fashion in the span of less than a decade. In less than ten years every human system would be isolated, alone and forced to survive solely on what resources existed in-system, and with what craft existed to exploit those resources. Habitats could theoretically last decades or even centuries before they failed, but there was the human element as well. Humans didn't react well to the knowledge they were cut off and doomed to slow death by habitat failure. Cardenia recalled what they knew of the fall of Dalasýsla. The humans malfunctioned long before their habitat did.

Feeling exhilarated about a confirmation of that fate for four dozen human systems and billions of individual humans was nothing to be proud about.

But Cardenia couldn't help it. She was exhilarated not because she was a fatalist or a misanthrope, happy that humanity was finally getting its comeuppance. She was exhilarated because *finally* the hazy nebulous shape of her reign, one whose meager main accomplishment was keeping parliament and the guilds from stomping on the unsuspecting planet of End with an influx of military boots, had suddenly snapped into focus. Cardenia now knew three things:

One, she would be the very last emperox of the Interdependency.

Two, the whole of her reign would be about saving as many human lives as possible, by any and every means possible.

Three, that meant the end of the lie of the Interdependency.

Which is what it was, and what Cardenia had learned that day she summoned Rachela I in the Memory Room and made her explain it all: how the vast majorities of the star systems accessible by the Flow were not easily habitable by humans but how they proceeded anyway, undeterred. How these independent systems began to trade and become dependent on each other for resources. How a group of merchants, spearheaded by Banyamun Wu, realized true power rested not in trade but in controlling access to the Flow, and set themselves up in the Hub system as armed toll collectors.

How they camouflaged and sold their resource grab under a manufactured religious ethos of "Interdependency," with Banyamun's daughter Rachela as the nominative figurehead of the new church and nascent empire. How the Wus and their allies paid off those who might oppose them with titles of nobility and commerce monopolies, creating the "house and guild" economic system that ensured a permanent caste system and actively discouraged the sort of economic diversification within each system that might now better position humanity to survive its imminent isolation.

How, in short, the Interdependency codified and manipu-

lated humanity's actual need for intersystem trade and cooperation, for the benefit of just a few at the very top. Starting with
the Wu family. *Her* family.

Cardenia had been shocked at the simple, unapologetic
bloodymindedness with which Rachela I had recounted the
Interdependency scheme. Until she remembered that the
Rachela I of the Memory Room was a computer simulation
without an ego. This version of Rachela I had no need to flatter
herself or rationalize the actions she, her father, and the early
Wu family and allies had taken. The computer simulation was
unashamed.

At that moment it had occurred to Cardenia that every emperox after Rachela had had the same moment she was then
having, the one where they had entered the Memory Room to
converse with their ancestors about the nature of the Interdependency, only to be told flatly that the founding story every
Interdependent citizen had been told and taught was a lie.
Cardenia imagined that nearly every one of them had had to
suspect—her own dream about Naffa telling her it was a scam
was a manifestation of her subconscious, not an actual ghostly
visitation, after all—but it's one thing to suspect it, and another
thing to be told it, by the simulated but verifiable representa-
tion of your ancestor.

Because she was curious, Cardenia had Jiyi call up emperoxs
at random to learn what they thought when they discovered—
or had confirmed for them—that the Interdependency was
founded primarily to benefit the Wu family and their allies. She
had wanted to know how it affected their own reigns. Some had
been surprised by their ancestors' duplicity and used it as a spur
to make the lives of the average Interdependent citizen better.
Some had been delighted by their ancestors' naked power grab
and had gone about making sure that it stayed secured for

further generations of the Wu family. Two were so appalled that they resigned, one self-exiling to End to become a farmer, and the other collapsing into nihilism, devoting himself to a life of "drinking and fucking," as his simulation put it.

But most emperoxs essentially shrugged and got on with the business of running the Interdependency. How it was created and who benefited from it was academic to the fact that it *did* exist and needed running, and that there was nothing anyone could do that would change that, not even an emperox. Emperoxs of the Interdependency were not meant to be radicals, in any political direction; ones that were found themselves discreetly removed and replaced by more tractable children or (if necessary) cousins.

Certainly Cardenia had spent the first nine months of her reign being confronted with the immense inertia of the office of the emperox, and how tradition and obligation had hemmed her in. Was she not, right now, traveling by shuttle to tour a spaceship she didn't care about, at the request of a politically connected family she disliked, with a man everyone but her wanted her to marry? Was this not, in itself, a metaphor of her entire life at the moment?

Now, however. The end of the Interdependency was not only inevitable as a matter of physics, but desirable as a matter of species survival. The monopolies would have to go as each system gathered resources and prepared for their isolation. The guild and nobility structures would have to fall, as impediments to the continuation of humanity. The lie of the Interdependency—that it was necessary and desirable—was coming to an end, and Cardenia, who had never wanted to be emperox at all, would be the one to end it. Would *have* to be the one to end it.

She was almost giddy about that fact.

"We're about to dock with the *Sing Out*," the pilot of the

imperial shuttle said over the speakers, and Cardenia nodded. She was traveling with a full complement of assistants and guards but at least some portion of the tour would be Amit and her alone, allowing the two of them moments of agreed-upon privacy to discuss whatever they felt like discussing. Cardenia assumed, on Amit's part, that would constitute some fumbling overtures of affection.

You don't have to pretend you might marry him now, a part of Cardenia's brain said, and that thought sent a pleasant shock through her system. It was true enough! The whole point of marrying Amit, or any Nohamapetan, would be to solidify the imperial house's position with regard to the guilds and parliament, and to keep that wildly ambitious house in line, at least theoretically.

But now there was no future to consider, at least as far as the Interdependency was concerned. Cardenia didn't need to worry about establishing imperial dominance for another generation, or currying favor with the guilds and the parliament. All that was going away. All that was left was striving to keep humanity alive after the fall. Cardenia was pretty sure she didn't need Amit, or any Nohamapetan, for that. If Marce Claremont was correct, and she strongly believed that he was, then within a few weeks everyone would have all the proof they needed that the universe was changing.

Cardenia thought briefly on Marce Claremont, with whom she had felt comfortable from the moment he entered her office and laughed at it. Cardenia had intended the meeting to be private but formal, but something about Claremont made her change her mind. She'd dropped the formal address and fairly hovered over him while they spoke, and then maneuvered it so they could speak again later, over dinner.

You're attracted to him, duh, her brain said. Cardenia couldn't disagree with that. He was smart, well-mannered, and cute enough, and it had been long enough since Cardenia had any sort of relations that that combination in any man within ten years of her age would have pinged her circuits. But it was something other than mere sexual attraction that Cardenia had responded to. As her shuttle docked she realized what it was: Claremont had reminded her, just a little, of Naffa. A little academic, a little sardonic, and someone who might see her as Cardenia, not as Emperox Grayland II. Or, at least, see her as Cardenia, too.

Maybe I just need a friend, she thought. She smiled wistfully at that and then she exited the shuttle, into the bay of the *If You Want to Sing Out, Sing Out,* where Amit Nohamapetan was waiting for her, along with at least two hundred workers who had built the ship.

They all bowed as she descended into the bay. "Your Majesty," Amit Nohamapetan said, as he drew himself up. "It is delightful to see you again." It was then that Cardenia caught the look on his face: a strained but pleasant mask. Hiding something that was obviously stressing him. In spite of herself, Cardenia felt a momentary stab of pity for Amit. Whatever was going on with him right now, it wasn't pleasant.

Cardenia returned the pleasantries and allowed herself to be introduced to the shipbuilders, shaking hands with the supervisors and greeting the rank-and-file workers. Cardenia had gotten used to this aspect of her job; she did a lot of greeting and waving, and would for the rest of her life.

Well, not anymore, her brain said.

She shushed it and turned to Amit. "Are you ready to begin the tour, Lord Amit?" she asked.

"Of course, ma'am," he said. Cardenia held out her hand, in

a formal but not unfriendly position. Amit gratefully took it and they walked out of the bay, followed by her retinue.

A tenner is a large ship, and there was quite a bit of walking planned. The tour would include the bridge and engineering capsule, in the main body of the ship, and then the cargo holds and factories in the rings. It was during the part in the cargo hold that Amit and Cardenia would be alone, with her guards positioned in the ring sections behind and in front of them. Her people would have already been on the ship for hours, making sure it was entirely secure before she set foot on it, of course. It would be relatively low risk for her to walk a hundred meters with Amit by herself.

The whole tour would take just under two hours, followed by an intimate tea service, also just between Amit and Cardenia. At which, Cardenia suddenly decided, she intended to tell Amit that he could forget about the whole marriage thing. That decision being made, Cardenia hoped she wouldn't be too awkwardly quiet during the course of the tour.

Ten minutes into the tour, however, it was clear that if either of them was being awkwardly silent, it was Amit Nohamapetan. He was offering the bare minimum of banter required before letting crew members stationed at their tour stops take over explaining the functions of the ship. Amit didn't ask any questions, which might be interpreted as politeness, except for the level of distraction he was showing; he seemed not to be paying attention at all to the crew members' explanations of their stations and duties. At one point Cardenia had to discreetly nudge him to get him to acknowledge and thank a crew member for their time.

By the time the two of them slipped through the door of the cargo hold, the vast expanse of which was clearly placed into their itinerary to give the two of them a few moments of alone time, Cardenia decided she'd had enough. "Lord Amit, if this tour was meant to show your warm personal side to me, I'm afraid you're failing considerably," she said, as they walked.

Amit smiled ruefully. "Yes, Your Majesty. Believe me, I am very well aware of that."

"Is there a cause for this?"

"I received quite a lot of bad news today, I'm afraid."

"I'm sorry to hear that. Was it something personal?"

"In a way. Mostly business, although as you know, business is often personal."

"I understand that better than most, I have to say."

"I have no doubt that you do," Amit said, and they walked a bit more in the cavern of the hold, quietly.

When they got to what Cardenia expected was the dead center of the cargo bay, Amit stopped and turned to her. "You don't want to marry me, do you, Your Majesty?"

Cardenia opened her mouth to say something placatingly but then "No, no, I really don't," popped out, and, well. There it was.

"All right, good," Amit said.

"Wait, what?" Cardenia said, entirely surprised. "Begging your pardon, Lord Amit, but I was under the impression, from your sister most of all, that I was here to be charmed and wooed by you. You now being visibly relieved that I don't wish to marry you is . . . *unexpected*, to say the least."

"I'm sorry, Your Majesty."

"I'm not," Cardenia said, and it was Amit's turn to be surprised. "I'm relieved that this tedious bit of politicking is over with. It means we might actually enjoy our tea together."

Amit laughed at this.

"But I don't understand why, after more than a year of a full push by your family, and by you, that you're now relieved to learn that I have no interest in marrying you."

"It's complicated," Amit said.

Cardenia motioned around them as if to say, *We are totally alone; this is the time.*

"The short version is that we have been made aware that other houses believe we already exercise too much influence over you. At this point we run the risk of *losing* influence rather than gaining it, through close association with you."

"Well, I don't know quite what to make of that statement, Lord Amit."

"I understand, Your Majesty. Suffice to say that guild and parliamentary politics are complicated enough now, and we have reason to believe they are about to become even more complicated in the future."

A warning went off in Cardenia's brain. "How so?"

"The matter of End, in the near term."

"And in the longer term?"

"Well, who can say in the longer term," Amit said, and started to walk again.

"No," Cardenia said, and stayed where she was, obliging Amit to stop walking. "Excuse me, Lord Amit. I don't believe you'd throw away your path to the throne because of the rebellion on End. I don't believe your sister would do that, either. There's something more to it, isn't there?"

Amit Nohamapetan looked for all the world like a child caught raiding the cookie jar.

"And this calling off of the marriage attempt isn't something that *you* want, is it?" Cardenia asked. "Which is to say, this isn't your idea. You're being made to do it. By your sister?"

"Not by her," Amit said.

"But *you* wouldn't abandon this on your own," Cardenia said.

"So whatever reason you have for it, *she* signed off on it. But she told me that she was willing to give up her seat on the executive committee for you if I chose to marry you. Because the House of Nohamapetan being on the executive committee is obviously trumped by the House of Nohamapetan marrying into the royal family and placing an heir on the throne. So something has happened between when I talked to her, and now. What is it, Lord Amit?"

Amit was silent.

"Is it about End?" Cardenia pressed.

"Your Majesty . . ."

"You're involved in it in some way, aren't you? The rebellion on End."

Amit looked exasperated. "Your *Majesty*. Why would we do that?"

Cardenia ignored the condescension inherent in the exasperation, because her mind was focused on the larger question: How *would* the Nohamapetans benefit from a rebellion on End? If they were engaged in it in some way it would mean they were either trying to win the favor of the sitting duke, install a new one, or possibly have a family member ascend to the throne—Ghreni Nohamapetan, the younger brother, perhaps.

But why? If the sitting duke was deposed and the action could be traced to the Nohamapetans, then the duke (or more likely his heirs) could force a suit in the Interdependency courts, along with a request to escrow the house's profits pending the resolution of the suit. That would be bad for business. If the Nohamapetans installed one of their own as duke of End, then they would ultimately have to give up their home base of Terhathum, where Amit's mother Jedna was the sitting countess—

Terhathum.

The part of Cardenia's brain in charge of gestalting slammed everything together and shoved it into her consciousness.

"Oh my God," she said, looking at Amit. "You know. You know about the Flow."

"I don't know what you're talking about," Amit said, but his look of absolute surprise when Cardenia mentioned the Flow called him a liar.

"You know it's about to collapse. You know that Terhathum is next. You're abandoning it for End." Cardenia stopped for a second, and then stared at Amit, not comprehending. "You know it's going to collapse but *you've done nothing to save your own people*. Why?"

"It's not collapsing, it's shifting," Amit started to say, and then clammed right the hell up.

Cardenia continued to stare, and then her brain kicked in and realized what he said. "No, Lord Amit. Oh, no. They're not shifting, they're closing entirely. Listen to me. You need to send a message to Terhathum today. Right now. They have to get ready. They have to prepare."

"Prepare for what?"

"For the collapse, Amit. For the collapse."

Alarms went off, and from behind and in front, guards came rushing at the two of them.

Amit looked around, shocked. "She wouldn't," he whispered. "She wouldn't. Not to me. Not now."

"What is it, Amit?" Cardenia asked.

He looked at her. "I'm sorry, Cardenia," he said, and then they were both grabbed by guards and pulled away, Cardenia in the direction they came from, Amit in the direction they were going to go.

Both groups got nearly to their respective doors when the cargo hold was torn apart by something slamming into the skin of the ship and driving itself at an angle toward the cargo hold deck. Cardenia turned as she simultaneously ran and was dragged, and saw what looked like the remains of a shuttle barreling across the cargo hold, tip over tail, toward the far wall where Amit and his guards were running. She screamed his name but it was lost in the shearing, tearing noise of the disintegrating shuttle and in the sucking noise of the air vomiting out through the gigantic hole in the cargo hold roof. For a fraction of a second she saw the back of his head, pushed down by the imperial guards as they ran. Then they were all mowed down by the threshing wreckage of the shuttle.

The ship, sensing the loss of atmosphere, began to drop pressure doors. Cardenia and her guards ran as fast as they could toward the falling doors but the gale-force winds of the ship's atmosphere sucking out the hole slowed them down. Cardenia screamed as the doors dropped lower, convinced they wouldn't make it.

They didn't. Not all of them. Cardenia's guards shoved her at the door and she tumbled, arms out. From the other side of the door, an arm reached out, a hand grabbed one of her hands and yanked her through the opening so roughly that she screamed out from the pain as her shoulder nearly dislocated. Then she was on the other side of the door, scrambling to get her foot out of the way as it slammed shut. Somewhere along the way she lost a shoe.

Cardenia was pulled up and dragged forcefully down the curving corridor, toward the ring spoke that would send them back to the main body of the ship. When they were in sight of one she looked at the three guards who were with her and was about to ask what happened when there was a crack and a shove that pushed her hard into the deck, fracturing her wrist and abrading her arms and face as they were dragged across the surface. The wind howled again. One of her guards, who had stood up after falling, was pushed out of the ring section and was carried away before more pressure doors slammed down.

When they were down, Cardenia counted to ten before getting up off the deck. She gasped desperately for air; the two ruptures had thinned out so much of the ship's atmosphere in the ring that Cardenia felt like she was suffocating. One of the remaining guards, gasping herself, located a wall-mounted emergency kit and broke it open, fishing out the two small pressurized containers of oxygen inside of it. She handed one to Cardenia and showed her how to use it. Cardenia sucked down a gulp of the oxygen and was so grateful for it that she started to sob.

The guard then checked on the other, who had not gotten up from the deck. Cardenia looked and saw a pool of blood surrounding the guard's head. He'd been pushed so hard into the deck that he'd hemorrhaged out.

All around them a huge creaking, popping sound moaned through the surfaces of their ring segment and into the attenuated air.

"What is that?" Cardenia asked.

"The ring was rotating to help give it gravity," the guard said. "Now it's been ruptured. The ring is tearing itself apart." She reached over to Cardenia, offering up her hand. "Come on, ma'am. We need to get you up that spoke."

The spoke was designed with push fields in mind; a wide walkway detoured off the main floor and up what appeared to be the wall of the ring segment and then into the spoke, with focused push fields securing crew as they walked up the "wall" to get to the spoke. The spokes emptied out into the main ship with push fields securing the path on that end as well.

"You first, ma'am," the guard said, and Cardenia limped up the wall, oxygen container in hand, and into the spoke, then turned back to look at the guard. "Keep going!" she said, looking up, motioning Cardenia forward, and then the groaning noise became much louder and from below the guard Cardenia could see the deck of the ring segment begin to buckle and tear. A pressure door, this one to seal off the spoke, irised closed. The last image Cardenia had of the guard was her yelling at Cardenia to run.

She didn't need the encouragement. She sprinted down the spoke until the push fields gave out, and then she was careening weightless down the spoke, first crashing into the wall and then dragging herself down it, trying to get to the far portal into the main ship.

As Cardenia careened down she passed a segment of the spoke with a transparent section. She looked out and saw the wreckage of the ship's ring, and the segment opposite her tearing away from the ship, rupturing the spoke that led from it, spilling debris. She watched it as she floated past and then it was behind her. In front of her was the portal to the main ship.

Which she now realized was sealed.

A sharp, jolting crack shoved the spoke around Cardenia, slamming her into a wall and spinning her around. As she spun she heard a high, chorused whistling; down the spoke was a rupture along the wall, little holes like pinpricks, strung out in a rough line at least three meters long. The spoke was losing atmosphere.

Cardenia clutched her oxygen canister tighter, pushed her way to the portal separating her from the main ship, grabbed a handhold on the side of the portal, and started banging on the portal with her canister. She kept at it as the air thinned and grew cold, taking occasional hits off the canister to remain conscious and banging. She kept at it until she either heard or hallucinated someone banging back on the other side.

She kept at it until the cold took her.

17

Imperial guards swarmed through the House of Lagos offices in the Guild House, prompting what Kiva thought was the only rational response to the event.

"What the fuck?" she demanded of Lord Pretar, who stood in his office while guards and investigators went through his files and tablet, along with the files and tablets of every other single person in the offices.

"There's been an assassination attempt against the emperox," Pretar explained.

"Which has fuck all to do with us how?" Kiva demanded.

"Lady Kiva, *please*," Pretar said, looking around at the guards. "Keep your tone respectful."

"Fuck *tone*," Kiva said. "Answer the goddamned question."

Kiva could see Pretar trying to decide if he, the senior director of the House of Lagos on Hub, could thump on the daughter of the matriarch of the house. After a second he decided against it, which Kiva thought was the correct although disappointing choice, because she was itching for a chance to grind him directly into the fucking carpet right about now. "The emperox was touring a newly completed spaceship," he said.

"Someone crashed a shuttle into the ring segment she was touring."

"Okay. And?"

"And, the shuttle is from one of our ships."

"What? *Which* ship?"

"The *Yes, Sir.*"

"You have to be fucking kidding me," Kiva said.

Pretar looked around them and arched his eyes, which Kiva found spectacularly annoying, as if to say, *These people wouldn't be here if I were kidding.*

"Lady Kiva," a voice said from behind her. She turned and saw a very officious-looking prick staring at her.

"Who are you?"

"Hibert Limbar. Chief of the Imperial Guard. I want to talk to you."

"Good, because I want to talk to you, too." Kiva turned to Pretar. "Out."

"It's my office," Pretar protested. "And you're not your mother, Lady Kiva."

"No, I'm not," Kiva said. "Call her and complain about me if you want. Until then, fuck off. I need your office."

Pretar stared for a moment, then exited. The guards and investigators in the office stared as he went.

Kiva motioned to them. "Tell the rest of them to fuck off, too," she said to Limbar.

"Everyone fuck off," Limbar said. "For the next fifteen minutes."

Everyone fucked off, and Limbar closed the door behind them.

"So how the fuck did one of our shuttles get jacked for this?" Kiva asked, walking over to Pretar's office chair and falling into it.

"It's funny you should ask me that, Lady Kiva," Limbar said. "I was going to ask the very same question of you. Possibly with fewer 'fucks' involved."

"Obviously I have no idea."

"You were the owner's representative on the *Yes, Sir*."

"Yes."

"And on the way back to Hub from End you stuffed your ship full of emigrants from End, allegedly fleeing the civil war there."

"Yes. So?"

"So it's possible one or more of those emigrants had plans once they got here."

Kiva snorted. "You're suggesting one of those assholes we shipped to Hub knew the emperox—a *brand-new* emperox, who was being crowned just about the time we left—was going to be on a particular ship at a particular time and then just *borrowed* a shuttle to take her out."

"I don't think that's likely. I think it's rather more likely someone here gave them instructions once they arrived, and scoped out the political landscape."

"What does that mean?" Kiva asked.

"Lady Kiva, are you aware of the ship that was attacked?"

"No."

"It was the *If You Want to Sing Out, Sing Out*, which was a new tenner commissioned by the House of Nohamapetan."

Kiva said nothing.

"Lady Nohamapetan tells me that not too long before her house's ship was attacked, you and your mother the countess threatened Amit Nohamapetan over a business dispute."

"We didn't *threaten* him. We just made very clear our displeasure over certain actions his house undertook against us on End, but offered to settle those issues out of court. You can ask him yourself."

"I would love to do that, except that he was with the emperox when the attack happened. The emperox survived. Amit No-hamapetan, alas, did not."

"Well, fuck," Kiva said, after a minute.

Limbar nodded. "I can show you the pictures if you like. There's not much left, however. Most of what wasn't smeared onto the ship deck was ejected out into space."

"You don't think *we* did that, do you?"

"Well, Lady Kiva, you tell me. You arrive from End with a business dispute against the Nohamapetans and with a ship full of emigrants from a planet whose rebels have been attack-ing targets all around the Interdependency—and who have at-tempted to assassinate the emperox before. So now here is an assassination attempt that not only targets the emperox but also gets rid of the heir to the head of the House of Nohamapetan, and incidentally does immense financial damage to his house by destroying its new tenner just before it's deployed into ser-vice. Do you not see how I could imagine that you and these terrorists from End might have decided to assassinate two birds with one stone?"

"You can *imagine* anything you like," Kiva said. "It doesn't mean that it's true. And it wouldn't make sense anyway. We needed Lord Amit alive to push through the settlement we wanted from him. Killing him before we got that wouldn't do us any good. Now they're not going to have a goddamn thing to do with us, especially if they think we're involved."

Limbar smiled. "That much I expect is true. Lady Nadashe is in a rage, and only the fact that she's currently whipping up support to send a troopship to End is keeping her full atten-tion from the House of Lagos."

Kiva opened her mouth to say something about the Noham-apetan involvement with the rebels on End and why the fuck wasn't Limbar looking into that, when she snapped her mouth closed so fast that her teeth actually clacked together.

"Yes, Lady Kiva?" Limbar said, noticing. "Something just occur to you?"

"I was wondering whether you have any evidence to back up your hunch here."

Limbar motioned around him. "There is a reason we're here. I don't imagine you or your mother is stupid enough to commit any plans like this to recordable media, if you were involved. But perhaps not everyone in your employ is that aware. In which case, we'll find out. In the meantime, Lady Kiva, you'll understand that I've restricted your movements to Hubfall for now and that you'll be discreetly monitored in your movement. It's not just you, of course. Your mother, Lord Pretar, and most of your executives here on Hub and on Xi'an are also being restricted."

"That's not going to go over very well with my mother."

"Then you may tell the countess, and you may quote me fully, that I don't give a fuck. Someone just tried to kill my emperox for the second time on my watch. You can be assured that I will find out who it is. And if it is you, or your mother, or anyone involved with the House of Lagos, I won't care how high and mighty you are, or how much you intimidate your underlings. I'll take you down, and your entire house, if I have to."

"I'll let her know."

"Do that. And now, Lady Kiva, if you'll excuse me, my people have to get back to work." He went and opened the door to let his guards and investigators back into the room. Kiva watched them file in and then got out of the chair, left the office, and headed toward the elevator bank. As she did so a guard detached herself from her duties and walked toward her.

"Oh, come on," Kiva said, to the guard. "Your asshole boss said you would be discreet."

"This is discreet," the guard said, standing next to her.

Kiva resisted the temptation to roll her eyes. "What's your name?"

"Sergeant Brenja Pitof."

"Well, Sergeant, am I going to get a moment to myself between now and whenever the end of this is?"

"Not really, no."

"So you're going to watch me when I take a dump."

"No."

"Good."

"As long as the bathroom doesn't have a window or a second exit."

The elevator door opened and Kiva stepped inside. Sergeant Pitof followed.

"Press the 'Ground' button," Kiva said.

"I'm supposed to follow you, Lady Kiva, not be your servant," Pitof said. Then she pushed the button anyway.

•   •   •

"Where are you?" Captain Blinnikka said to Kiva, over her tablet, the one the Imperial Guard hadn't confiscated.

"I'm in my hotel room bathroom," Kiva said.

"What's that noise?"

"It's the shower."

"You're calling me from the shower?"

"No, I'm running the shower so I can talk to you. I have a fucking guard in my hotel room."

"What's the guard doing?"

Lying on the bed after a particularly exhausting bout of screwing,

Kiva thought, but did not say. Kiva decided that as long as she was going to be that closely watched, she might as well get something out of it. "Waiting for me to be done showering, so maybe let's get to the subject. Which is, what the fuck happened with our shuttle?"

"It was coming back from Imperial Station when the communications went dead and it piloted itself to the dock where the *Sing Out* was being built and rammed itself into the damn thing. Imperial Guard craft opened up on it as it came in but they didn't manage to destroy it before it hit."

"Who was the pilot?"

"Ling Xi."

Kiva grimaced. Xi was completely competent and wholly uninteresting and had no personal politics as far as Kiva knew. "It doesn't make sense she would jam a shuttle into that ship."

"I don't think she did," Blinnikka said. "We have the data from the shuttle's control panels. It shows a lot of activity during the trip, but not piloting data—or more accurately piloting data that corresponds to the trip. Everything we see is what you'd see from a pilot trying to take *control* of the shuttle, not actively piloting it."

"So you think it was hijacked."

"Yes. I think it was hacked into somehow and then either autopiloted or remotely piloted to the *Sing Out*."

"Did you tell that to the Imperial Guard?"

"They didn't ask, and I decided I'd let them figure it out. They just came onto the ship, downloaded everything they could, and set up shop in one of the cargo holds. They're still there. They questioned me and the senior staff, but that was hours ago. We're not allowed to leave. I don't know what they're up to right now."

"There was no one else on the shuttle except Xi?"

"No."

"What about before? She piloted the shuttle to Imperial Station, yes? Was anyone with her then?"

"Hold on," Blinnikka said. Kiva waited, and while she waited, decided that she really did need a shower; she and Sergeant Pitof had been pretty exuberant. She stripped down, put her tablet into speaker mode, and got into the shower.

"There were a couple of passengers," Blinnikka said when he came back on. "Three, actually. A husband and wife named Lewyyn, and a man named Broshning. They were departing the *Yes, Sir* for good."

"Do we know where they were going?"

"I have no idea."

"But *someone* does, yes? Isn't there some way to find out?"

"I don't know. I'm a captain, not a private investigator."

"Ask Gazson Magnut. If they had cargo in the holds that they didn't take on the shuttle with them they would have to arrange to have it sent somewhere."

"We just offload it. Imperial Station handles it from there."

"Then have someone ask *them*."

"Easier said than done."

"We've got the fucking Imperial Guard thinking we are trying to assassinate the emperox," Kiva said. "I think we can make a little *effort*."

Blinnikka was quiet for a moment. "Do you have me on speaker?"

"Maybe."

"I thought you said you were trying to avoid being heard."

"I decided I needed an actual shower more."

"I wish I didn't know that."

"Find those people for me. Tell me where they are."

"No promises."

"Then I guess I'll see you in prison."

Kiva heard Blinnikka sigh. "I'm not calling you back. I'm afraid of what you'll be doing when you pick up. I'll send you a message."

"Encrypted."

"Obviously," Blinnikka said, and disconnected.

Kiva finished cleaning up, turned off the shower, toweled off, and opened the door to find Sergeant Pitof directly on the other side.

"You know there's an easier way to find those people," Pitof said.

"You fucking listened at the door?" Kiva said, incredulous.

"Yes."

"What did you hear?"

"Most of what was said after you turned on the speaker."

"You're unbelievable."

"Just because we had sex doesn't mean I stop doing my job, Lady Kiva."

Kiva opened her mouth and then closed it. "I have no good response to that," she said, finally. "Now tell me what you mean about there being an easier way to find these people."

"Everyone who arrives at any imperial station for permanent immigration has to let customs know where they are staying. Immigration needs to keep track of them until they are cleared for permanent residency."

"So customs knows where they are."

"Probably."

"Sometimes people lie about where they are going."

Pitof shook her head. "You have to present your hotel reservation or the name and address of the people with whom you are staying before you leave customs, and check in once you arrive."

"And then you walk out the door and are never heard from again."

"At the very least you'll be one step closer to finding them than you are at the moment."

"So how do I talk to customs?"

"You don't. I do."

"Why would you help me?"

"There's no reason I couldn't help you. Just as long as you know that I'm going to report everything I do for you to my boss."

Kiva arched an eyebrow. "Probably not everything."

"No, I'll report the sex too."

This gave Kiva pause. "Isn't it actually unethical to fuck the person you're trailing?"

Sergeant Pitof shrugged. "I was told to keep you close."

Kiva laughed at this. "I think I like you, Sergeant Pitof. You're my kind of asshole."

"Thank you, Lady Kiva. Now tell me those names again. I couldn't really make them out over the sound of your showering."

•   •   •

Taffyd and Chun Lewyyn were staying on Imperial Station, at a moderately priced hotel called the Primrose. That was no good for Kiva; she was stuck on Hub. She'd deal with them later. She was waiting for information on Geork Broshning when she heard a crash and then screaming in the hotel lobby. Kiva reached into the closet for a robe and then opened the door and looked down three floors into the hotel atrium, and the crumpled body there, looking up at the ceiling of the hotel, sixteen stories up.

"Found him," Sergeant Pitof said, from the room. She put on the other robe and walked out into the walkway to show Kiva the information on the tablet, which included a picture of Broshning.

Kiva looked at it. "Pretty sure I just found him too," she said, and pointed to the body on the atrium floor, surrounded now by people, and which had now begun to leak. Then she noticed something else and started walking down the hallway in her robe, toward the elevators. Pitof followed.

On the lobby floor, Kiva walked into the atrium, past the dead body and the scrum of people around it, and over to one of the planters there, stuffed with attractive artificial plants. In the planter was a keycard, nestled into the leaves of a large, fake succulent. Kiva snatched it up, walked again past the dead man and his admirers, and headed over to reception, where she got the attention of a very shaken-looking hotel assistant manager.

"Would you be a dear and ping Geork Broshning for me? He's expecting me but I've forgotten his room number."

"Yes . . . of course," said the hotel assistant manager, activating his screen to search for the name, and then swiping over to a communication panel to punch in the room code. "No response, ma'am," he said, after a minute.

"I don't suppose you could just tell me the room number?"

"I'm sorry, ma'am, I'm not allowed to do that."

"Of course," Kiva said, and then turned just as Pitof walked up to her. Kiva walked straight past her minder and back onto the elevator, pressing the button for the twelfth floor as Pitof walked on. Pitof noted the floor but didn't say anything.

On the twelfth floor Kiva got off, walked to room 1245, the number she had seen the assistant manager punch into his screen, and pressed the card to the door. It unlocked.

"You probably shouldn't follow me in here," she said to Pitof. "You might be accused of tampering with the evidence. In a bathrobe."

"Shut up and open the door," Pitof said. Kiva shrugged and went in.

The bed in the room was rumpled but the sheets were not pulled back; someone had lain on the bed but maybe hadn't slept in it. Otherwise the room was neat with suitcases and other effects unpacked. Kiva looked to the desk and found a notepad and a pen there, with letters on the sheet on the top of the notepad. She went over to the desk and without touching it read the words, written in a tight, small script.

I grew maize and banu on End, it said. *The banu died because of a fungus. They say citrus caused it but I think it was from the maize. It failed too. I lost everything and then the war forced me out. I tried to leave but I couldn't afford it. Then Ghreni Nohamapetan asked to see me. Told me he'd pay my way. Said he felt responsible for what happened to my banu. Said I had been a good franchisee.*

He said when I arrived at Hub to contact a customs official named Che Isolt who would tell me what to do from there. Isolt came onto the ship and gave me a transmitter box. Told me to leave it on the shuttle when I departed. I did. Then when I came to the hotel I turned on the monitor and found out what happened to the shuttle.

I know they'll figure out how it happened. I know they'll find me. I know no one will believe me. I've already lost so much and have been played for a fool. I thought I might have a chance for a new life on Hub. I was wrong.

Sorry for the mess.

"Motherfucking Nohamapetans," Kiva said, and turned to Pitof. "Do you have your tablet?" Pitof held it up. "Call your boss."

"What do you want me to tell him?"

"Tell him I found something that gets me and my house off the goddamn hook."

"He's not going to be convinced by a suicide note," Pitof said.

"It's not just a suicide note," Kiva said.

"It's still going to take some time."

Kiva nodded. "Yeah. When you're done, let me use your tablet."

"Why?"

"Because I need to call my captain and tell him to stop looking for Broshning. And then I'm going to call someone else."

"Who?"

"Someone I'm pretty sure can speed up the process of getting my house off the hook a whole fucking lot."

The imperial guard pushed the door open and Marce Claremont walked into the ornate and cavernous room where the
executive committee was having its first meeting of the morning. Marce sported a folder and eyes as large as plates as he took
in the baroque design of the immense room and realized that
no matter how long he stayed at the imperial palace he would
probably never get used to its ridiculous sumptuousness. It was,
in a word, excessive.

He reached the table where the executive committee sat, save
the emperox, who was still recovering from her assassination
attempt. The member at the head of the table, the one Grayland
II told him would be Archbishop Korbijn, essayed him quietly.
Marce bowed to her and briefly scanned the table for the other
person he was looking for, Nadashe Nohamapetan. He'd never
seen her before but he recognized her quickly enough—younger
than any other member of the executive committee, and bear-
ing a strong family resemblance to her brother Ghreni. She
looked back at him, neutral, as she should have, because she
had no idea who he was, or what he represented.

"You're new," Archbishop Korbijn said, to him.

Marce nodded. "Yes, Your Grace. I am Marce Claremont, the

emperox's new assistant for science policy. I was hired just yesterday on my arrival from End."

This got Nadashe's attention, but she hid it well; if Marce hadn't been directly looking for a reaction, he would have missed it.

Korbijn smiled and acknowledged the committee. "This might be a lot for your second day."

"Yes, Your Grace. It's a lot. More than you know."

"I understand you have an update for us on the emperox's condition," Korbijn said.

"I do, and I have another piece of business that the emperox wished me to present to the committee, if you will indulge her wishes."

"Of course."

"The emperox's condition is improving," Marce said. "She's still suffering from the effects of cold and hypoxia from being trapped in that leaking tenner spoke, but fortunately her guards—or what remained of them—were able to retrieve her before she suffered any genuinely life-threatening injuries. She was lucky. Luckier than the five guards who were lost protecting her, and the four guards who were lost trying to rescue Lord Amit Nohamapetan." He turned and nodded to Nadashe. "My condolences, Lady Nadashe, for your loss."

"Thank you," she said.

"Of course." Marce turned back to Korbijn. "Dr. Drinin has told her that he wants to keep her on bed rest and observation for a few more days, to let her body heal further, and suggested to her that this executive committee be allowed to handle any issues that come up. I believe he was hinting to her that this committee should take on the parliamentary authorization of force against End and its rebels."

"What did the emperox say to this?" Korbijn asked.

"She said that absent her presence, the committee may act in her stead to implement the authorization—"

"No time like the present," said Upeksha Ranatunga, who in parliament had voted to send the troopship *Prophecies of Rachela* to End.

"—but only after I presented this committee with the second piece of information she wished to share with you."

"And what is that?" Korbijn asked.

"This," Marce said, and opened the folder he was carrying, which contained nine printed documents, each containing a substantial number of pages, stapled together. He began distributing the reports to the committee members.

"What is this?" Ranatunga asked.

"It's an early draft of a scientific paper my father received several years ago, from a doctoral candidate named Hatide Roynold. She'd sent it to him because, although my father was the imperial auditor on End, he was there performing another task given to him by Emperox Attavio VI. My father was a Flow physicist, as I am, and the late emperox had him collecting data on the health of the Flow streams inside the Interdependency. Attavio VI was concerned, despite the best assurances of nearly all reputable Flow physicists, that these critical trade routes might collapse."

"And will they?" Ranatunga asked.

"It's happened before," Marce said. "Most obviously we lost the Flow stream to Earth, our ancestral home, more than a millennium ago. Another stream collapse, involving the Dalasýsla system, happened a couple hundred years later. However, since then, the Flow streams have been remarkably stable, a fact which has allowed the Interdependency to thrive and prosper."

Korbijn shook the report, which she was not bothering to flip through at the moment; others on the committee had also set them down; Nadashe Nohamapetan had put hers down to make some notation on her tablet. "Does this paper suggest the Flow streams are collapsing?"

"No," Marce said. "The paper actually proposed that the streams are likely to undergo a radical shift, rearranging themselves over the course of a very few years. Most of the Flow streams that we have now will go away, but they'll be replaced by emerging ones that will allow trade in the Interdependency to continue—but with End the nexus of the new Flow stream network, not Hub."

"Is that accurate?" Korbijn asked.

"That's what Roynold wanted to know, which is why she sent the draft to my father, who had written an earlier paper along the same lines, the findings of which he discussed with Attavio VI, with whom he shared a friendship. It was by Attavio's request that he stopped publicly researching the topic, but the early paper was still out there. Roynold supposed that he was the only person who would take her seriously on the topic."

"And what did he say?"

"Nothing; he was researching privately for the emperox. The only person I think he ever shared the draft with was me, because I was working with him on his research. And publicly, at least, Hatide Roynold stopped researching on this topic. Her doctorate addresses another vector of research entirely. But the imperial guards have just spoken to her overnight. It turns out that like my father, Roynold had a private patron who allowed her to continue her research on the topic of the Flow streams shifting. Nadashe Nohamapetan."

All eyes turned to Nadashe, who smiled. "I *knew* this was coming," she said, and addressed Korbijn directly. "Hatide is a friend of mine from university. She came to me in financial straits and wouldn't take charity. So I funded her research on this topic instead. I gave her a stipend to finish this and her other work, and she gave quarterly updates. Which I never read because that was never the point."

"I'm sorry, Lady Nohamapetan, but there is reason to believe otherwise," Marce said.

Nadashe turned to Marce and would have glared a hole in his chest if she could. "And what reason is that, Mr. Claremont?"

"It's *Lord* Claremont, Lady Nadashe," Marce said. "And because your brother suggested otherwise."

"To whom?"

"To *us*," said Emperox Grayland II, from the doorway. Everyone stood, except for Marce, who was already standing. He smiled at Grayland's sudden appearance. They had not planned it when they had spoken earlier, but he could tell she had been agitated when he came to her and disclosed what Kiva Lagos had told him, along with his own personal information. When the emperox told him the things she knew, everything, appallingly, fell together. After she had made calls to follow up on loose ends, the two of them planned this presentation, which Marce was to deliver.

But she also made him wear a microphone so she could hear the entire exchange, which is why she had a response to Nadashe Nohamapetan when she was too far away to possibly have heard what she was saying as she walked through the door. Marce had to admit it made for a nice psychological effect.

Grayland walked slowly to the table and waved at everyone to sit. Archbishop Korbijn moved to sit elsewhere besides the head of the table, but Grayland signaled she should stay where she was. She reached Marce and leaned on him instead.

"Your brother, Lady Nadashe, revealed to us that your family knew about Dr. Roynold's work," Grayland said. "He told us that just before he died, torn apart by that shuttle that crashed into your new tenner. We didn't know what he meant at the time. But then we had a conversation with Lord Claremont here, and he knew what your brother was talking about, because he'd seen her early work. He knew what it said, and he also knew it was wrong."

"It *is* wrong," Marce agreed. "The math was sloppy. I haven't seen her latest work yet, but if she's still suggesting a Flow shift, then she never corrected her initial errors."

"But you wouldn't know that," Grayland continued, to Nadashe. "So you and your family worked from the assumption that End would become the new center of the Interdependency. You worked so that when it happened, you, and not the House of Wu, would be the ones to control Flow access. You promoted rebellion on End, sent your brother Ghreni there to administer it, developed an agricultural virus to exacerbate it, and blamed it on the House of Lagos to cover your tracks and to get back at an enemy house."

"Here at Hub you pushed for military aid to End's duke and then used pirates to take those weapons for your family, pushing the duke to more desperate action," Marce said. "And you kept the pressure on for more military intervention by planning and executing terrorist attacks here and in the rest of the Interdependency."

"That's a lie," Nadashe said.

"We have Che Isolt in Guard custody, Lady Nohamapetan," Grayland said. "Your man at customs and immigration. He gave you up almost immediately. He told us how he identified and acted as a go-between between you and immigrants from End. How you would either use them or frame them for the terrorist events. He even told us about the attempt yesterday. How he gave an unwitting immigrant a transmitter that hacked into the shuttle through a maintenance program and sent it into your own ship. Do you know why he gave you up so easily?"

"Because he found out you intentionally killed your brother to make it look like an attack on the Nohamapetans," Marce said.

Grayland nodded at this. "Apparently fratricide was too much even for him. Although he did approve of you attempting to frame the House of Lagos for all of this. He said it was a clever move."

"The House of Lagos isn't happy about it, however," Marce noted.

"No," Grayland agreed. "No, they are not. And neither are we, Lady Nadashe. About any of this."

There was dead silence around the table as the entire executive committee stared at Nadashe Nohamapetan.

"I am grieved that you would believe any of this, Your Majesty," Nadashe began.

"Oh, cut the shit, Nadashe," Grayland said, irritated. "It's over."

"No, Cardenia," Nadashe said, and there were several gasps as she used the emperox's personal name, in a flagrant breach of protocol. "It's not over. Perhaps for me. Not for the House of Nohamapetan." She took her tablet, which she had kept in her hand this entire time, and tossed it onto the table. She pointed at it. "The minute your lackey here put Hatide's report in my hand, I sent a message to the *Prophecies of Rachela*. The troopship with ten thousand marines and all their equipment and weaponry. By the time you showed up and started your tirade, the bridge crew had locked itself in and begun moving the ship toward the Flow shoal. It was already positioned for immediate transfer. In less than fifteen minutes the *Rachela* will be through and on its way to End. It's too late to stop it."

Grayland glanced over to Korbijn, who grabbed her own tablet, leapt up from the table, and started making calls. Then she turned her attention back to Nadashe. "Your bridge crew can't stay there forever."

"Don't be stupid," Nadashe said. "They're not the only ones I have with us. I've been working on this for years. When the *Rachela* comes through to End, we'll control the system. We'll control its imperial station first, and if my brother doesn't control the surface of the planet by then, we'll control it soon enough. Then it's simply a matter of waiting, isn't it? Now we can defend the exit shoal to End easily enough. We've planned for that. And when the Flow streams shift, we'll start negotiations."

"You don't understand," Marce said. "Roynold was wrong. There's no shift coming. There's a *collapse* coming. Every single Flow stream is disappearing in the next decade."

"Excuse me, what?" said Upeksha Ranatunga.

"That's why I'm here," Marce continued. "My father confirmed it. We confirmed it with data taken from ships coming to End. It's all shutting down. All of it. End is about to be as isolated as every other system."

"That's your interpretation of the data," Nadashe said.

"It's already happening," Grayland said. "The stream from End to Hub is already closed. The stream from Hub to Terhathum is next. Your family's home system, Nadashe. *Your* home system."

Nadashe shook her head and smiled. "No. And it doesn't matter anyway." She pointed at Marce. "If he's correct, then billions are about to die. End is the *only* system in the Interdependency with a habitable planet. Every other system is man-made habitats. They'll last for years or even decades. But eventually they'll fail. They'll all fail. Except for End. Which the House of Nohamapetan will control, if it doesn't already."

The door to the room opened again and four imperial guards

came through and marched toward the executive committee table. Hibert Limbar followed behind them.

Nadashe looked at them, and then at the emperox. "Are those for me?"

"Yes, they are," Grayland said.

"Let me give you a piece of advice, Cardenia," Nadashe said, as the guards crowded around her. "Keep me alive and treat me very well. The end of the Interdependency is coming one way or another. However it comes, the House of Nohamapetan is going to be there, waiting for its tribute. It's not going to look kindly on you if something happens to me."

"We'll keep it in mind," Grayland said. "In the meantime, thank you for your service on the executive committee. You're dismissed."

Nadashe laughed, stood up from the table, and walked out, accompanied by the guards. The entire executive committee watched her go.

Then when she was gone, Upeksha Ranatunga cleared her throat. "I want to get back to this thing about the Flow streams collapsing in a decade." She looked at Marce and Grayland. "Is it true?"

"It's true," Marce said.

"And you're only telling us *now*?" Ranatunga said, disbelieving.

Marce heard Grayland sigh, saw her glance over at him for just a moment, and then turn to Korbijn, who was returning to the table.

"The *Prophecies of Rachela* is gone," Korbijn said. "Through the Flow shoal. On the way to End."

"It's only ten thousand marines," Marce said. "And there can't be that many more at the imperial station there. You have hundreds of ships and hundreds of thousands of marines."

"All of them have to go through the bottleneck of the Flow

shoal," Grayland said to him. "A few ships and weapons are all they need to defend it."

"You seem sure about that."

Grayland laughed, bitterly. "How do you think the House of Wu became the imperial house a thousand years ago, Lord Claremont? We did the very same thing here. In the space above Hub. Controlled the shoals and made everyone who wanted to come or go through them pay a price. We made them pay, Lord Claremont. Just like the Nohamapetans plan to make anyone going to End pay. And at the end of it, they'll be the new emperoxs, or so they believe."

"Then seal off End entirely," Korbijn said. "If the Nohamapetans want to self-exile, let them."

"It's not that simple," Marce said.

"Why not?"

"Because Nadashe was right," Grayland said. "There's only one system that will support human life on its own once the Flow collapses. And that's End. We can prepare every system for the collapse. Give them everything we can to last as long as they can. But it's End where humans will survive when everywhere else has gone dark. We need that planet. We need to get at least some people from every system in the Interdependency to it."

"And it's the Nohamapetans who stand in our way," Marce said.

"Yes," Grayland said, nodding.

"So what do we do?" said Upeksha Ranatunga, after a minute. "What do we do now?"

EPILOGUE

"Don't you have better things to do than to sit around here?" Attavio VI asked Cardenia, as she sat in the Memory Room.

"Are you expressing judgment?" Cardenia asked.

"I remember asking you that question once when you were spending time with me as I was dying. It's assonant to ask you again now. It gives the appearance that I care. Which is a thing you need."

"You know you ruin it when you put it like that."

"I apologize. But the question still stands."

"I do have better things to do," she said. "But I'm going to sit around here anyway."

The simulation of Attavio VI nodded and then sat next to her—or at least, the simulation of him gave the appearance of sitting next to her. "I came here too," he said. "Whenever I was overwhelmed or exhausted or just needed to be away from other people. I would come here and talk to my mother or grandfather or any of the other emperoxs."

"Did it work?"

"It worked about as well as it's working for you right now," he said. "But I decided it was good enough."

Cardenia smiled at that. "It is good enough," she agreed.

"You haven't been in the Memory Room as often recently."

"Do you miss me when I'm gone?"

"I don't exist when you're gone, so, no," Attavio VI said.

"I'm busy with the end of everything," Cardenia said. "I had Lord Marce give a presentation to parliament. I've ordered the military to create a plan for taking back End. I've suspended the operations and monopolies of the House of Nohamapetan and given them to the House of Lagos to administer."

"I'm sure that went over well."

"It went well with the House of Lagos, at least." Cardenia remembered the meeting with the Countess Lagos and her daughter Kiva, both of whom were profanely delighted at the fall of the Nohamapetans, and the rise in their own fortunes. The countess gave Lady Kiva responsibility for the Nohamapetan monopolies, with Cardenia's permission. "Marce's presentation was not nearly as successful. He laid it out as simply and in as straightforward a way as it could be done, and the majority of the parliament still thinks it's nonsense even though we have proof."

"But you don't have proof yet," Attavio said. "It hasn't been more than two weeks since Lord Claremont arrived. The ships from End could still be delayed by the civil war. The Flow stream to Terhathum is still open."

"I don't know that it will matter even then," Cardenia said. "I'm continually confronted with the human tendency to ignore or deny facts until the last possible instant. And then for several days after that, too."

Attavio VI nodded. "This is why I never said anything about it."

"Yes, and I'm getting a ration of shit for *that*, too, thank you very much, father of mine," Cardenia said. "I have seventy percent of the parliament angry with me because they don't believe this collapse is coming, and forty percent angry with me because I didn't tell them about it sooner."

"That math on that is bad," Attavio VI said.

Cardenia shook her head. "No, because some people are both. And then there are the allies to the Nohamapetans who either believe Nadashe has been framed either by me or the House of Lagos, or have decided that a little bit of treason and rebellion isn't that big of a deal. Which is another thing I get to thank you for—letting that house become as influential as it did."

"I can't be blamed for that."

"Of course you can be blamed for it. I just blamed you. I'm getting blamed and now I'm passing some of that blame on to you. I hope you feel bad about it."

"I'm dead. I don't feel bad about anything."

"Must be nice."

"It's not," Attavio VI said.

Cardenia closed her eyes for a moment and rested back against the wall of the Memory Room. "I didn't want to be emperox, you know," she said.

"Yes," Attavio agreed. "I remember."

"You didn't want me to be emperox either."

"I remember that too. But regardless of what either of us wanted there is the fact of what is. And the fact is, you are emperox. Probably the last emperox of the Interdependency. And the question you might ask yourself is whether you would want anyone else to be that person."

"No," Cardenia said. "No, I wouldn't."

Attavio VI nodded. "Remember there's a reason I suggested the name Grayland to you. To remind you what had to be done. And to inspire you to be the person to do it."

"Do you think it's working?"

"I don't have opinions anymore," Attavio VI said.

"Well, pretend that you do."

"You're asking a heuristic computer network for its opinion."

"Yes I am. Do you think it's working?"

There was a pause and Cardenia could have sworn she saw the image of Attavio VI flicker for the barest fraction of a second. Then, "Yes. I think it's working."

Cardenia smiled. "There. That wasn't so hard, was it?"

"In fact, yes, it was."

Cardenia laughed at this and then grew silent again. "The Interdependency was built on a lie, you know," she said, to Attavio VI.

"Yes, I know. If not a lie, then perhaps on the least malignant projection of its original intent."

"It's a lie," Cardenia said. "I know it. You know it. Every emperox knows it. All of the major houses, the ones that have been around since the founding of the Interdependency, know it, and the minor ones are pretty sure about it too. We've all been agreeing to live with this and continue this lie. For centuries."

"Yes," Attavio VI said.

"It feels like the lie is coming due now," Cardenia said, and then held up a hand. "I want to be clear, it's just a feeling. There's no rationality behind it. But the feeling of it is so strong within me. Knowing that we created the Interdependency for our benefit, and pretended it was something that benefitted everyone. It makes this collapse feel like it's the universe commenting on our choice."

"It's not."

"I know. The Flow has nothing to do with us. It doesn't care about us. It's just something that is. But I still can't shake that feeling."

"That's the human brain," Attavio VI said. "It creates patterns when there aren't any. Imagines causality when there is none. Imagines a narrative where none exists. It's in the design of the brain itself. It's primed to lie."

"And primed to believe the lie."

"Yes," Attavio VI said.

And then Cardenia had an idea.

"Huh," she said, after the idea had unpacked itself in her head.

"What is it?" Attavio VI asked.

"The Interdependency began with a lie."

"Yes."

Cardenia smiled. "I think it needs to end with another one," she said.

ACKNOWLEDGMENTS

As ever, I think it's tremendously important to note that there is more to a book than simply the words that go into it—it passes through many hands after it leaves mine and before it gets to yours, and all of those hands make it better. Therefore, let me acknowledge the following: Patrick Nielsen Hayden, my editor (who was promoted to associate publisher at Tor while I was writing this—congratulations, Patrick); as well as Miriam Weinberg, who had the thankless task of checking in on me about when the manuscript would be in; Tor art director Irene Gallo and cover artist Sparth for a fantastic cover; copy editor Christina MacDonald for catching my many errors; text designer Heather Saunders; Alexis Saarela and Patty Garcia in Tor publicity; and of course Tom Doherty, who runs Tor.

I am especially grateful to them because I turned in this book rather later than I intended to—the second book in a row I have done that for—and no doubt tried their patience in having done so. To each of them I can only say that I am heartily sorry to have been a pain in the ass for a second time in a row. I did have plans to get this in early. Also, if I turn in a third book late, I think it would be fair if everyone involved in the production of the book gets to punch me hard in the arm.

(As a side note, and this is not an excuse, but holy buckets, did the 2016 presidential election make it hard to focus on writing a novel, because I felt like I needed to check in every five minutes to make sure we didn't find a way to blow ourselves the hell up. I'm writing these acknowledgments in October of 2016, so the outcome of the election is still in doubt, and I'm still worried about everything ending in fire. But at least now I don't have to try to write a novel around the worry, too.)

(As a second side note, I will also note that the title of this book—*The Collapsing Empire*—was not intended as a commentary on the current state of the United States, the UK, or of Western Civilization in general. I thought it up years ago. It just happened to look like commentary because, let's face it, 2016 was a *historically* fucked-up year, and I can only hope 2017 is going to be better. Because if it's not, it really is time to head to the bunkers with our barrels of beans and rice.)

Coming back to acknowledgments, I'd like to give thanks to Ethan Ellenberg, my agent. I always give thanks to Ethan, but at the moment I'd like to give a special moment of appreciation. As some of you may know, this book represents the first book of a ridiculously excellent multibook, multiyear contract with Tor, which I was extraordinarily happy to get (Hey! I get to write novels through 2027 at least! That's pretty good!), and which Ethan was an exemplary shepherd of during the negotiating process. I got very lucky when he became my agent, and I'm grateful with every book that he does such a fine job for me. Thanks also to Bibi Lewis, who handles my foreign language contracts; to Joel Gotler, my film/TV agent; and to Matt Sugarman, my entertainment lawyer. In other news, I am now a person who has lots of agents and lawyers. I know, I think it's weird as well. Finally, a big wave of appreciation to Steve Feldberg at Audible, who handles the audio versions of my work.

The number of friends who kept me grounded while I wrote this book are too many to be counted in these acknowledgments, so let me resort to the old phrase of "you know who you are" and say thank you. (If you don't know if this includes you, hey, just assume it does. Thank you! You're awesome.) Also, thank you, readers. Yes, you! You let me write for a living. How great is that? I have a house and food and pets that won't eat me out of gnawing hunger because of you guys. I don't want you to think I don't appreciate that. I do. I really do.

Additionally, I'd like to thank the administrators and volunteers of the 2016 edition of HawaiiCon for having me as a guest. I got a surprising amount of this novel done while I was on the Big Island of Hawaii for their convention, and I think getting as far away as humanly possible from the mainland, and its constant news feed, made a huge difference. Not to mention, you know, being in paradise. Thanks, folks.

I'll close these acknowledgments as I usually do, by thanking my wife and daughter, Kristine and Athena. They actually have to live with me while I write these novels, and it's not always a happy walk through the poppies. I can be cranky and snarly, especially when (as in this particular case) I get a little behind and I'm uncomfortably reminded that novels are actual work. They love me anyway, even when I only debatably deserve love, and my appreciation for them is nonending and immense. I love them more than pie and churros combined. I think you all know how much I love pie and churros. They're even better, trust me.

—*John Scalzi*
October 5, 2016

extracts reading groups
competitions books new
discounts extracts extracts
competitions events discounts
books extracts
new events
events books
extracts new reading groups
new title reading groups
interviews events new
events extracts extracts
discounts events books
new books events interviews
new
events new
books extracts

www.panmacmillan.com

discounts extracts discounts
extracts events reading groups books
competitions books extracts new